ADRIE

UNDER THE
ORANGE
MOON

for

KRISTI-

Who loves my characters as much as I do.

Thank you for reading everything I write.
I would be lost without your endless brainstorming
and your thoughtful words of encouragement.
You are a true friend, indeed.

Prologue

"Please don't do this tonight." Ben McKenna heard his voice crack along with his pleading, adding to the weakness he felt deep in his gut. He swallowed hard and attempted to ignore the stinging in his chest that intensified with each horrible word she said. "It's my last night here. Please."

"You're just like him!" she screamed, her voice becoming more vicious with each drink.

Ben sank lower as his mother's terrible words filled his heart. It never got easier.

"I regret the day I had you," she slurred. Her body swayed until she leaned against the wall with a flat, unsteady palm. "That's all I needed: another McKenna man to curse my life and abandon me."

"Mom, I'm going to *college*."

"On the other side of the country!"

"I'll be back to visit as soon as I can," he lied.

"Where do you think you're going?" she asked as he rose from the chair and stood taller than her. There was a time long before when she could speak down to him, but it was now his turn to stand above her.

"I'm not doing this with you tonight."

She pushed herself from the wall and moved close enough that her boozy breath wafted into his nose, causing him to lean back.

"Oh yes, run to that bitch and play house with the Mathews. Perfect little Linda Mathews," she sneered. "She thinks she can steal my son!"

"She didn't steal me, Mom. You're the one that makes it that way—" There was just no point in reasoning with the irrational. "Just go to bed," he demanded and pushed past her.

He closed his heavy eyes as he heard the shattering of picture frames, bottles, and glass ... whatever she could get her hands on to throw in her fit of rage. He wouldn't dare turn around; he couldn't stand another minute with her.

Ben slammed the door with enough force that he could hear the cracking of the window behind him as he walked away. His mother's hysterical screams shot through the night and he wondered what the neighbors might say behind their backs tomorrow. It didn't matter now; by then, his mother and this nightmare of a life would be far behind him.

He just needed one more night with the one person who made him feel alive.

He needed one more moment with the one person a McKenna man could never be good enough to have.

After his short walk through the yards that led to the only place that had ever made him feel wanted, Ben crept into the Mathews' home. There was so much movement there that he knew no one would ever tell the difference between him and one of the loud Mathews boys. It was safe to come and go in that house—not that anyone would care if they did catch Ben walking around at one in the morning. For whatever reason, pity, most likely, he was just as important to them as they were to him.

For this one night, it would be worth the risk of being caught and questioned. He had to be next to her one more time before he left this life behind. He needed to spend his last night in Phoenix lying beside her and basking in the arousal it sparked. He needed anything that would quiet his rampant emotions and she was the only one who could do just that ... whether she knew it or not.

This was the case whenever it came to her. No one would ever know—or *understand*—how much he needed her presence.

It didn't even make sense to him. She looked and acted nothing like the typical girly-girls that Ben slept with. She was a natural beauty. She didn't need to wear heavy makeup and dresses to turn him on; her usual jeans and T-shirts never hindered his attraction to her. Beneath it all, there was a true magnificence about her; she had a calming effect that he would always crave.

Even worse, her family meant more to him than his own. And, when it came to his late-night visits to her room, he betrayed them on a regular basis.

He just couldn't help himself.

Ben opened Dylan's door and stepped into her dark room. He removed his shirt and slid under the sheets, careful not to shake the bed and startle her. He moved close, just close enough to feel her breath on his chest. He moved his hand into her soft hair, gently twirling it between his fingers and letting the ends stroke his calloused skin. It was a perfect representation of them: her deep, flawless beauty against his sharp, jagged, and utterly damaged existence.

As the moonlight illuminated her face, he stared down at her and felt that familiar calm sweep through him.

"Ben?" he heard her ask sleepily, her eyes fluttering open.

He didn't say a word. He never did when she woke up. Like every time before, he only sighed and pressed his lips to her head. He pulled her closer to his body and felt her relax against his chest.

"It's your last night," she whispered against his bare skin.

Ben closed his eyes and moved his hand up the back of her nightshirt, pulling her closer and squeezing for dear life.

"Ben?" she asked quietly. "What happened?"

He shook his head gently. He felt a humiliating tear form in the corner of his eye and prayed that she didn't notice.

Dylan took a heavy breath and exhaled with a sigh. In a sudden movement, she sat up and looked at him with a sweetness and understanding that would haunt him for years. He never needed to tell her anything; she always just knew.

"You don't have to talk," she whispered, and carefully lifted her shirt over her head.

Ben sat up and swallowed hard as he stared at Dylan's body, now covered only by a pair of purple boy shorts. This was a first. She had never been so bold, not even in his fantasies.

With a gentle movement, she raised her chin to meet his eyes, causing the ends of her hair to brush across her bare shoulders and drape over her breasts. It was absolutely beautiful; she was exquisite. As she placed her shirt on the bed, her trembling hands revealed the nerves she attempted to keep in check.

He reached out and touched her, watching as she sighed heavily and closed her eyes. He traced his fingers over her breasts and ran his thumb over her nipple, feeling the way the peak hardened beneath his touch. Without another thought in his raging head, he pulled her into his lap and settled her onto his hard body. He placed his hands on her hips and thrust himself upward, laughing to himself as her innocence showed in her widened eyes. He pulled her even closer and leaned his head slowly until his lips barely brushed her breast, his warm breath clearly driving her mad as she writhed above him. Within seconds, he took it all into his mouth, his tongue playing with the tip and his hands traveling up her back and into her hair.

Dylan's panting grew heavier as she bucked against him. She latched her fingers onto his shoulders and then into his hair, urging him to keep going.

He pressed harder and moved his hands down her back and into the back of her underwear. With both hands, he grasped her bottom as he contemplated taking off the boy shorts that separated him from everything he had spent a lifetime fantasizing about.

"Take them off," she said into the air above them, her voice hoarse.

Ben pulled his mouth away from her chest. He looked up at Dylan—his perfectly sweet, innocent *Dylan*—and shook his head, bringing himself back to reality.

"It's okay," she assured. Her chest rose and fell with each sharp breath she took.

He shouldn't have thought about it; he was angry at himself for allowing his brain to function now, of all times. Nevertheless, he *had* to stop. This wasn't Dylan, and he certainly couldn't allow a one-night stand to be his last memory of her. Not her. Not ever.

And nothing, not even Dylan, was going to get in the way of his escape.

Ben looked into her eyes and slowly shook his head, a silent *no* that he knew ripped her to pieces. She couldn't possibly understand what was going through his head, but he had to save her from the destruction that he left on everyone who had ever been foolish enough to love him—even his own mother. He was his father; his mother had always been right about that. He was selfish, heartless, and incapable of putting anyone before himself. Dylan was too good; she was too pure and flawless to end up as miserable as Ruth McKenna.

He said nothing as he suddenly lifted her from his body. He refused to look at her face. He couldn't bear to see the unforgivable amount of pain he knew would be in her eyes.

He pulled his shirt over his head and fled like the gutless dog he knew he was.

CHAPTER

ONE

Ben McKenna sank deeper into the leather chair he had rested in for more than six hours. He watched the red letters on the large informational screen above him switch from "boarding" to "delayed" too many times to keep track of. He seriously wondered if this was a divine indication that he should not be getting on that plane.

Selfishly, he hoped his flight would be canceled. He wanted nothing more than to go back to his apartment, eat a steak, drink a beer, and get back to work. It seemed like now, as during the childhood that shadowed him, he was only weighed down by the irritations that went along with his life back home. He found himself completely aggravated, as usual.

"Damn," he muttered, his voice practically a growl.

As his phone rang in his pocket, he was reminded of the source of his frustration. Without looking, the caller was obvious to him. No one else would call three times in a row.

"Hello, Mother," he answered grudgingly.

"Benjamin? Where are you?" she asked fearfully. This wasn't motherly fretting, of course. It was simply the panic that came from the knowledge of her son's obvious reluctance to come home. "You're still coming, right?"

"I'm just waiting for this screen above my head to tell me to board my plane. If that ever happens, I'll be on my way."

"It's still delayed?"

"It snows here in Massachusetts, Ruth."

"You know I hate that."

"Sorry, *Mom.*" He sighed deeply and closed his eyes. "I'll call you when my plane lands."

Ben slid his phone back into his pocket and leaned his head against the uncomfortable chair. He despised the holidays, but, most of all, he hated going home to his past life. He would never do this of his own volition. Only a mother's guilt could pull the unwilling home.

Technically, it was his holiday break, but he knew better than most that truly successful men never take breaks. That was what he was raised to believe, anyhow.

This waste of a trip was a meaningless way to appease his unhappy mother and, even more so, anger his disapproving father, a Supreme Court judge. Even now, he could hear his father's voice rambling on about the importance of representation and the behavior of a truly driven man. The voice was always domineering, even when it was only imaginary.

He was, indeed, focused. His life was planned down to the very last detail: flying through his first year at Harvard Law School, approaching a promising career in the legal world. He had always been expected to succeed, only because he had never failed. He worked harder than anyone in his class, even earning an internship at one of the most successful law firms in the country beginning in the spring. He would forever credit his father's influence with that achievement in the back of his mind, holding it there and dwelling on it in secret.

"Flight two-sixty to Phoenix, Arizona, is now boarding," a woman announced over the intercom.

Ben got to his tingly feet and grabbed his carry-on. He boarded the plane at last and sat beside a window.

He sighed long and heavy before nuzzling up to the window. It was uncomfortable, but, then again, so was the whole damn trip. His only solace was sleep. He would sleep through the agonizing flight as it led him away from the flurries of snow and into the warm Phoenix sun for the holidays, a place he hasn't been in five years.

* * *

"It's about time." Jonah Mathews stood by the baggage claim with his hands stuffed deep inside his pockets. He looked exactly the same as he had the year before when they had met for Spring Break. "Nice suit," he taunted, in true Jonah fashion.

"Nice haircut," Ben joked, before giving Jonah's arm a manly smack. "You've been watching the Disney Channel again, I see."

"Just keepin' up with the stylish times, asshole." Jonah twirled his keys. "You ready?"

"Nope." Ben sighed and picked up his suitcase.

During the drive, Ben watched out the window and noticed nothing new. It was the same as he left it: sky, mountains, cacti, and sand. When he was a child, he'd thought of his city in simpler terms: blue, red, green and brown. It wasn't that he despised where he was from or thought of it as ugly. He'd always just seemed to need a bit more from the seasons: dramatically cold winters, wet springs, humidity in the summer, and crunchy red leaves that fell to the ground in autumn. He loved his desert, but not enough to live in it.

"How's California?" Ben asked casually.

"I'm livin' the dream," Jonah answered with a lazy grin. "I changed my major again."

"Again?" Ben laughed. "Man, you better be careful. Your mom is going to cut you off soon."

"Nah, she's happy enough that I'm still going. Besides, I work at the dealership part time."

"Bar money," Ben said through a burst of laughter.

Jonah was spoiled rotten. As long as his mother paid his rent and took care of him, he would change his major repeatedly, extending his education for a free ride.

"Sorry, Mr. Law School, where's your job?" Jonah blurted with a smirk.

Ben shrugged and shook his head. "Touché," he answered, knowing the situations were hardly similar. He decided to end it there and avoid insulting Jonah, which he would have, had their banter continued.

"Charlie's save-the-date card came," Ben remembered out loud, grinning at Charlie Mathews' womanizing reputation when they were younger. "What the hell is that about?"

"I don't know," Jonah answered with a chuckle as he merged onto the freeway. "He's all about this girl."

Ben laughed. "He's only three years older than us, though."

"Hey, you don't have to tell me that. Believe me, I know. If I ever try to get married at twenty-five, lock me up."

"So, is your whole family coming in for the holidays, then?"

Jonah gave an easy smile. "Yeah, my mom's been floating around the house like she's on a cloud."

"I bet." Ben chuckled, picturing his self-proclaimed second mother in pure holiday bliss. "What about Weed?"

Jonah crinkled his nose at the mention of the cruel nickname he and his brothers had given his twin sister while growing up. It was bad enough she was a girl with a boy's name, surrounded by boys, and then labeled not as a flower, but as a weed.

"She's good. Still living at home, but doing well." Jonah turned to glance at Ben. "By the way, you know what she'd do if she heard you call her that."

"I'm not scared. I wore a cup today, just in case."

They both erupted into laughter and a small piece of Ben warmed at the familiarity of home and his lifelong friendship with Jonah. He decided at that particular moment that if he had to be home, he was at least happy to have Jonah with him.

Ben's eyes swept over the Mathews house, and he had to smile as they pulled into the driveway.

He sighed heavily. "Home, sweet home," he caught himself saying aloud.

"Tell me about it," Jonah agreed.

Growing up, Ben loved the never-ending chaos that swarmed the Mathews' house on a regular basis. It made him feel surrounded and secure, just the opposite of his own dismal home, filled with only pretentious decor and a depressed, neglected mother. This was more his home than any place he had ever known.

Almost immediately, Linda Mathews was out on the porch with her hands in the air, waving with a smile. She was warm and looked like a real mom, Ben had always thought. Her hair was always back and the only places she ever seemed to be, when she wasn't teaching her Kindergarten class, were the kitchen or her garden. Her arms were always wide open for Ben, which he supposed was due to the lack of loving arms in his own home.

Ben smiled at Linda and sighed. "There's Mom Two," he said with a laugh.

"She's been waiting for you all damn day," Jonah grumbled. "She's happier to see you than her own sons."

Ben missed Jonah's last sentence. His stomach flipped when he caught sight of the person standing just to the side of the house. She was barefoot, carefully stirring a bucket of paint. She gathered the end of her white skirt in her other hand and held it between her long, tan legs. Her light brown hair hung loosely over her face and curled slightly at the ends. Her mannerisms and paint-splattered arms gave her identity away, of course, but Ben still couldn't seem to believe his eyes.

"Oh my God. That's ..." Ben squinted his eyes and leaned forward. His mouth hung open as he stared long and hard.

"Who?" Jonah stared ahead with squinted eyes of his own. "Weed?"

"What?" Ben flinched with disbelief. "In a dress?"

"Man, you're checking out my sister." Jonah chuckled.

Oh Lord. "She looks like—like, uh—"

"You really have been gone a long time, brother."

* * *

Dylan Mathews stirred her paint and frowned at the color that was forming. She had been going for a purplish-gray, like a rainstorm, but it seemed to be getting a bit too dark.

She knew that Jonah had gone to get Ben from the airport, but she couldn't bother to get as excited about his arrival as the rest of her family. So she stood, bent over her bucket, and pretended not to notice his presence.

As if that were possible.

"Dylan, look who's here," her mother called from the porch. "Aren't you going to say hello?"

"He's not even out of the car yet, Mom. I'll let you do the honors of jumping him."

Linda waved her hands at Dylan and rolled her eyes. She ran off the porch and wrapped her arms around Ben's neck. He wasn't her biological son, but she loved him enough that he could be.

Dylan stood upright and let the end of her skirt fall. She moved her long hair out of her eyes and placed her hands solidly on her tiny hips. She could easily imagine how much paint she had managed to splatter on her face, arms and legs. Not like she would ever worry herself over washing up for Ben.

"Hello, Ben," she said, standing firm and allowing him to come to her.

"Dylan." Ben's eyes moved up and down her body, an automatic movement that seemed to catch even him off guard.

Still a pervert, she thought.

"You look like a car salesman in that suit," Dylan teased. She enjoyed making him suffer, even now.

"Uh, yeah what's up with that suit?" Jonah finally asked.

Ben smoothed out his unwrinkled jacket. "Nothing. I had something I needed to take care of before I left and it happened to require a suit."

"Well, go get normal clothes on," Jonah demanded.

"I will, loser. I have to see my mom, anyway." Ben swung his carry-on over his shoulder and gave a casual grin.

Jonah let out an exasperated laugh. "Hey, Princess, your other hand looks a little light. I take it I'll be bringing your suitcase to your mom's at some point?"

"Thanks, buddy," Ben answered with a smirk. He turned and began to walk the familiar path behind the house and into the neighbor's yard by leaping over the concrete wall that separated it.

The grass and AstroTurf that stretched between the Mathews' and McKenna's had been worn down to dirt. It had been a shortcut to them as kids, but a pain for the surrounding neighbors who guarded their landscaping with their lives. On any given day of their childhood, an angry neighbor could be heard screaming from a window because one of them had blindly hopped onto one of their plants or small palm trees from the other side of the wall.

"Careful, Mr. Raymond is still there and he still hates when you walk on his grass," Dylan warned.

Ben waved away the thought. "It's faster to go this way. I don't want to walk all the way around the block when I can just hop a few walls. I'll be back in thirty minutes or so."

Dylan watched him leave and rolled her eyes at his nonchalance. Even now, when he was supposed to mature with age, Ben remained unaffected by and totally oblivious of the world around him. He only cared about one thing: himself.

"Dylan, enough with the paint already," her mother called. "I need help with the potatoes."

Dylan dropped her stick robotically and jumped up on the porch. There was no point in arguing. With everyone home again, not only was the house going to be a whirlwind of commotion, but there were going to be easily fifteen pounds of potatoes to peel.

Being the only girl in the family, Dylan got the dubious honor of being her mother's assistant in the kitchen. Fortunately for her, Charlie, Dylan's second oldest brother, was getting married in the spring. That meant Dylan would soon have an ally and, more importantly, someone else to peel the potatoes, for once.

"Is Ben joining us for dinner?" Linda asked, pulling down the dinner plates from the cupboards.

"Does Jonah's bottom drawer hold about fifty porno magazines?" Dylan replied. The twins never seemed to mature when they were in their mother's home.

"Dylan," Linda said firmly.

"Sorry, Mom," Dylan said through a small sneer.

"Ben didn't recognize you when we pulled in, *Weed*," Jonah teased. He elbowed her as he reached over to grab a piece of green pepper from the counter.

Dylan glared at Jonah. She hated that name and loathed all of her brothers for torturing her with it her entire life. It was a cruel name, even if they had intended it to be funny.

"Shut up, Jonah," Dylan hissed.

"I'm sorry. You're not a weed anymore," Jonah apologized with a cocky grin.

"I never was a weed, idiot!"

Charlie hopped up on a stool between Jonah and Dylan. Always the bully of the family, he pulled Jonah into a chokehold, and said, "I think Weed's new name should be Bubble Butt."

"Adult children of mine, please behave." Linda tasted her gravy to make sure it was perfect. "Your sister is neither a weed nor a bubble butt."

"Come on, Mom. She has to be one or the other." Charlie grinned menacingly. "What was that about Ben?"

Jonah laughed. "He checked her out when we first pulled in."

"He did?" Linda turned, intrigued.

"Yep." Jonah elbowed Dylan again.

"Well, our little Weed is growing up," Charlie teased.

"Charlie, shut up!" Dylan screeched. "Why are you even here? Go back to your apartment!"

"Sorry, Weed. I'm here until the wedding. Besides, I want to bond with my baby sister before I become a husband," he teased, pinching Dylan's cheeks. "You're going to miss me when I'm gone."

Dylan squirmed out of his hold and punched him in the arm. "Ugh, I so won't."

"Okay, that's enough," Linda commanded with her hand over her smile. She loved the sound of her children bickering. Most would agree that made her a lunatic, but the familiar feeling warmed her heart to no end.

"Mom, stop laughing!" Dylan hollered.

"Oh, honey, you're beautiful. That's a nice compliment that Ben was attracted to you."

Dylan scowled while she tried to calm her flaring temper. She had half hoped that after five years of silence, the constant teasing about Ben would be ancient history.

Charlie smacked Jonah on the back of the head. "Quit it."

"What? You were teasing her more than I was," Jonah replied, rubbing his sore head.

"Shut up, Jonah," he said plainly. Charlie put his arm around Dylan. "I'm sorry, baby sister. I'll stop."

Dylan rolled her eyes and grabbed the giant pot of water from the counter. She struggled to carry the dreadfully heavy thing out back. She slumped onto the deck behind her house to begin the endless job of potato peeling.

*   *   *

Ruth McKenna held her arms out to her son as he moved up the stairs to greet her. She hadn't changed much over time. Clad in her usual pajamas, she still looked sad and pathetic, the only way that Ben had ever known her.

"Hello, Mom," Ben said, cringing at the feeling of her cold hands on his face.

"Benjamin, how was your flight?"

"It was an airplane—same as always."

"I'm happy you came home. How is school?"

"Fine." Ben's one-word responses were subliminal messages that he sent to people he didn't wish to speak to on a regular basis.

"Just fine?" His mother's eyes scanned his blank expression, hoping there would be a bit more chatter on his part.

"That's what I said, right?"

"Okay. Fine." She pointed up the stairs. "Your room is just how you left it."

A light breath escaped Ben's lips as he made his way up the wooden steps. She said the word "left" like he had abandoned it when he took off for school. What was even more entertaining was the way she managed to make it sound like he left her as well. Everyone leaves Ruth.

Ben opened his door and looked around before stepping inside and setting down his bag. Besides the few random boxes that his mother had stored in there, it was just as he left it. He smiled at the Harvard banner that hung over his bed. Seeing it there gave him a sense of validation, knowing he had made it.

He sat on the edge of his lumpy mattress and looked around the room. He pulled open his bedside drawer and examined the items that were left behind: remnants of his glory days in high school, magazines, phone numbers, condoms, and a foul ball from the last Diamondbacks game he'd gone to.

He changed into more comfortable clothes, slipping into a pair of expensive, but faded, jeans and a gray Harvard T-shirt. He fell back against his bed before running his hand through his hair and laughing to himself when the reality of it all set in. He was home. Seeing the Mathews is what had brought this into focus for him. Not his mother or her house. It was the Mathews family that made him feel that pleasant, good-to-be-home feeling.

It was like old times. Only Dylan did not look like the old Dylan.

Dylan. She was absolutely fascinating. He couldn't control his smile when he thought of her, the only girl born to Linda Mathews, who came out with a knack for doing boy things better than most boys. Her baggy clothes hung on her petite body, she loved art, threw a football like Brett Favre, and had no problem taking her brothers down by kicking them square in the balls.

He thought about her eyes—her emerald green eyes. Those were the same. Her hair shined the same, too, he noticed. Sparkling wisps of auburn still shone through the light brown when the sun hit it a certain way. Her olive skin made her look somewhat Mediterranean when she tanned, he remembered.

She could hardly be described as a weed anymore.

Her fiery nature was the same as when he left, too, only she seemed to have let the best of herself come out with age. That damn dress. This new development could be a problem, making his stay a bit more difficult than he had originally thought. He was, after all, a man with eyes and a very healthy sex drive.

Ben sighed at the memory of how her dress had bunched between her legs and he nearly scolded himself out loud for even allowing thoughts about Dylan's legs to enter his mind.

Here we go again.

"Knock, knock." His mother opened the door without any response from Ben, which was not just annoying, but typical. "Are you going to be here for dinner?" Already she was making his visit complicated.

"I don't believe so. Why?"

"I thought about cooking." She half frowned. "No big deal." Her expression suggested otherwise.

"Tomorrow?"

"I thawed the chicken already. Maybe it will keep until then."

"I'm sure it will be fine, Mom." Ben sat up and stared at her disappointed face. "Ask me."

"What?"

Ben rolled his eyes. "Ask me what you want to ask me. Get it over with."

"Fine. How is he?" Her eyes watered and her voice choked.

"He's the same as always. He's busy, selfish, and bitter." The three adjectives Ben used to sum up his father, Warren McKenna, were harsh, but true.

"Ben, you shouldn't say those things."

"Then you shouldn't ask." Ben stood. "You've wasted about two decades of your life waiting for that man, Mom."

16

"I haven't waited." Her voice went quiet, sending Ben the familiar signal that tears were coming.

"I'll see you later." Ben walked by her, gently placing his hand on her arm as he passed. "We'll have dinner tomorrow night."

He hated when she cried. Not because it made him sad, but because it truly irritated him more than he could tolerate. It seemed his mother cried every time they spoke. No one should ever see a parent cry, a theory he wished his mother lived by.

Sometimes it was hard for him to draw a line between his parents. He wasn't sure where his anger began. Was he mad at his selfish father for leaving to have his affairs out in the open? He hadn't even filed for divorce. It was as if he pressed the delete button and erased his wife from his mind completely. She was an afterthought, only on his mind when he wrote the monthly check that would keep her satisfied enough to let him live in peace. His mother, on the other hand, would wait forever for her husband to realize he had made a mistake. Ben didn't believe that her waiting revolved around love, of course. It was about her pride, and that, alone, infuriated him.

However, the ridiculousness of their marriage would soon be ending and Ben could finally feel at peace. He was even more thankful that he would be back in Cambridge when his mother received the papers.

*　*　*

Dylan sat on the edge of her back patio. Her legs were spread as she peeled each potato and let the skin fall into the garbage between her feet. She fought hard against the potato, taking all of her frustrations out on the defenseless spud.

The sun beamed down on her skin and a soft wind soothed her nerves as she attacked the potato in her hand. She took in a large breath and released it slowly, loosening her tight grasp on the peeler. Breathing was essential in this moment.

Why did he have to look so good? Was there simply nothing ugly about him? And why had he looked at her like that? It was amazing that he had even looked at her at all. Normally, he seemed to practically look right through her unless they were alone, when the dynamic changed into something bizarre, but brilliant.

She gripped the peeler with such force that it dug into her skin.

She would always be pathetic over him, with or without his presence. Even in his absence she stupidly related everything to him. Like, when her mother wanted to replace the diving board on the pool, Dylan used what she secretly thought of as her Ben-timeline to determine that it hadn't been replaced since he had mastered a back flip, over twelve years earlier. She was such a loser.

It was easy to see his younger face in his now-manly one. It seemed as though, while everyone else went through the unpleasant ugly phase of pubescence, Ben had glided through it with grace and perfection. Dylan felt no surprise that he was even more handsome than before. He had aged beautifully. His light brown hair was careless, but stylish. His eyes were a deceiving, child-like blue. But there was no innocence about him. There never had been.

It wasn't a simple thing, pushing Ben out of her mind while he was away. Of course, she hadn't forgotten him. She never would. She had hoped that he would never come back, though. Sadly, that just wasn't a logical wish.

"Need help?" Ben stood in front of her with a cheesy grin and a hand shading his unadjusted eyes from the Arizona sun.

"No," she answered quickly. She refused to look at him too long out of fear she'd say something stupid.

"How have you been?"

"Great."

"Are you mad at me?"

She stared into his eyes—*hard*—as if to freeze him in place with only one icy look. "I haven't seen you in years."

Ben leapt up and sat next to her. "Well, that's just it. You don't seem very happy to see me."

Dylan stopped peeling and stared at him. He was so full of himself that sometimes she wanted to slap her own cheek for ever holding him in the high regard that she did.

She gasped dramatically. "Oh my Lord! Is it really you, Ben McKenna?" She covered her mouth. "My life makes so much more sense now that you're home. Take me Ben. Take me now." She let out a fake, girlish yelp and went back to her peeling.

Stunned and put in his place, he slowly reached down to grab a potato from the pile. "That's better. Thank you."

"Any time."

"You're still painting, I noticed."

"You say that like it's a bad habit, like I'm smoking or something."

"I'm just trying to make conversation. Wait. *Are* you smoking?"

"No—God!" She tried not to laugh by biting her lip. "Yes, I'm still painting. I'm an instructor at the new art institute in Scottsdale."

"What?" He snapped his head back in disbelief, smiling proudly.

Dylan laughed and shook her head. "I can assure you that it's not all that glamorous. Most of my students are a bunch of old people from the retirement home at the 101 and Scottsdale Road."

"Still ... that's great. You should be proud."

Dylan shook her head. This was how they were and she knew now that it would never change, not even with age. Ben was only the Ben she knew when he was sure no one else would see. Like the night before he left for college. When someone else was looking, Dylan changed from the friend he congratulated to Jonah's twin sister, Weed, whom he teased or ignored.

"How did you end up teaching?" he asked as he tossed a potato in the air and then caught it.

Dylan looked up into the sky and sighed. "Well, let's see. I studied Fine Arts at Arizona State. I met an instructor named Scarlet, who let me apprentice under her for three years until she moved to New York. I loved every second of it and I guess it made me want to become an instructor, too."

"That makes sense."

Dylan nodded and smiled. "Yeah, I guess."

"So, do you do anything else, other than teach old people how to paint?" Ben asked.

"I've gotten close with Charlie's fiancée. I spend a lot of time with her."

"What's she like?" he asked.

Dylan shrugged. "She's nice. She's good for Charlie."

"Nice? That's kind of like the go-to word for when you want to say something good, but you don't have anything real to say."

"You're such a lawyer," she teased.

Ben laughed and nudged Dylan's arm. "I just call it like I see it."

"No, really. I do like her. You will, too."

"I'm sure I will," he said with a hint of sarcasm.

"You're back, with normal clothes on," Jonah said as he stepped through the French doors that led into the kitchen.

Dylan snuck a look over at Ben. She had tried so hard to not look at him that she hadn't even noticed his new, more familiar outfit.

Ben hopped back down to the stone path that led around the pool. "So, what's the plan for tonight?"

"I think it's a good bar night," Jonah replied, patting Dylan on the head. "Dylan is a part-time bartender at Ollie's."

"Really? You left out the part about moonlighting as a bartender," Ben said as he smiled at Dylan. "Are you working tonight?"

Dylan stood up and lifted the pot, now even heavier with potatoes. "I have to work at eight."

Ben reached out and pulled the pot from her hands. "Then we'll see you at nine, *Weed*."

CHAPTER TWO

Ollie's Bar looked like a hole in the wall and smelled like old, stale beer. Dylan had grown accustomed to the male patrons who screamed and hollered loudly at the losing team on the TV screens above her head. She found the blaring volume of the games rather soothing because it reminded her of being in her grandfather's kitchen, listening to baseball games turned up loud, since her grandfather was nearly deaf.

She loved this job. She loved the ripped jeans she got to wear and the free shots she got to do. Not to mention the added bonus that the more attitude she gave, the higher her tips seemed to be. There was an uncanny mix of alcohol, testosterone, and witty comebacks that seemed to turn men on at sports bars. It was something Dylan never understood, but thoroughly enjoyed when it came to her tips.

The bar was conveniently located in the middle of Tempe, filling the place from wall to wall with college students just about every night. In the summer, it was slow and almost not worth Dylan's time. Still, she went because she enjoyed the atmosphere and good conversation.

"There's our favorite bartender," Ben exclaimed, smacking his open hands down on the wooden bar.

Dylan poured three shots and slid two over to her brother and Ben. She lifted her glass and smiled mischievously. "Cheers."

"What are we drinking to?" Ben asked, pressing the glass to his lower lip, but holding off until Dylan answered.

Jonah blurted, "To getting laid."

"Whatever," Dylan answered with an eye roll, and then downed her tequila.

Jonah walked away to greet a crowd he recognized, leaving Ben and Dylan alone and awkward, although neither one would ever admit discomfort.

"How's school?" Dylan asked.

Ben nodded before taking a sip of the beer that Dylan handed him. "It's good."

"Good."

"How long have you been working here?" Ben asked.

His eyes moved around the room, a maneuver Dylan decided was for her sake. For some time, he had been staring at her tight, black T-shirt that had "Ollie's" written across the chest.

"A year."

"What made you decide to be a bartender?"

Dylan smiled, amused at their second attempt to make small talk. "I came here for my twenty-first birthday and drunkenly asked for a job."

"That's funny."

Dylan didn't respond. She only stared at him with a puzzled look, a silent request for him to elaborate on his humor.

"You acquired a job as a bartender while you were drunk?" He stared at her with his familiar cocky smile. She pretended as though it irritated her and, in a way, it did. She despised how much that smile, a look meant to frustrate her, only seemed to make her more attracted to him.

"Yes, when you put it that way, I suppose I did."

"How many times has your boss tried to hit on you?"

"He doesn't. He hasn't."

"He will."

"And if he does?"

"Shouldn't I ask you that?" Ben noticed that Jonah was just a few feet from them, and lowered his voice. "What if he does?"

"I don't know."

"What don't you know?" he asked with narrowed eyes.

"What I would do if he did. He's a nice enough guy."

"You and Olerson?" Ben erupted into wicked laughter.

"What's so bad about that?"

"He's a meathead."

"No he isn't!"

"Yes, he is."

"Why?" Dylan asked, shaking her head.

"Do you remember when we were younger? He thought he was the shit."

"Kind of sounds like someone else I know," she said, staring pointedly at Ben.

"Awww, Dylan. That hurts."

"You're not insulted and he's not a meathead, so stop it."

"It's okay. You're just defending your man," Ben teased with his eyebrows raised.

"Why are you standing here bothering with Dylan?" Jonah called. "There are people here who want to see you, man." Jonah pulled Ben's arm and led him away.

As they moved toward the crowd of old friends, Ben raised his bottle in the air and winked at Dylan, a gesture she took to mean he intended to finish aggravating her later.

She was startled out of giving him a look that would have killed him by an eruption of screaming testosterone. The Phoenix Suns were playing on TV and, for the fifth time in the first half of the game, a bad call was made.

Through the crowd of hollering men appeared Hugh Mathews, another brother to add to the long list. He smiled when Dylan realized he was there. Only about a year older than the twins, he was sometimes mistaken for Jonah or for their triplet. He was the one who came into town the least. He lived in Washington and never had a steady job, but always seemed to get by, possibly on his good looks and flighty personality.

"When did you get in?" Dylan asked, leaning over the bar to hug him.

"Just now. I haven't even unpacked," Hugh answered. He looked around and smiled. "Where's the crew?"

"Where else?" Dylan joked, pointing to the swarm of girls that surrounded Jonah and Ben. "Do you want a beer?"

Hugh shook his head. "I just came to say hello. I partied way too hard last night. I almost threw up on the plane."

"Wow. I'm shocked, Hugh," Dylan began with widened eyes. "Are you losing your touch? Are you pregnant?"

Hugh put his hand up and smiled. "Hey, my touch is not lost, and if I'm pregnant, God is playing one cruel joke on me that I just may deserve. Don't you worry about me, little sister; I'll be back tomorrow night with every intention of drinking you under the table."

"I'll believe it when I see it," Dylan said as he stepped away.

Dylan frowned as her brother joined the others. She was stuck on the other side of the bar, serving, as usual. Most of the time she didn't mind, but tonight she felt restrained, unable to join the sibling reunion that was going on right in front of her.

"Dylan, get out of here," Michael yelled from the kitchen.

Michael "Ollie" Olerson grew up with Charlie Mathews, Dylan's second oldest brother. He was a local football legend who had suffered a career-ending injury in college, came home with a business degree, and opened the bar when he was only twenty-three. He had been overjoyed when Dylan asked for a job a year later.

"You don't need to stay all night," Michael said, walking toward her. "Why don't you take off when the game is over? Have some fun for once."

"Who says I'm not having fun?" Dylan flirted with Michael, but only because she knew he liked her. Ben was absolutely right about that. She couldn't say that she'd never considered Michael, but she didn't think it would be fair of her to force feelings she just couldn't seem to conjure up, no matter how right he would be for her.

"Go hang out with your brothers." Michael rubbed her shoulders as he stood with her behind the bar. "Finish up back here with the NBA crowd and then I'll close the place down tonight, okay?"

Dylan tried to act nonchalant about her release. "Whatever you say, boss."

Michael cringed. "I hate when you call me that." He rubbed the top of her head as he headed to the beer cooler in back.

"Weed, grab me a beer, would ya?" Charlie asked with an inquisitive smile. "Ollie's still got a thing for you, huh?"

Dylan handed Charlie a beer, ignoring his comment. "Where's your wife tonight?"

"No wife yet, baby sister." Charlie took a large swig from his bottle. "Only a fiancée, who's home at the moment."

Charlie was easygoing, the polar opposite of their oldest brother, Brandon. He had been a football hero in high school who, for reasons no one could understand, dropped out of college his freshman year to become a construction worker. He carried huge loads on his tan shoulders all day long and enjoyed every minute of it. He simply loved the hard labor and the hot sun on his back.

The biggest surprise to the family had been when playboy Charlie came home to say he was engaged. Dylan and her mother had only met Meredith once, making it hard to take him seriously for a while. Now, six months later, with the wedding set for the spring, it seemed as though he wasn't kidding after all.

"When are you going to get a boyfriend?" Charlie asked, half smirking at the thought.

"When men aren't pigs," Dylan answered, raising another shot of tequila to her lips. "So I guess never."

Charlie watched his tiny sister throw her shot back like a pro. "Anyone in particular we're talking about right now?"

Dylan only glanced Ben's way. "Nope."

* * *

Ben could feel Dylan's glares without even getting a solid look at her. He positioned himself in such a way that he could watch the bar out of the corner of his eye, a way to see her every movement without being obvious about it. After watching Michael Olerson drool all over her, however, Ben was beginning to rethink his decision to spy.

He cringed as Dylan fluttered her long lashes at Michael, and thought, *Look at me like that.* The only thing he found remotely entertaining about the grotesque display behind the bar was that, despite her girlishly stupid smile, he still knew her well enough to know that she was completely uninterested in Michael and his attempts to flirt.

He had to laugh at his ability to unconsciously infuriate her. He enjoyed irritating her for reasons that he couldn't even explain to himself. It was a turn-on, perhaps.

There was a wit about her that enthralled him to no end. Even her quirks were endearing, from her fear of birds to the strange way she despised the feeling of holding chalk. He still remembered clearly how much trouble she got into in fifth grade when she refused to write on the board. She stubbornly sat with her arms crossed until the teacher could no longer legally hold her after school. He had found it adorable, though he wouldn't have dared admit it out loud.

Ben nodded along to some redhead that remembered his name, but, for the life of him, he could only remember her lopsided chest. He was a champ when it came to appearing as though he was listening. Throwing out an "uh-huh," an "oh?" and a nod every few minutes seemed to satisfy this one very much.

He had been stuck listening to her for what seemed like two NBA games. A quick glance at the TV above Dylan's head proved him wrong when he realized the Suns were still playing, though long into the fourth quarter.

Charlie finally stood up, leaving the path to Dylan perfectly clear. Ben took his chance the moment it presented itself and left the lopsided girl in mid-sentence.

"How's the legend, Olerson?" Ben asked, as he slid onto the stool in front of Dylan, praying he didn't sound jealous.

"He's fine."

"You know there are laws about sexual harassment that he should probably look into."

"Oh?" Dylan smiled. "I thought sexual harassment only applied when it was unwanted."

"Are you saying you like it when he rubs your shoulders and pats your head?" Ben felt ill at the thought.

"I don't dislike it."

"You like being a barmaid that gets love taps like a dog, then?" he asked with narrowed eyes.

"I suppose I do."

"Well," Ben leaned forward, "then you work for the right man."

"Well, okay." Dylan shrugged and flashed him a smirk.

"Could I get two shots?" he asked, smirking devilishly in return.

"Make it three," Jonah called from behind him.

Defeated in having his moment alone with Dylan, he obliged. "Make it three."

Dylan poured the shots and slid them over to Ben. "She doesn't look like a tequila girl," she said as she shot a glare at the redhead. "This should be interesting."

"Retract the claws, crazy. I didn't order the shot for her." Ben slid one back to Dylan while he watched her with one mischievous eye. "I actually wanted this one for my favorite tequila girl."

Jonah laughed. "Quit hitting on my sister."

"I would never." Only Ben knew that he was. He figured Jonah would never expect it and, even with it in front of his face, he would more than likely shrug it off as a harmless, drunken joke.

Jonah lifted his shot. "Here's to the sexy brunette over there." He slammed his glass down on the bar and staggered drunkenly to his newest victim.

"Your redheaded girlfriend over there looks upset," Dylan teased, clearing away the empty shot glasses. "You might want to go back to her."

Ben told himself to walk away. The worst part of him refused to listen most of the time and, when there was liquor involved, the devil on his shoulder had a way of taking over.

"I don't even know her name," he said.

"I'm sure every girl in here could say that she's made out with you, Ben. I truly believe that you couldn't tell me half their names."

Ben leaned over the bar on his elbows. "I know your name."

"I said girls you've actually kissed, smartass." Dylan crossed her arms and shot him a warning look.

He scanned the room to make sure that Jonah was far enough away. With a teasing spark in his eye, he lowered his voice, and said, "We've made out before."

Dylan's face flashed with anger. "No. We've never *made out* before, Ben." She threw back her last shot and slammed the glass back down on the bar. "For you to say otherwise is just insulting."

Not really all that thrown off by her reaction, he watched as she closed down her register and grabbed her bag.

"Are you leaving?" He wanted to chase after her, but he realized he wasn't that drunk yet.

"Michael said he's going to close up tonight and, quite frankly, I have no reason to stay."

As Brandon Mathews stepped into the bar, Dylan pulled him right back out the way he came. Brandon was their oldest brother and, to no one's surprise, the most successful, with a career as an architect in California. He never really argued with the idea that he was the man of the family.

"Drive me home," she ordered, yanking him along with her.

"What?" Brandon's confused eyes narrowed on Ben. "What's wrong?"

"I just want to leave," she hissed, and stepped outside.

"Okay." Brandon turned and followed his little sister's lead.

"What did you say to her, McKenna?" Michael asked Ben from behind the bar.

Ben refused to turn around to look at him. "Bag it, Ollie. You just worry about getting me another beer."

Michael sent a beer sliding down the bar, intentionally unopened. Amused by Michael's attempt to irritate him, Ben smirked as he slammed the bottle against the side of the bar, scratching the wood and sending the metal cap flying.

"You know what, McKenna?" Michael asked.

"I don't know that I care, Olerson."

"You're still an asshole."

"What's wrong with Weed?" Jonah asked as he stepped to Ben's side.

"Who knows?" Ben answered innocently. "Brandon's driving her home."

"I think it's time to follow. I'm drunk," Jonah slurred. "I wish we would have caught a ride with them."

"Lightweight," Ben teased.

"I had more shots than you. Shut up."

Ben wanted to leave as well, but he couldn't let Jonah know his motives. "I'm crashing at your house tonight."

"No shit."

The two paid their enormous bar tab and hopped into the first cab they could find. As they rode back to the Mathews' house, Ben quietly hoped that Jonah didn't take too long to pass out.

* * *

Dylan tossed angrily in bed, frustrated not only at herself for allowing Ben to get to her again, but for the mere fact that he didn't remember something she thought about on a regular basis.

Why do you keep letting him do this to you? she thought, as she pulled the pillow over her head.

She had gotten on just fine without him around and now his beautiful face was not just in her mind and memory, it was real and saying things that her imagination had not allowed before. This was his game and she would always be the fool that let him win her over. Even five years later, he still managed to aggravate her, hurting her more than anything. She had always wondered what a run-in with Ben would do to her and now she knew. He was the same Ben that he always had been, with no glint of hope for a change.

Dylan pictured him talking to the redhead with her cleavage flopping out of her shirt right in front of his eyes. She thought of herself, on the other end of the spectrum: ordinary, like the weed that she had always been known as. Ben had always wanted the perfect girls, the fake bimbos who knew more about lip-gloss than they did about art, culture, and the environment.

She promised herself that tomorrow would be different. She would ignore him for the next three weeks and hopefully she would be stronger when she saw him again in another five years.

However, all of a sudden, in a moment of symmetry that seemed to take her back in time, there he was again. Dylan felt him slide next to her beneath the blankets. She knew she wasn't dreaming. He was really there and, somehow, she wasn't the least bit surprised.

His arms wrapped around her torso and he pressed himself to her. His open hands moved along her skin, and she shuddered against him as he pulled her closer by her hips. He wasn't trying to be gentle; this was different. Like his looks, the mannerisms of his late-night bed invasions had matured into something more masculine.

She didn't tense up, push him away, or even turn to face him. She only lay perfectly still, knowing if she made any controlling moves he would leave instantly.

He nuzzled her hair, inhaling as he pressed his lips to her neck. He whispered through a haze of alcohol, "I know we didn't kiss that night, Dylan."

Her lips formed a smile that she would not dare allow him to see. She knew him well enough to know that this would be the extent of his admissions for one evening. Ben always left her wanting more. Tonight, however, that quiet statement was enough for her, and she could sleep.

CHAPTER THREE

Dylan awoke to the sound of Ben leaving. She opened her eyes just in time to see his bare back as he snuck out her door. She imagined him fearfully looking around to make sure that not a soul would see his secret departure. If he were to get caught, she was sure he would hope for it to be by Hugh, out of them all. Hugh would give him the least grief.

No one would believe that nothing had happened while Ben slept in her bed and spooned her. It was difficult even for Dylan to understand. With his hands all over her, his discipline had been something she couldn't comprehend. She had felt his arousal against her, but he hadn't acted on it.

She rolled over and sighed as she looked out her window. The sun had not risen and her day was far from beginning. Despite the fact that it was still early, she could not manage to make herself go back to sleep.

She stood and slid on a pair of oversized pajama bottoms. She slipped a sweatshirt over her head and walked out of her bedroom and down the stairs.

In the kitchen, the lights were all off, but the dawn sky was just enough light for Dylan to see. She stood over the sink and watched as Ben disappeared over the wall, heading for his mother's house.

He was still shirtless. His body had improved over the years—not that it had needed to. His chest was more chiseled now. His muscle tone was sharp, his body angular. His pelvic bone made a faultless V as it traveled down into his pants, driving her mad as she tried not to look at him.

"Morning," Linda called from behind Dylan. "What are you looking at?"

Dylan nearly jumped out of her skin. "Nothing. I'm just looking."

"Are you hungry?"

"Not yet."

"I'm going to make a big breakfast in honor of your brothers being home. Did you see Hugh and Brandon last night?"

"Yes. Hugh only stayed a few minutes and Brandon brought me home. I have no idea where Charlie went."

"Charlie's here. Why did Brandon drive you home?" Linda poured her coffee and raised an eyebrow at Dylan. "What was wrong with your car?"

"I did too many shots."

"Oh, Dylan," Linda said, shaking her head.

"Jonah left his car there. Are you going to be angry at him?"

"I'm not angry. I just don't understand how you can go to work and come home drunk," Linda answered, unprepared for her daughter's snap.

"No one was *drunk*, Mom."

Linda lifted her hands in peace. "All right, I'm sorry." She quickly changed the subject. "Do you think Ben will have breakfast?"

"How should I know what Ben will have?" Dylan felt attacked even though she wasn't.

"Well, isn't he here?"

"No. Stop asking me questions."

"I think you should go back to bed, Dylan. You're being really snippy." Her mother narrowed her eyes and stared. "What's wrong?"

"I just want you to let me breathe without hovering over me every five seconds," Dylan hissed. "Get a boyfriend or something."

"Oh yes, I'm the one who needs a boyfriend," Linda snapped. "I'm not the one flipping out on people for no reason."

Immediately, Dylan felt strong, stinging guilt spread through her chest. Her mother, wife-turned-widow when her father, Carl Mathews, lost his battle with cancer more than nine years before, would never replace her husband.

"I'm sorry, Mom. I just want you to stop hovering."

"I wasn't trying to hover," Linda replied. "I don't even know what I said wrong."

"Nothing. You said nothing."

Linda put her arms around Dylan's shoulders and surrendered. "I'm sorry. I just love you." She waited for Dylan's inevitable smile. "Help me with breakfast?"

"Fine," Dylan answered, attempting to cover her childish grin.

* * *

Ben stepped through the sliding glass door just in time for breakfast. He was showered and dressed in clean clothes. His brown hair was still wet and looked towel-dried.

"Where'd you go?" Jonah asked.

Ben smiled. "You were snoring, so I left."

Dylan felt her cheeks flush. She refused to look at his face while he stood above her, grinning mischievously. She was angry that he had snuck into her bed, but she was furious at him for leaving. She thought about tying him up next time.

He was back now, nibbling sausage and glancing her way with a satisfied smile, daring to remind her that he had been in her bed.

True to their constant battling and bickering, Ben challenged her like this regularly. As much as she felt unworthy in his presence, she had always accepted his dares with the hope that one day she would feel more like his equal. Nevertheless, that day had never come.

Dylan could still clearly recall the way she had overcome her transition from training wheels to two wheels. She had been five and just couldn't seem to get the hang of balancing on only two wheels. Ben had teased her relentlessly one day, zooming past her like a pro and even skidding to a stop that splashed a puddle in her face. Call it will, tenacity, or just plain old bravery, but she had finally ripped his bike from his hands and taken off with a speedy grace. It hadn't been her brothers' cheering, her mother's happy tears, or her father's proud smile that day that had made her pat herself on the back. It had simply been overcoming Ben's taunting and proving him wrong.

Ben sat in the chair beside Dylan and picked up her juice. She could feel her anger rising. She knew this was all to irritate her and what made her the angriest was that it was working.

Dylan stood up to get a new glass of juice. She took her time pouring it, listening to the boys' conversation around the table. It was as if no one had ever left and their lives were exactly as they had always been. The quiet mornings she spent with her mother were always pleasant, but extremely empty. There was a void at the table and, despite the fact that only two sat around it regularly, the leaf was always in, as if there were six. Neither she nor her mother needed to say out loud that they were delighted to fill the empty chairs.

"Did Dylan tell you the news, boys?" Linda began, smiling behind her coffee mug.

"What news?" Brandon asked.

"No news," Dylan snapped from the refrigerator.

"Why are you being so modest?" Linda asked.

Dylan huffed loudly and rolled her eyes. "It's really not a big deal."

"Of course it is!" Linda sounded irritated and thrilled at the same time. "What has gotten into you today?"

"What do you mean?" Charlie asked. "What's wrong with her today?"

"She has been so crabby all morning," Linda complained. "Honey, you need a nap. You must not have slept well last night."

Ben choked on his stolen juice and all attention shifted to him. Realizing it, he slammed on his chest with his fist, and announced, "Wrong tube."

"Uh-huh," Brandon said with his brow raised at Ben. He slowly turned his attention to Dylan, and asked, "Weed, what's the news?"

Dylan said nothing while she stared at her mother, waiting for her to jump in and tell them for her. The interruption was inevitable, so Dylan thought she would just let it happen to begin with.

Linda impatiently waved her hands at Dylan and said, "She's been asked to do a gallery showing of her work."

"What?" Jonah asked, shocked. "How long ago? You never said anything."

"It only happened a month ago." Dylan felt her face blush when she realized that Ben looked pleased and, in a way, proud. "I don't even know the man that wants to hold it. His name is Norman ... something. He's seen my work and asked if I had enough pieces that I would be willing to do a show."

"That's awesome, little sister." Brandon winked at Dylan and gave a satisfying grin before taking in a heaping mound of eggs. "When is it?" he asked with a full mouth.

"June. The gallery is in Lower Manhattan," Linda answered for Dylan. "He has a store in Greenwich Village, which I hear is super trendy!"

"We'll all have to come. Ben, do you think you can spare a weekend in June?" Jonah asked.

"We'll have to see. I'll buy a painting, regardless," Ben answered, before taking a dramatic drink from Dylan's new glass of juice.

Dylan ripped the glass from his hand. "*You* couldn't afford me," she snapped.

* * *

Ben climbed the rugged, brown trails of Papago Park. He grew up exploring the many holes and twists of Phoenix's paths and hills, but he found, in this particular moment, that five years had given his feet just enough time to forget which way to move along the rocks.

He wouldn't admit to a soul that the desert sun on his face was calming and had somehow quieted the stresses that constantly plagued his overworked mind. He enjoyed being home, but knew he would be quite ready to go back to Cambridge when his three weeks were up.

He stopped when he saw her. She stood on the edge of the giant rock and looked out over the Phoenix Zoo. Ben almost winced at how much of her beauty she allowed to be seen now. Why did she have to be wearing another dress?

As the breeze whipped up, it lifted the hem of her dress and flapped her skirt against her legs. She bent to the side, one paintbrush in her mouth, another behind her ear, and a third between her fingers. She touched the bristles to the canvas and drew a long, black line down all the way to the bottom.

Ben couldn't tell what her painting was going to be, but since he knew her talent, he was sure it would be a masterpiece. He watched quietly and took a great deal of satisfaction in how perfect she looked when she did what she loved most.

He took a seat on the first boulder he could find and watched as Dylan continued to paint. He looked around and realized where they were. He remembered this place very well, like he had been here yesterday.

Carl Mathews, Jonah and Dylan's father, had seemed to go quickly, but painfully, when he died of cancer. He'd gone to the doctor with constant headaches and left with grim, unexpected news: three to six months to live. After his funeral, Dylan had closed up. She'd run around the house, only thirteen years old, organizing and cleaning for her mother. She'd made sure that there was enough food for the guests who came back for the wake and handled everything else that went along with it. She didn't cry and she hadn't allowed anyone but her mother to cry to her. She was a rock.

After the wake was over and the guests had left, Ben found her weeping on the very rock he sat on now, which wasn't a surprise; she could see the giraffes from there. He'd only been thirteen at the time, but he had understood how Dylan worked, even when her twin brother hadn't. Ben had sat beside her in silence and hadn't said a word as she sobbed into her hands, eventually falling into his lap. He'd rubbed his fingers through her hair and continued to say nothing as he quietly comforted his Dylan. In that moment, he'd truly felt as though she was *his* Dylan.

In those very few, rare moments in their backwards relationship, he found it interesting that she knew he would be there for her. She hadn't resisted crying in his lap like most teenagers would have; she had known that he would allow it. But her confidence in him only scared Ben more.

Now, watching her in all her sun-drenched beauty, looking out over the scenery below, he only regretted more the way he acted when her brothers were around. He wondered if she knew how he really saw her: faultless and fascinating. He wondered if it was written all over his forehead as he imagined it was whenever he spoke to her. Even five years later, that spark—that *fire*—still burned only for her.

Beauty was not hard to come by. Ben could find it easily wherever he happened to glance. It was all around him on a regular basis. Dylan was more than just beautiful, though. She was resplendently perfect. But he could never have her.

With each stroke on her canvas, her painting was brought to life. In very little time, it began to take shape perfectly. The longer he stared, the more he came to recognize his own face on the canvas. He smiled in bewilderment and slowly crept away from her, having managed to go unseen and unheard for the entire time he had sat behind her, watching as she painted him.

* * *

On Saturday afternoon, Dylan and Meredith walked into their fifth bridal shop of the day. Dylan had cleared her entire schedule, so she didn't mind modeling the endless array of bridesmaid dresses that her future sister in-law pulled from the racks.

"That one's pretty, but not all the girls look good in everything like you," Meredith pointed out. "My sister is a bit ... uh ... rounder."

Dylan smiled and shook her head. "Then maybe your sister should have come instead of me."

"No. That won't work, either. She bothers me and you don't," she answered simply. Meredith put her finger to her mouth and looked around the store. "I think I might just have you all wear different styles, but in the same color."

Dylan sighed deeply and stared into the mirror. She did enjoy the way the dress fit her. The long, light pink fabric hugged all the right spots and showed off her defined collarbone and shoulders. Although the sparkly accents were something she could have done without, she knew that she looked good in the dress and secretly hoped Meredith would agree.

She stood on the highest part of the floor, next to the window, and turned halfway to look at her bare back in the mirror.

A knock on the window startled her. She spun around and felt her face flush when she realized that Michael Olerson was on the other side, grinning at her from ear to ear.

"Nice," he yelled through the glass, pointing up and down with his finger.

Dylan smiled as she lifted her skirt and curtsied exaggeratedly for Michael.

He raised his curled finger and motioned for her to come outside. "Just for a minute," he pleaded loudly when she shook her head and frowned.

Dylan nodded as she gave in and hopped down the steps. As she walked to the dressing room, she unzipped the dress and began to pull it off, unaware that Michael was still watching and nearly collapsing from the unintentional show.

She walked outside barefoot.

"Hey," Michael said, attempting to regain his composure. "Bridesmaid duties?"

Dylan glanced back into the store and sighed. "Yep."

"I see. I won't keep you, then." He fiddled around with the bag in his hands. "What are your plans for tonight?"

Dylan raised one eyebrow. "Uh, nothing. Why?"

"I'm not going to ask you to work. Don't worry." Michael stammered and fiddled some more. "I told Charlie I may swing by tonight to have a few beers with him. That's all."

"And?"

"Well, are you going to be there—home, I mean?" he asked, sounding hopeful and humiliated at the same time.

"Most likely," Dylan answered carefully. She knew he was attempting to see her, but she felt too awkward to help him out.

"All right then," he replied. "Meredith looks like she's going to go Bridezilla soon. You should get back in there."

Dylan glanced back through the window and waved at Meredith's nagging glare. "Yikes. I have to go," she said to Michael, and practically sprinted back into the store.

Back inside, Meredith grinned. "He won't give up, will he?"

"He hasn't even started," Dylan answered with a smirk. "He's too shy to even begin."

"Would you go out with him?"

"I know I should, but—" Dylan shrugged. "I don't know."

"Don't force feelings you don't have," Meredith warned. "You'll just hurt him more in the end."

Dylan nodded as she put on her shoes. "I know."

* * *

Linda Mathews didn't go out very often, but when she did, she was well aware that the boys would stay in and drink themselves stupid. She didn't mind. Just the thought that they were noisily filling up her home once again sent warm feelings through her heart.

Charlie passed around bottles of beer as they all relaxed in the living room. With everyone present, even Ben, Dylan knew this was going to be a long night full of boozing and vulgar language.

"Where's Mom at anyway?" Jonah asked, sitting on the couch with his legs stretched out into the middle of the room.

"She went out with a few friends," Brandon answered. He slapped Charlie on the back of the head. "Use a coaster."

"Isn't Michael coming?" Dylan asked.

"Who invited him?" Ben asked with a scowl.

"I did," Charlie announced. "He likes Weed. I thought I'd help him out."

"That idiot? Seriously?" Ben snapped before he could catch himself. His voice grew calmer as he asked, "You want your sister with that guy?"

"Why not?" asked Hugh. "He's a good guy. Successful."

"He owns a bar," Ben half-laughed, choking on his resentment. "I wouldn't call that successful."

Dylan sighed and rolled her eyes. "Why is this in discussion right now?"

"Because we want you to date Olerson, that's why," Jonah teased.

The doorbell rang, causing Dylan to jump to her feet and Ben's throat to tighten. She turned and warned them, "Behave," before heading to get the door.

She returned with Michael, who smiled as everyone greeted him loudly, except Ben, who wouldn't lower himself to say hello. There was simply no point in acting as if you liked someone you despised.

Dylan sat on the floor beside Brandon. Ben watched as she stretched out in front of him. He wanted to punch Michael in the face when he realized that, like him, he was admiring her long, tan legs.

The group sat and chatted for hours, drinking until the beer was just about gone. They had a lot to catch up on. The fond feeling of history repeating seemed to hang over them all as they understood that these times didn't come as often as they should.

This was their club, in a way. Once a group of boys that would build pipe bombs and ramps in the garage, they were now a coterie of men that had a unique history and a bond that could never be broken.

Despite the lack of blood, Ben was just as much a part of this brotherhood as Jonah and the rest; this was his family as well. But Ben looked at Dylan in such a different light. Could he go that far and get away with it? No. He knew he could not.

The more that Ben drank, the more irritated he was at Michael's presence. Every so often he would glare over to where he sat with Dylan, exiled from the reminiscent conversation and forced to come up with their own topics of discussion.

The night came and consumed the desert sky with black. Michael looked out the window and Ben knew without a doubt that his brain was in motion. Ben thought this would probably be the moment the asshole would turn to Dylan and suggest a walk or something romantic like that.

He watched as, like clockwork, Michael finally worked up the nerve to whisper to Dylan, and they walked out of the room. They disappeared into the kitchen and Ben wanted nothing more than to follow them and listen to every word that Michael used to seduce her. He stood up and followed them, pretending to use the bathroom so he could hear what they were saying.

"I like hot cider better than tea," he heard Michael say.

He couldn't help but roll his eyes and mouth the word "pansy" from the other side of the bathroom door.

"Well, I'll make both, then," Dylan said politely. "I'm sure you want whisky in yours?"

"Yes please," Michael agreed. "You know me so well."

Ben wanted to gag. He decided he had heard enough and flushed the toilet to keep up his charade. He quickly slipped back into the living room and took his seat on the couch.

Dylan and Michael appeared in the room with thermoses in their hands. They put their shoes on and headed for the door.

"Where are you guys going?" Jonah asked.

"The moon is orange." Dylan grabbed a blanket and turned to look at all of them. "There's enough tea and hot cider for everyone. Did you drunks want to join us?"

Michael shook his head at them from behind Dylan, a silent but obvious request to be alone with her. If it had been anyone else, the Mathews boys would have all gone outside and hovered over their sister, protecting her from the perverse idiot that wanted alone time with her. But this was Michael Olerson and, for whatever reason, only he could successfully ask them to back off.

"I'm going to bed," Charlie answered with a drunken grin. "Goodnight."

"I'm going to throw up," Brandon announced as he staggered up the stairs.

Hugh said nothing as he climbed the steps behind Brandon.

Jonah leaned back against the couch with a smile. "Thanks for the offer, but Mom will be home soon and I want food before I sleep."

"I'll go," Ben announced, defying Michael. He stood and grabbed his sweatshirt. "What are you drinking, Dylan?"

The disbelief in Michael's eyes shifted to rage. Everyone knew that Ben could be a jerk. Stooping this low was not out of the norm for him, so he couldn't understand the look on Michael's face.

"Tea," Dylan replied. "Do you want some?"

"Yes," Ben answered with a devilish smile, an air punch into Michael's gut. Serves him right. Ben knew what he was up to. "I'd love some."

Dylan poured the hot tea into a thermos for Ben and smiled, looking a little confused. "I didn't know you liked tea."

"I like it better than cider," he replied flirtatiously. He could feel the evil glares from Michael, which only satisfied him that much more.

Jonah shook his head and chuckled at Ben's rude behavior, but he would never dare tell him to stop. Jonah would always agree with Ben. "Have fun watching the moon."

They walked through the sliding glass door and headed into the backyard. Dylan sat down on her blanket with a guy on each side. She looked up at the moon and sighed delicately.

Michael pointed up, and said, "There's the constellation Fenix." His finger traced a shape that Dylan tried to see. "Do you see it?"

Dylan laughed. "No."

Ben watched in amusement as Michael worked hard to keep Dylan's attention. He knew better than anyone that constellations were not the way to impress her. This was a definite one-up in his direction, knowing her inside and out from a history that went as far back as he could remember.

"Hey, did you know that the moon looks orange right now because of the pollution in the atmosphere?" Michael asked stupidly and with growing desperation.

"Really?" Dylan asked, looking up into the sky. She was obviously trying to be polite. "That is interesting, but sad at the same time. I like an orange moon for different reasons. I'd rather not know about the scientific explanation for it."

Feeling evilly triumphant, Ben smiled victoriously and scooted closer to her, practically flipping Michael the bird. The rare appearances of the orange moon reminded her of her father. Ben knew this well, and he knew exactly why Dylan looked at the moon the way she did that night. Normally, this would make him sad for her, but he secretly thanked Carl for granting him this triumph over Michael.

"Olerson, shut it. You're ruining the moment," Ben harassed.

"What moment?" Dylan asked with a careful smile.

Michael laughed uncomfortably, stiffening in frustration. "Ben here thinks everything with him is a moment. He doesn't realize that we could care less if he's here or not."

"*You* may not care that I'm here," Ben jabbed. He grinned at Dylan as if to point out her smile. "Dylan's always happy when I'm around."

"Sure," Dylan teased, elbowing Ben and leaning into him with a lighthearted laugh.

Fueled by Ben's hovering and constant teasing, Michael swallowed hard like a nervous loser and reached over to pull Dylan's hand from her lap. Ben waited for Dylan to let go awkwardly, but she didn't. She actually hung onto Michael's hand and continued to watch the orange moon, sickening Ben to the point of seething aggravation.

Not quite defeated, Ben scooted even closer to Dylan and allowed his arm to just barely touch hers. He matched her breathing and moved with her as he hoped she would find the feeling of him beside her as pleasant as he did. *That's my hand*, he thought.

Dylan could feel the silent competition between the two of them. She understood the threat that Michael was feeling, but, for the life of her, she could not figure out Ben's motives. She chalked it up to intoxication.

Michael sighed loudly. He looked Dylan's way and smiled. "Do you want to go for a walk *alone?*" She knew that last part was meant for Ben's ears.

"That's a terrible idea. Her brothers wouldn't like that," Ben answered for her. He looked Michael up and down with a suspiciously raised brow. "You never know with certain people."

"What?" Dylan laughed in disbelief. This was getting ridiculous. "Ben, shut up," she said.

Michael stood up and held out his other hand. "Let's go," he continued politely. He looked at Ben and said, "You're not invited."

Dylan knew what he wanted. The thought of kissing Michael made her stomach sink. He was already displaying actions that made Dylan rethink everything she thought she knew about him. The hand-holding alone was enough to make her want to crawl under a rock and stay there; she had been thankful when he let it go to stand. The sweat on his palms was too annoying for words. Or maybe that was her sweat, a reaction to the hand she didn't want to hold.

"Michael, I'm tired. I was thinking about just calling it a night," Dylan said, taking the coward's way out.

"Some other time, then," he said, disappointedly.

Ben stood up and flashed a wide, satisfied grin. "Have a good one, Ollie." He pulled at Dylan's shirt and headed up the patio steps.

"I'm going to walk him to his car," Dylan said, pulling her shirt from his hand and cutting an evil glare his way. He was like a dog chewing on her pant leg.

Ben froze on the steps. He glared at them both and pressed his teeth onto his lower lip, a mannerism that Dylan knew well. He was trying to shut himself up.

"I'll be there in a minute," Dylan snapped at Ben when he hadn't moved.

As Dylan and Michael headed around to the front yard, Dylan could feel him moving closer. She prepared herself for his attempt and contemplated dodging it when it finally came.

"So, thanks for having me," Michael said when they reached his car. He moved in close, and Dylan turned her face away. He kissed her on the cheek and pulled back with a smile. "Goodnight."

"Goodnight," she replied, wishing she felt disappointed. "I'll see you at work tomorrow."

As Michael drove off, Dylan walked back into her dark house. Jonah was snoring away on the couch and Ben was nowhere in sight. She sighed as she walked up the stairs to her lonely room where she got ready for bed and slid between cold sheets.

The sound of her door opening and closing wasn't a shock. It was only a matter of seconds before Ben was sliding under her covers. He pressed against her and moved her hair from her face.

"Why did you do that to me?" he asked in a low whisper.

His fingertips traced along her jaw and down along her neck, causing a tremble she couldn't conceal.

"I didn't do anything to you," she whispered.

"You don't like him," he said, rubbing his nose to hers. His hand moved along her hip and down to her thigh. He lifted her leg and pulled it around his body, a move that stunned her beyond anything she could have anticipated.

Ben's hand moved over Dylan's shoulder, and he slid his smallest finger under the strap of her top. "Michael Olerson doesn't deserve you," he whispered.

"Do you?" she asked boldly.

Ben's lips brushed against her neck as he pulled her closer. He was hard against her and wasn't trying to hide it. "No," he whispered, sending a gust of warm breath into her ear. "Nobody does."

Dylan moved her hips with him and tried to prepare herself for what she was sure was going to happen next. Was she ready? Of course she was! It was all she had ever thought about. Even in Ben's absence, she had dreamed of this moment.

His hands moved around her curves, exploring over what little clothing covered her. She thought of urging his hands on, pulling him into her. Could he really be so closely controlled that he could resist making love to her if she was to undress completely? She felt like she was at a fork in the road and whichever way he wanted to go, she would happily go that way as well.

Nevertheless, this was Ben she was dealing with, and he always kept her on her toes. When she realized that was as far as he was going to let things go, she relaxed into his arms and closed her eyes. His heart thumped through his chest and slammed against hers until it slowed to a soothing beat.

This was her comfort, sleeping in his grasp. She hadn't forgotten how much she loved his warmth and his skin against hers. The days were growing too long now, as she waited to be back in his hold. Sadly, it was all she looked forward to anymore.

She slept soundly and happily, waking up every once in a while to stare at Ben's perfect, angelic face. She pulled him closer and nuzzled deeper into his arms. This was her peace, her only perfection, an escape from reality. She would enjoy it until the sun came up and pulled him away.

CHAPTER FOUR

Ben walked through his mother's front door as quietly as possible. The sun was still buried in the horizon and he was sure Ruth would still be asleep. The pills she was taking these days wouldn't allow her to wake up before the sun rose, anyway. Ben wondered if she was even awake when she was vertical. She seemed to be in a fog most of the time and, odds were, in her hallucination of drugs and alcohol, she assumed he wasn't even there.

If he crept up the stairs quietly enough, hopefully she would believe he actually spent a night there. *I slept here the other night*, he would lie when she confronted him about not staying home. He walked into his room, pleased that he now had something to throw back at her when she nagged him to near death about being so neglectful.

He fell back against his bed and felt peace when he realized he could still smell Dylan's perfume. He couldn't remember her ever wearing any before, another sign of her maturity after all these years. Perfume or none at all, he was drawn to her naturally.

Ben rubbed his hands over his face and found himself wishing that he kissed her. She would probably have been angry at him for doing it when he'd had so much to drink. He wondered what her lips felt like; he could only imagine after all this time.

It had been harder for him to move from Dylan's bed that morning. She was so tangled up in him—almost holding him there—that he hated to pry himself away. But he knew he had to and she should know it as well. If Jonah or any of the others caught him there, if they knew what he thought about when she was next to him, in nothing but her underwear and a small top, they would kill him for sure.

The Mathews boys were his brothers, but Ben was on thin ice in this particular area. They knew him inside and out. They knew what a pig he was and how he treated all the women in his life, including his own mother. They would justify killing him because they would fear him hurting their sister. And that was exactly the point. He *would* hurt her; he destroyed everything in his path.

He couldn't watch her get closer to Michael Olerson. That was asking too much of him. He thought of himself as strong, but he wasn't *that* strong. There was never competition before. He never had to watch her hold hands with anyone, flirt with anyone, or, for God's sake, talk about constellations and tea with anyone!

His head spun with these thoughts and he quieted them when he realized he was getting nowhere. He thought about staying away from Dylan. Last night was close enough. If she had kissed him or done anything inviting, he couldn't have stopped himself as he had the last time. He knew this. If it weren't for his mother's guilt trips he would hop on the next plane to Massachusetts and never come back, just to avoid it all.

Ben tossed and sighed loudly into his pillow. He knew he just needed to sleep it off.

"Benjamin?" His mother's knock on the door woke him, but he said nothing back.

She opened the door and sighed loudly. "It smells like a bar in here."

Ben sat up and stared at her tired face. He looked around sarcastically. "It's a good thing I don't see one. I could use a shot."

She squinted at him. "Your father sent these." She held out a white piece of paper. The longer blue paper at the bottom was a dead giveaway. Ben knew what they were, but he stared at them and said nothing.

"Did you know?" she asked, and it sounded like she was talking through a lump in her throat. "Is this why you finally came home?"

"Mom, please. I didn't."

"Divorce papers? It's Christmas." She squeezed the papers, crumpling them between her fingers. "You didn't know?"

"How could I?" Ben sat on the edge of the bed. He held out his hand, and asked, "May I see them?"

She handed the papers to Ben. She leaned against his door and cried into her hands. She sobbed loudly and even let out a muffled scream. She tried to catch her breath dramatically. It was an Oscar winning performance.

Ben never could tell the difference between a genuine cry and an attention-seeking tantrum. It didn't matter, anyway; neither one made him feel sorry for her. Was this for his benefit? Was this so he would call his father and convince him to change his mind? Either way, how could she use him this way?

He scanned the papers. His father cited irreconcilable differences. *Coward*, Ben thought. He wished there was a box for "fell out of love," "never loved her," or, more appropriately, "selfish bastard." That would tell the truth.

"Mom," Ben began carefully, "don't you want this to be over?"

His mother caught her breath and stared. "Why now, though, Benjamin?" She shook her head in a fit of rage. "After all these years of separation, why now?"

"It's like you've been divorced all this time, anyway. You haven't even seen him, Mom." Ben wasn't sure why he even tried. She wouldn't see it this way. "This means closure."

"Closure?" Ruth's face flashed with anger. "Oh, I should have known you would agree with him. You're just like him!" she screamed.

Ben sat back and sighed. He allowed her to go off on him. He would play the villain. The real monster was somewhere else, off living his life with the new girlfriend who was probably half his age, while Ben sat and cleaned up his father's mess.

An hour later, Ben ran from his mother's. She took the pills that were supposed to calm her down, but they seemed to turn her into a zombie more than anything. He would gladly take that over her screaming, crying, and blaming. He would be her punching bag forever and he knew it. He was his father's son and she would remind him of that every day.

Ben sprinted through the foothills on the trails that ran behind his old neighborhood. He had no destination; he would go wherever his feet took him. He was used to the treadmill at his gym now and, as he ran, he found it quite sad how deprived he was of beauty back at school. He never enjoyed the outdoors, the fresh air, and scenery. His busy life consisted of school, the gym, the library, and his apartment, all indoor facilities.

He could feel his heart hammering, his pulse racing, and sweat forming. He couldn't remember the last time he ran like this. It was almost painful, but good. He ran off the anger, the frustration, and, most of all, the guilt.

* * *

Dylan opened her paint box and ran her fingers along the faded wood. She chose her colors carefully, scanning each jar, just hoping inspiration would flow through her. She loved this spot and all its privacy. It was peaceful, quiet and, most of all, away from her family.

She dabbed her brush into a deep red she had mixed the day before. She loved to play with colors, blending and combining until she found a shade of her own. Her mother's garage was filled with unused colors. She couldn't bring herself to ever throw away her past concoctions, because she figured she might need them one day.

She began her work with a short brushstroke and then a line, long and soft. Then another stroke and more lines; more color would come soon enough. Her trance began and she was thoughtfully brushing, curving and lining. She added a dab of midnight blue; she brushed, stroked, and blended. She moved the hair from her face, completely focused on her vision, her dream. Now black, now gray. She felt what she was creating. She *was* what she was creating.

She stretched her folded arms above her head and let her eyes close. The sun beamed down on her face, warming her lips and cheeks. It was the memory of her vision that she blended with a longing inside herself; allowing it to escape onto her canvas made it true somehow. Her vision was as real as it ever would be. She opened her eyes and added one last touch of black, completing her moment. She stepped back. Paint smeared her forehead, her cheeks, and even her hair. With her number two brush in her mouth, she sighed into the breeze and loved her newest creation.

Footsteps approached behind her. She could hear them, a heavy breath with each quick stride. She turned to stare at the trails that led to this place. She waited for the person to turn through the rocks, shrubs, and small cacti that blocked her view. As he appeared, he blurred with an array of colors that she recognized instantly.

"Ben?" Dylan called, as he raced by her. "What are you doing?"

Ben slowed until his feet froze in place and he bent forward to catch his breath. He almost seemed annoyed that she'd stopped him. He stood hunched over with his back moving up and down as he caught his breath.

"Are you okay?" Dylan asked, concerned.

"I'm fine," he lied. "What are you doing up here?"

"Painting." Dylan dropped her paintbrush by accident. She was acting like a bumbling fool.

He knew this was her favorite spot to paint and it frustrated her that he pretended he didn't. Of all the hills in Phoenix, this seemed to be the one that the tourists avoided. It was remote and peaceful. Ben knew this place as he knew her.

Ben pulled off his wet shirt. "That felt good," he said as he breathed heavily. He stretched his muscular arms above his head and looked out at the view.

Dylan's eyes widened and she looked anywhere that wasn't Ben. She hated how absurd she felt around him. Why couldn't she just act normal? Because now this man, who was too beautiful for words—the man she dreaded even looking at—was sweating and shirtless as he panted heavily in the sun. *Ugh.*

Ben looked around, stopping when he saw the painting she had just finished. "Who's that supposed to be?" he asked, still breathless.

Dylan glanced over at her newest piece and felt herself blush. She had never intended for him to see the painting of a night sky filled with stars stretching above a naked man and woman sitting intertwined, their lips almost touching.

"No-no one," she stammered. She gave herself a moment, closed her eyes, and drew in a long breath. She still looked bashful, but she smirked. "Why does it have to be anyone?"

"It doesn't." Ben let out a small chuckle as he looked away and raised his arms above his head again. His face relaxed in the sun and he sighed heavily.

"Help me carry this stuff back down to my car," Dylan demanded, still trying not to look at him. "It took me two trips to get it up here."

Ben groaned loudly and grabbed her bucket and easel. "Good thing I came up here for you."

"Don't be a jerk," she said.

They walked back down the long trail that led to the dusty car lot below. Dylan chewed on her lip, wondering if Ben was going to mention the things he said to her in bed the night before. She almost admired his ability to dismiss it the following day. He would never acknowledge it until they were back in the world where only they existed, when, *poof,* he was hers again. She only wished she had his talent.

He set her things down and stared at her with pain in his eyes. His mind was obviously racing, and he seemed overwhelmed by whatever was going on in there. He looked as if he could have blurted something out at any moment, releasing the words he couldn't decipher so maybe someone else could make sense of them for a change. He wouldn't dare, Dylan knew. He was a locked vault of emotion.

"Is it your mom?" Dylan asked against her better judgment. "Did something happen?"

"Dylan, don't act like we're friends." He closed his mouth too late to stop the words, and realized it with a long sigh. "It's nothing."

"We're not friends, Ben?" Her heart ached. Why did he want to hurt her all the time? She made it too easy for him. He knew she would always forgive him, she would always come back for more, and she would most definitely accept him without an apology.

Ben's face hardened. "No."

"Then what are we?" She felt the stinging in her eyes and silently scolded herself for allowing her eyes to even water in front of him.

Ben stared at her and exhaled loudly. He seemed to think hard about what he wanted to say. It was almost as if he were arguing with himself about whether to speak, a battle his big mouth would win, no doubt. "You're my best friend's sister, Weed. That's it."

"And at night?" She wasn't sure why she pushed for these cold answers. She knew nothing nice would come from him. "In my bed?"

Ben shook his head and shrugged carelessly.

Dylan wanted to punch him, but she decided he would probably enjoy that more, like foreplay. She headed for her car, leaving Ben and all her belongings, including her painting, at the bottom of the trail.

Michael Olerson couldn't have pulled up at a better time. Dylan watched him look from her to Ben until he stopped the engine and got out. He looked uneasy until he got close enough to see from their expressions that he was hardly interrupting a happy moment.

Dylan heard Ben swear behind her and that pleased her very much. She wasn't proud of what she was about to do, but she wanted Ben to suffer at any cost.

"Hey," Michael said, handing her a bouquet of flowers. "I, uh, was just driving around and saw your car."

"With a bouquet of flowers?" Ben called from behind them. "Convenient."

Michael ignored Ben, something he did well. He smiled at Dylan and asked, "How would you like to go out to dinner with me tonight?"

"I have to work tonight, remember?" Dylan pursed her lips.

"I know your boss, remember?" Michael said with an adorable smile. Dylan couldn't tell whether she only thought it was adorable because she was angry with Ben. It didn't matter. The point was, in that moment, she thought it was adorable.

Dylan turned and stared at Ben. He was still watching, not smiling, and it even looked as though he was shaking his head. She knew he would never bring her flowers. She was positive he would never ask her on a date.

She looked back at Michael. "Like a date?"

Michael blushed and looked down. "Yeah, like a date."

Dylan thought long, but not too long. It pleased her to know that Ben was witness to this. "I'd love to," she answered, her voice unexpectedly girlish.

She heard Ben swear again and then, out of the corner of her eye, she watched him storm back up the trail. He was going to have a temper tantrum, but she couldn't bring herself to care.

Michael glanced at Ben's back as he disappeared and shook his head. "Asshole," he said with a smirk. He looked back at Dylan. "I'll pick you up around six?"

Dylan nodded, knowing she was a terrible person. "Perfect."

* * *

The phone only rang twice, which didn't give Ben time to rethink his decision to make the call. When his father answered, Ben's heart sank. He never stood up to this man. He never voiced his opinions and he would be damned if he was going to share his feelings with anyone.

"Benjamin?" Warren McKenna answered, sounding angry. He never tried to conceal the fact that Ben was the last person he felt the need to speak to.

"Dad, hello." Ben could feel the lump in his throat rising.

"What is it, son?" Warren was an impatient man. He hadn't spoken to his son in weeks, but he still managed to make it sound like it had only been five minutes, as if Ben called him too much. The truth was that Ben was never the one to initiate any phone contact with his father. He would happily accept a life of emails.

Ben found his bravery; it was easy when he was angry. "I thought you were going to wait until after the holidays to send the papers, Dad."

Warren paused. "Well, I decided against it. I thought it would be better if you were there with your mother."

"You could have warned me."

"Son, I'm skiing with Jackie and her children. I didn't have time to call."

Ben sank to his bed. He could have done without that information. His father would take Jackie's children skiing; he would avoid important phone calls for Jackie's children. But when it came to his own son, he would dismiss him like garbage.

"Take care of your mother, son." Warren waited for a few moments. When Ben didn't respond, he hung up.

After Ben realized the line was dead, he threw his cell phone at the wall, shattering it. Warren was the source of most of Ben's outbursts.

From the moment Ben was old enough to remember, it had been drilled into his head that feelings were a weakness that truly strong, successful men should do without. It was weak to love, to cry, and to show compassion. A good defense attorney did not have empathy for anyone. A good judge only saw black and white. According to Warren, Ben would live in this empty, colorless world if he wanted to succeed. And only then would his father be proud.

And Ben's latest encounter with Dylan was just about enough to put him over the edge. *That damn painting.* He didn't need to say it; he knew exactly who it was in the painting. He wouldn't admit that it turned him on, either. For some reason, even the smears of paint on her face turned him on more than he could handle; he didn't need her imagination coming to life. Knowing that's how she imagined them together was enough to drive him crazy with lust.

He didn't mean to say those things to her, and it nearly killed him to walk away from her again. He was getting tired of being the reason for the sadness in her eyes. He knew that if he had stayed it would have been worse for them both. He contemplated a redeye flight home just so that she could be happy again.

Ben looked down at the remnants of his phone. He needed Jonah: someone who would never ask a question, knowing he wouldn't get a response. He needed to get ridiculously drunk.

CHAPTER FIVE

Dylan regretted wearing the skirt she had on. She felt as though she had given Michael the wrong idea again. Only, this time it was her fault and she knew it. She sat as close to the car door as possible, praying the dinner would go by quickly so she could get back to her bed and foolishly wait for Ben to come to her room in a fit of jealousy. Hopefully, this would make him see how capable she was of replacing him. But, of course, she could never truly replace him.

"I'm happy you said yes, Dylan." Michael smiled as he drove. He glanced over at her a few times, only looking at her eyes, never her legs, as Ben did on a regular basis.

"Me too," she agreed, calling herself a liar in her head.

They pulled into the parking lot of the restaurant. Michael shut off the engine and turned halfway toward her. He looked at her for a few moments.

"You look really pretty," he said sweetly. "Are you ready?"

Dylan nodded and opened the door. She felt relief when she realized he wasn't going to kiss her right away, as she had suspected. Still, she knew that moment was coming, and she was not thrilled about it. In fact, she feared it immensely.

Michael held her hand as they walked to the restaurant, and opened the door for her. She felt as though he was putting her on display, acting like they were a couple. She wondered why she was so offended by this and wished she could find some way to enjoy herself.

They ordered their food and sat in silence. The candle glowing in front of them added unwanted romance for Dylan. She seriously thought about blowing it out, but decided against it at the last minute.

"Are you excited for Charlie's wedding?" Michael asked.

"Yeah," Dylan nodded. "I still don't know who I'm walking with."

"Probably me," Michael answered. "You know he asked me to stand up, right?"

"Yep." Of course Dylan knew this. She had already begged Meredith not to pair them up, secretly hoping that would leave Ben as her only choice, since she refused to be paired with any of her brothers.

"Who does he have standing, anyway?" Michael asked, looking deep in thought. "There's Brandon, Hugh, and Jonah. Who else?"

Dylan sipped from her glass. "Ben," she said softly. "And you."

"Ben." Michael rolled his eyes. "I didn't think he was going to accept."

Dylan laughed. "Well, he actually hasn't said yes or no to Charlie quite yet."

"He's such an ass," Michael said, shaking his head. "Why does your family put up with him?"

Dylan felt protective, despite Ben's undeserving behavior. "Because he's part of our family, Michael; he's one of us."

Michael smirked. "Right."

"What does that mean?"

"I don't want to argue about this, Dylan." He smiled and grabbed her hand. "I'm sorry I brought it up."

Dylan pulled her hand back and looked into the soft glow of the candle between them. She wanted to go home.

*   *   *

Ben, Jonah, and Hugh stepped into State's bar, the third stop on their evening pub-crawl. Jonah was well aware of Ben's rage and knew it was only getting worse as they kept drinking. He had no clue why Ben was so angry; Ben would never give details. One thing was for sure, though: this was going to be an unpredictable evening.

When Ben wasn't within earshot, Hugh turned to Jonah and whispered, "Man, he's on edge tonight. I bet you twenty bucks we get into a fight because of him."

"No deal," Jonah replied quickly. That would be a losing bet. Ben was ready to slam his fist into something, and he would soon enough find a reason to accomplish this. He kept his destructive personality in check most of the time. None of his professors or acquaintances from school would ever guess he had such a fondness for fighting. But he had quite the temper.

The few that knew him well often wondered if Ben sometimes enjoyed a good punch in the face. Too many times to count they had witnessed him take the first hit. He would almost smile before spitting blood on the ground and returning the punch. It was like taking the first hit was his polite way of fighting. If someone didn't know him, they'd think he was crazy. Maybe he was.

Ben ordered shots and looked around anxiously. He told himself to loosen up and enjoy his rare night out with Jonah and Hugh. He wanted nothing more than to calm down, but he was well aware that all alcohol ever did was enrage him more. He tried to push thoughts of Dylan out of his head, but it only seemed to irritate him, reminding him she was on a *date*.

"Where's Dylan at tonight?" Hugh asked, as the three of them sat down. "She wasn't at Ollie's."

Jonah answered, "She's probably off painting on a mountain."

Ben felt his lip curl. "She's on a date with Olerson," he grumbled, before taking his shot.

Jonah and Hugh both shot Ben a surprised look. "What?" they asked in unison.

Ben nodded, staring forward, half-ashamed at the blatant display of jealousy that he prayed they didn't pick up on. "He stalked her favorite painting spot today and asked her."

"Holy shit," Hugh said with a chuckle. "That's great."

"Weed with a boyfriend," Jonah said in disbelief. "Pretty cool."

"One date does not make him her boyfriend," Ben barked. "It's just dinner. She could do a lot better than him and I'm sure she has."

Hugh and Jonah both erupted into laughter.

"What's so damn funny?" Ben asked.

"Weed? Someone before Olerson?" Jonah laughed again. "Man, she's never even been on a date before."

Ben sat up, half curious and half elated at the possibility of his Dylan being completely untouched. "Never?"

Hugh shook his head. "She's never shown any interest in any guy. Ever. Trust me, many have tried, too."

"Why?" Ben asked.

"I don't know." Jonah shrugged. "She's just always been so independent. She's never even talked about guys. Honestly, I don't think she wants the hassle of Brandon and Charlie's wrath, for one thing, and for another, I think she's too picky."

"That's true," Ben nodded, and sipped his beer. "Brandon and Charlie would be all over that if they didn't know the guy."

"But this Ollie thing is pretty cool. Charlie will like that," Hugh said. "She needs a good guy."

Ben looked away and hid his disgust. Michael may have been a good guy, but he wasn't good enough for someone as perfect as Dylan. He imagined his hands on her and nearly became sick with jealousy.

He turned his attention to the other end of the bar and realized there were four girls with his name on them. *A perfect distraction*, he thought.

He ordered a tray full of shots, the lemony, girly kind that was sure to make these prissy girls' faces sour up.

"Ladies," he said, handing each of them a glass. "How are we tonight?"

"Great," said the only blonde of the group. "We're just great."

Jonah introduced them all and waited for the girls to respond with their names. The girls all eyed one another, snickering as if they knew something the guys didn't.

"You don't remember me, Hugh?" a brunette finally asked. "You seriously have no clue who I am?"

Ben laughed. "Only you buddy," he said, placing his hand on Hugh's shoulder.

"Oh, like you can talk, ass," Hugh snapped at Ben, grinning. He turned his head and flashed his white teeth back at the ladies, clearly wishing he had more time to think. "Sure I do," he lied.

"What's my name?" she asked, smiling coyly. "Can you at least tell me when we met?"

"It's on the tip of my tongue," Hugh said, chuckling nervously. "I swear I recognize you."

"I'll give you a hint," she said, flashing a seductive smile. "It was about a year ago and there was a pool involved. There may have been a blindfold. I'm not sure, though. You were a bit drunk and I was a bit naked."

Hugh's eyes lit up and he grinned, reminiscing. He pointed to her and laughed, covering his mouth with his other hand. "Whoa!" he practically shouted. "My midnight pool girl! Didn't you get arrested?"

"Almost," she answered with a giggle. "Thanks for bailing on me like that, by the way."

The girls did their shots and laughed. They whispered into each other's ears, making Ben want to gag. He wondered which one he could see himself taking home, but he wasn't interested in any of them; they weren't Dylan.

"Guys?" a voice called from behind them. "*We're* with them."

The three of them turned and stood face to face with four guys who looked ready to pounce. They weren't small men, either. They reminded Ben of four Michael Olersons; they were football-playing meatheads who needed to be taught a lesson.

Ben's smile widened and Hugh and Jonah didn't have to wonder what was coming next. They braced themselves and watched as the menacing flicker in Ben's eye grew brighter. A door had been opened and Ben was ready to fight with pleasure.

"Not *now*, you're not," Ben answered with a smirk.

"Listen, dude, we don't want any trouble from you. Just walk away and we'll all have a good night," the largest of the group warned.

"See, that's funny to me. When four guys walk up to me and stand the way you assholes are standing, all tough and shit, that makes me think trouble is exactly what you're looking for." Ben flashed a grin that wasn't meant to be friendly.

"We just wanted to let you know that these ladies aren't alone. That's all, dude," said the smallest one, who wasn't very small, as luck would have it.

Ben took a long sip from his beer and then slammed his shot. "Hey, you know what? You can have the sloppy seconds. I'm pretty sure we're done with them anyway."

"How the hell are they your sloppy seconds?" another one asked, fists at his sides. "You just met them, dude."

Ben hated being called *dude*. He especially hated the kind of guy that would use that word as many times as they had in the last five minutes. Ben, wanting more than anything to have a good ol' bar fight, couldn't back down now.

Ben, Jonah, and Hugh exchanged looks that said *Are we really going to do this?* But they already knew the answer.

"Really?" Ben said. "Let me explain how this works. Clearly you don't know, so I'll help you out a bit. Your girl here was just telling my friend here about how she remembered a night not too long ago when he gave her the best fuck of her life. That makes her sloppy seconds and you a piece of shit in bed," he shrugged and added, "dude."

Before Ben could say another word, a fist was barreling into his face. This would begin the bar brawl that he so desperately wanted in order to take his mind off Dylan and her date.

*   *   *

Dylan and Michael walked through downtown Phoenix and admired the Christmas lights that decorated the city. Dylan didn't want to take this evening stroll, but guilt refused to stop punishing her for using Michael to get Ben's attention.

Every so often, Michael's hand would skim hers and she would pull it away, preventing him from any more hand-holding.

"Did you enjoy dinner?" he asked quietly. "You barely ate."

Dylan held up her tinfoil swan full of leftovers. "I'm sorry. I wasn't as hungry as I thought. I would say I'll eat it later, but with my brothers all home, nothing stays in the fridge for long."

Michael laughed. "I don't know how you do it, Dylan."

"Do what?" Dylan never understood why people felt sorry for her for having four brothers. They would do anything for her. As long as she had been alive, they'd been wrapped around her finger.

"They sure do hover, don't they?" Michael stopped. "All I ever remember is them swarming around you."

Dylan shook her head. "No, they didn't. I just followed them around everywhere."

Michael stopped in his tracks. He turned to face her and grabbed her hand, which Dylan hadn't expected in the middle of a conversation about her brothers.

"Dylan," he began. "I'm really into you and I just need to know if I have a chance."

Dylan sighed and tried not to feel guilty.

"I get mixed signals from you, though, so what is it?"

"Michael, I think you're great," she whispered. "I'm just having a really hard time making decisions like this. I've never dated anyone before."

Michael smiled. He seemed to think that was a good response. "We'll go as slow as you like," he promised. "No pressure."

Dylan nodded, not at all satisfied with her cowardly answer. She wanted to say, *I think Ben is interested in me, so I'm using you while I wait for him to make up his mind.*

The drive home was quiet, but Michael seemed more relaxed. Dylan knew that he was under the impression that she would eventually come around. She liked that he had granted her a slow courtship, buying her a bit more time to figure things out with Ben.

They pulled into the Mathews' driveway and Michael parked his car.

Dylan put her hand on the door, ready to bolt into her dark house. She turned her head just in time for Michael's lips to meet hers. She froze in shock when his tongue slid into her mouth.

Michael seemed oblivious to her alarm, despite the fact that she didn't participate as eagerly as he did in the kiss. She sat, dumfounded, and quite possibly appalled if she could think clearly enough to be so.

"Goodnight," he said, smiling. "I'll see you tomorrow at work."

It wasn't her first kiss, but it weirded her out as if it were. Her first kiss had been with Carter Miller in high school, during a game of spin the bottle at Lucy Reynolds' house. Her second, and last, kiss had been with some guy she would never see again. He was cute and she was drunk. It had seemed like a good idea as they danced at a club, but terrible when she remembered it the following morning.

Dylan nodded. "Night," she said, and ran to her front door.

She climbed the dark stairs and wondered if Ben would be gracing her with his presence, but froze when she opened her door and saw her bed. Ben lay flat on his back on her bed, fully clothed, battered and passed out cold on top of her comforter.

Dylan sighed as she made her way to him, sitting just on the edge of the mattress and staring down at his bashed-in face. "Oh, Ben," she whispered.

She left to get a wet washcloth from her bathroom and returned to his side. She ran the cloth along the gash above his eye and then down to his fat lip. She frowned at the thought of his beautiful lips being damaged. She lifted his right hand and cleaned up his cut knuckles, mentally cheering him on for giving a few punches in return. She kissed the open gashes and placed his hands back down on his chest.

Ben's heavy, bloodshot eyes opened slightly and he tried to look up at her. "I hate how much I love you," he slurred.

"Me too," she whispered with a smile. Her heart nearly exploded, but she couldn't allow herself to get too worked up over that lovely admission. This was Mr. Unpredictable himself in her bed. If she were to release even the tiniest of happy tears, there was a good possibility that Ben would be scared sober and flee from her room forever.

Dylan got ready for bed, brushing her teeth and getting undressed. She turned off her light and slid under her sheets next to a very drunk Ben. She rested her head on his chest and enjoyed the slow rise and fall his breathing created beneath her cheek.

She allowed herself to unbutton his shirt so her hands could rest on his warm skin. She smiled as she pressed her body to him and felt the control that she always allowed him to have.

This was her vulnerable Ben, her open-book Ben. In this state, he would tell her anything, without any recollection of having done so tomorrow. One drunken admission was enough for her tonight, though. It wasn't the words she cherished the most, but the feeling of him in her bed.

"I love only you," she whispered, knowing he couldn't hear. She closed her eyes and happily drifted off to sleep.

CHAPTER SIX

Ben watched Dylan's eyelids flutter. She was waking up, but he wanted to let her do it in her own peaceful way. So many times he had watched her sleep, her eyes rolling under her lids, her pink lips puckering every now and then. It was beautiful.

He noticed the wet cloth that hung over the bedpost and realized, despite his blurry memory, that she had used it to clean him up. His hands and jaw throbbed, but he knew it could have been a lot worse had Jonah and Hugh not been there.

"The sun is up," Dylan whispered.

Ben laughed. "Yes."

"You're still here?" Dylan asked with wide eyes.

"Yes."

"How are you going to leave?" She seemed worried, which Ben found adorable.

Ben sighed as he flipped onto his back and pulled her down to his chest. He stroked her hair and teased, "I suppose I'll just have to surrender."

"You got beat up last night?"

"No," he answered quickly. "Jonah and Hugh helped me out."

"I'm sure they did," Dylan joked. "Camaraderie rule?"

"The very one."

Ben tightened his arms around Dylan. He caught himself contemplating kissing the top of her head, but his brain screamed until he decided against it. He smelled her hair and felt the sensations run through his entire body, consuming his heart as well, causing it to thump relentlessly in his chest, loud enough that she was sure to hear.

"Do you remember coming in here last night?" Dylan asked. "Do you remember me finding you?"

"I don't even remember how we got here last night. Matter of fact, I don't even know if your brothers came here with me." Ben chuckled. "I remember someone's fist going into my face."

"Oh," Dylan answered, disappointed.

"How was your date?" Ben asked with a sneer.

"Awful," Dylan groaned. "He kissed me."

Ben wanted to vomit. "Don't tell me that."

"Why?"

"You know why," was all he could say. Asking him to elaborate would only be for her own satisfaction.

"Maybe I need to hear it," she confessed quietly.

"You don't." Ben stretched his arms out over his head. "Why the hell would you go out with him, anyway? You're just asking for him to get the wrong idea. And for what? That isn't you, Dylan."

"You don't know anything about me, Ben. How would you know what kind of behavior is me and what isn't?"

Ben smirked at her. He was ready for this dare. "I don't know you?" he asked.

"Nope," she said simply, with a smile of her own.

"Hah. Okay," he began, preparing to blow her away. "You love pink but won't admit it because you're afraid it will make you sound too girly. You're afraid of moths because you think they'll eat your hair, and you hate chalk. I stopped skateboarding because you were better and I was embarrassed. You even throw a football better than I do. You secretly love *Harry Potter* movies, and when you were ten you fell off your bike and I carried you home. When your dad died, you only wanted me and you cried in my lap."

Dylan's mouth fell open, but she closed it immediately with a small, startled gasp. "I don't *love* pink," she mumbled with a red face.

"Yeah you do. Should I keep going?" Ben asked confidently.

Stunned, Dylan could only slowly shake her head.

Ben smiled, proud of himself, and pressed his back against the pillow. "I know you better than anyone, Dylan. I don't have to live here to prove that."

Dylan stared at him in utter confusion. She seemed to be deep in thought as she blinked heavily.

"I gotta get out of here," Ben announced through a yawn.

Dylan sighed loudly, shaking off the verbal whiplash he had just given her.

"What is it?" he forced himself to ask.

"I hate when we're not in this room," she admitted. "It all becomes different."

Ben said nothing. She was right. He sat up, sliding her from his chest. He turned and looked down at her as she looked up at him. He stared for a few moments, wondering if he could ever really be with her. Even now, with her messy hair going every which way and her eyes full of sleep, he thought she was perfect. It was hard for him to dismiss her with so much of her exposed. If she welcomed any kind of physical contact, if she made that kind of move, she would surely see his weak side.

"What are you thinking about?" she asked quietly.

"Nothing," he said, shaking his head and pretending to be annoyed. He was really in a state of anxious panic to get away from her half-dressed body. "Please just go see if anyone's out there," he practically pleaded, motioning toward the door.

Dylan stood, all but growling. She stared at Ben as she pulled up her oversized pajama bottoms, covering her gray and pink striped underwear. She pulled on a sweatshirt and yanked the hood over her long hair.

Ben watched in amusement as Dylan childishly stomped to her door and opened it just a crack. She looked around as much as she could and gently closed the door.

"You're good," she announced, and walked back over to the bed. She crawled under the covers again and lay against her pillow behind him.

Ben turned and looked down at her again. He let himself push back a piece of her hair that had fallen over her cheek. "Thank you for taking care of me last night."

Dylan sat up quickly. "Ben?"

Ben sighed. "Yes?" he answered, genuinely annoyed this time.

"I'm ready whenever you are, just so you know."

Ben nodded. "Okay," he answered, not wanting her to elaborate.

"I mean it. Even if we never see each other again."

Ben's stomach sank with fear. "You're serious?" he asked, trying to find the line between what she said and what he thought. There had to be an in-between.

"Yes. Very," she confirmed. "I want you to be my first."

Scared, but unable to admit it, Ben got to his feet and headed for the door. He stopped with his hand on the knob and his eyes down. "This is a terrible idea, Dylan."

"I know."

Ben opened the door and snuck out of her room without another word.

* * *

Dylan wiped down the already-clean bar in order to avoid Michael's gaze. She hoped he didn't think of last night's kiss as a step forward in their relationship—although she was sure he did.

She found herself wishing the day would go by quickly. Maybe she could sleep the day away and stay awake all night to savor every minute that Ben spent in her bed. She thought of ways to seduce him into kissing her. What could she wear that would really get him going? She'd noticed that the night before, when she touched the nape of his neck, he seemed to shiver. Maybe she would try that again. Oh, she really was losing her mind, but she didn't care.

"Last night was fun." Michael finally spoke those inevitable words. "We'll have to do that again."

Dylan froze mid-wipe with her bar towel in hand. She sighed and closed her eyes when she felt the feeling of guilt turn to nausea. She fidgeted and took a deep breath.

"You do want to, right?" Michael asked softly.

Dylan turned and leaned against the bar. "Michael—"

"Ben?" he asked with a defeated look on his face. "I should have known."

"It's not just Ben." She paused, wondering how much she could say without him going straight to Charlie—or, God forbid, Brandon. "It's a lot of things, Michael."

"Like what?"

"Well," she stammered. "You're my boss, for one."

"I don't have to be. We both know you don't work here for the money." Michael leaned against the bar like they were going to argue about this. "You make enough at the school."

Dylan laughed. "I don't work here for fun, Michael."

"Okay, but you have to know, I wouldn't fire you if it didn't work out."

Dylan sighed and looked down to the floor. "Please don't," she whispered.

"He'll hurt you, Dylan," he warned.

Frustrated, Dylan snapped her head up to glare at him. "I didn't say this was about Ben. You're the one who's assuming it is."

"Well, you haven't corrected me."

"Do I need to?"

"I wish you would."

"I can't," she answered shamefully.

Dylan looked up and met Michael's sad eyes. He looked as if she had kicked him in the gut and ripped his heart out of his chest. It was the first heart that Dylan had ever broken and, suddenly, she was very aware of the horrible responsibility that went along with it.

They seemed to have a staring contest for minutes. Dylan half wondered if she would give dating him a try just so he wouldn't look at her like that anymore. It was killing her to have to know that she was the reason his eyes looked that way.

The door to Ollie's opened, and Dylan felt a rush of relief. As Michael escaped to the kitchen, she hoped that the bar would be abnormally slammed with customers just so she could think of something besides her ridiculous love life. Unfortunately, the Monday crowd was good, but not that good.

"What do you say, little sister," Hugh called from the end of the bar. "Grab me a beer."

"Nice shiner." Dylan flipped off the cap for emphasis and set the beer down in front of her brother.

Hugh grinned. "I hit him back."

"Are you alone?"

"Nope," he warned with a smile. "They're *all* coming up."

"Everyone?"

"Yep." Hugh leaned forward, and whispered, "Did Olerson make his move last night?"

"Gross." She despised even the thought of this conversation taking place. "Don't ask me that!"

"I just meant if he kissed you?" Hugh corrected with a cringe. "Now you're making me feel weird."

"I don't like him like that. I wish you all would stop forcing it on me."

"Are you a lesbian?" Hugh asked. "I mean, seriously?"

Dylan stared at him for a few seconds. She chewed on the inside of her cheek, contemplating whether to bash him over the head with his bottle or just chuck the jar of bar cherries at his face. She had always been a tomboy, but what choice did she have with four brothers?

"I'm not even going to dignify that with an answer," she said.

"Well." Hugh laughed, before taking a swig of his beer.

The rest of her brothers and Ben walked through the door loudly. It wasn't as if they wanted everyone to notice them, they were just loud by nature and made no attempt to be otherwise.

One by one they each took a stool in front of her. Dylan, knowing what they all wanted, slid beers to them in the order that they sat.

"She's not a lesbian, guys. Don't ask her if she is," Hugh joked. "I did and now I'm a dead man."

"What?" Jonah asked, confused. "Why would you ask her that?"

"Because she turned down Olerson," Hugh answered quietly. "All the girls like Olerson. He's *Ollie*."

Ben sat up and met Dylan's eyes. Dylan stared back and waited for Ben to smile, make a sarcastic comment, wink ... *something!* He did nothing but stare.

"Maybe she's already dating someone we don't know about," Charlie suggested.

"Yeah, maybe she's dating someone from her class," Jonah offered.

"An artist?" Brandon nearly choked. "No way."

"I'm not dating—ugh. Stop it!" Dylan wasn't sure if she was more mortified by her brothers talking about this like she wasn't there, or the fact that Ben was there to hear it all.

Michael stepped out from the kitchen. "Mathews," he addressed everyone but Ben with one word. "How's it going?"

Dylan could see the lingering pain of rejection in his eyes. She knew that her brothers would see something was off. They were all so filled with testosterone, though; there was no way they would peg it as a broken heart.

Dylan stood just in front of Ben. She smirked at him and thought that maybe she should just name that particular smile after him, the only person she ever gave it to. She reached over and pulled the empty bottle from his grasp. Ben's remarkably soft eyes connected with hers. He let her slide the bottle from his battered fingers. His hand looked as if it had gone to war.

"Would you like another one?" she asked, intrigued by his silence.

Ben nodded and looked down the row of oblivious Mathews men who were chatting away with Michael. He looked back at Dylan and smiled. It was a peaceful expression, one she'd never seen on him.

Dylan set his full beer in front of him and smiled back.

Ben couldn't believe how beautiful Dylan looked as she gazed at him from behind the bar. Her hair was pulled back messily. A few tendrils had fallen down and hung around her face. Her jeans were ripped stylishly and her shirt was tight and white with a wet spot on the bottom. She had to know how hard he struggled when he was next to her.

"Will we see you tomorrow night?" Dylan asked.

"Christmas Eve?" Ben shook his head. "I doubt it. I promised Ruth I'd stay with her."

Dylan looked disappointed. Ben could tell she was trying to hide it, but he could see her deep, unintentional sigh, nonetheless.

Ben chuckled. "You know I'll be over for the lights. I just have to wait for her to pass out from her pills."

The light show was a tradition that the Mathews had been putting on for years. It all started with Carl and his love of Christmas lights, but had transitioned into a much-anticipated event that included fireworks for the entire neighborhood to enjoy. When Carl passed away, Brandon took over the job, naming it "The Annual Christmas Carl Show" in honor of his dad.

"You haven't been to one since our senior year in high school."

"Anything new in it?"

Dylan laughed. "No."

"I still miss it," he said with a frown. "It was always a good time."

Dylan smiled. "The last year you were here was the best."

Ben remembered but didn't comment on it. He drank his beer and nodded, hiding his grin.

It had been his favorite year, too. He remembered all too well when he and Dylan lay side by side and looked up into the sky as the fireworks shot above them in red, green, and gold. They had been hidden from the rest of the world, even Jonah. Ben wasn't sure what had made him crawl over and lie flat on his back beside her. It was probably one of his rare weak moments of giving in to his desire to be near her.

He remembered turning his head and secretly admiring her face as it lit up from the Christmas colors in the sky above them. She had been smiling giddily, probably feeling her dad's memory all around her, as they all had on that night. Ben could even recall what she was wearing: baggy jeans and a small, gray, Michigan State T-shirt from her father's alma mater.

As they watched the sky, Dylan had taken his hand and held onto it tightly. Ben remembered being taken aback, but refusing to let go. They'd held hands until the show ended and Jonah called out Ben's name. He'd sat up and run from her, only to end up making out with Chrissy Turner an hour later to try and get Dylan out of his mind.

Caught up in his reminiscing, Ben looked up at Dylan and spoke quietly, unable to control what he was saying. "Do you have to close tonight?"

Dylan shook her head. "Not if I don't want to."

"Come over." He felt brave and defiant as he put himself out there and waited for her to reject him, destroy him with one single "no."

Dylan stared at him, her eyes wide. "To your house?"

Ben nodded, despite his conscience screaming for him to stop.

Dylan glanced at her brothers to make sure they weren't listening. She looked back at Ben and smiled, intrigued. "Why do you want me to come over?"

Ben grinned. "I want to be alone without any distractions." He jerked his head at the Mathews boys. "Why else?"

"Please don't freak out when I get there, Ben."

Ben shook his head. "I promise."

"No games, Ben. I mean it."

He chewed on his lip and waited for her to laugh. When she didn't, he realized she truly was frightened he would run. "How can I convince you?" he asked sweetly.

"You can't," she admitted. "Just know that if you run tonight, or flake out in the least, I'll never speak to you again."

"You could never keep that promise," he joked. When he realized she still wasn't laughing, he tried to sound a bit more convincing. "I won't flake out," he promised again.

"And your mom?"

"Pill popping on a regular basis now; I'm not even sure that she knows I'm still in town."

Dylan laughed and covered her mouth. "I'm sorry. It's not funny."

Ben's heart ached at her laugh. Even as a child he had loved it. He remembered it being soothing music to his ears that always warmed him up.

"Then you'll come?"

Dylan nodded slowly. "Okay."

Ben threw a ten-dollar bill onto the bar. "I'm outta here," he announced. He knew this would cause questions, but he was ready with answers.

"Where the hell are you going?" Charlie asked, stunned. "We just got here."

"I have to go see my mom. I promised her I would come home early."

"Since when do you care about that?" Jonah asked, also appearing quite taken aback. "You always promise her."

Ben shook his head and laughed. "I'll see you guys tomorrow." He turned and walked out the door.

* * *

Ben's hands shook as he cleaned up his room. He pulled out the movies he thought Dylan would like to watch. He even made his bed, but then messed it up again, thinking that would be too obvious.

He changed his mind over and over again. He checked to make sure the condoms were still in his bedside drawer and he loathed himself until he remembered that he was waiting for Dylan. His beautiful *Dylan*. She was relying on him to make this moment mean something. He had to make it right—to make it *count*.

And, with that understanding, his uneasiness drifted away.

He would make it perfect for her.

He thought about Dylan and the way she looked in the morning. He smiled when he realized he could sleep with her comfortably now. He could wake up with her in his arms and not worry about his friends, her brothers, lurking outside the door. He could laugh with her all morning and even make her breakfast. Why hadn't they done this before? His house would have been so much easier.

Ben realized that he was smiling like a child waiting for his presents on Christmas. He found it to be a fantastic coincidence that this happened to be the holiday season. Dylan would be his present, beautifully wrapped in whatever she chose to put on.

* * *

Dylan's heart slammed against her chest. She could have thrown up at least ten times as she got ready for Ben. She showered, shaved, and washed her hair so it wouldn't smell like beer. She thought of what to wear and decided against a dress. It was midnight. Yoga pants and a tank top were appropriate for this. She was sure Ben would be in pajama bottoms as well. She giggled when she thought of it as a sleepover.

She drove to Ben's, knowing that it wouldn't be ideal to go without her car. Her brothers were not the brightest men in the world, but they would know exactly where she had been if she happened to stroll through the yards in the morning.

She pulled into Ben's driveway and smiled when she saw that he had left the garage door open, a sign to hide her car there.

She climbed the stairs and felt odd that his house was always so ... cold. She had been there as a child, but not nearly as much as one would suspect. She knew the familiar scent of his house and she knew where every room was. But this was Ben's mother's home and he had never liked to be here, even as a child.

Dylan paused at his bedroom door. She tried to slow her racing heart before she walked in. She thought about what he might be doing on the other side. Had he changed his mind? Oh, please don't do this to me, she silently pleaded. Not now, of all times. Not for my *first* time. Be perfect.

"Ben?" she asked, opening the door.

He stood in the middle of his room, wearing black and gray pajama bottoms, like she had suspected, and a pleasant smile on his face. His arrogant expression was surprisingly absent as well.

"Hello," he said, walking to take her bag from her hands.

Dylan smiled. She felt the awkwardness disappear with his greeting. Her fear of rejection had dissipated along with the protective wall that usually surrounded him. This was the Ben that only she knew existed, and she was happy for his rare appearance.

"How did you get out of work?" he asked, pulling her onto the bed to sit with him.

Small talk was good, she thought.

"I just said I couldn't stay." Dylan smiled. "Don't worry, my brothers are still there."

"I don't know your brothers tonight," Ben teased.

"Right."

"Do you want to watch a movie?" he asked.

Dylan looked at Ben and smiled. She slowly shook her head. No answer had ever been more obvious.

Ben nodded shyly. "Right."

Dylan stared at him and silently willed him to move toward her. She needed his control tonight, if only because she was clueless on how to begin.

"Did Olerson give you any problems about leaving?"

"No. I think he was actually happy to see me leave for once." Dylan didn't laugh this time. She felt so much guilt when she pictured Michael.

"He did look a bit grim when I saw him." Ben smiled. "You must have told him not to kiss you again."

"Pretty much."

"Good. Did he ask why?"

"He knew why," Dylan answered. She searched for any reaction in his expression. She looked at his mouth and waited for his usual arrogance to emerge, but it didn't come.

"Tell me." He smiled at her, his lips twitching as he attempted to hide his smirk. He would tease her about this in his own playful way; he just couldn't help himself.

Dylan decided against being bold, despite his luring expression. "Why do you think?"

Ben leaned forward slowly. He drew her hand into his and held it as he pulled her closer. He kissed her cheek and set his hand on her thigh. He moved his mouth to her ear, sending so many sensations shooting through her that it was hard to keep up with them all.

He gently placed his lips against her neck, and urged, "Tell me why, Dylan."

She paused; the feeling of his breath against her neck was more than she could stand. She wanted him to put his hands all over her and she was anxious now, knowing that he wanted the same and wasn't hiding it.

She refused to close her eyes.

"Because," she began. She felt his tender hands sliding up her back, beneath her shirt, as she whispered, "I only want to kiss you."

In a moment that sent her head spinning with surprise, Ben swiftly wrapped her legs around his waist and settled her in his lap. He ran his hands through her hair and adjusted her head so that she was looking straight into his eyes. His thumb caressed the back of her neck as his breathing intensified to match her own. "What do you want me to do, Dylan?" he asked quietly.

"Kiss me," she whispered between breaths. She was overjoyed at the thought that his lips would finally be on hers. She wasn't sure which part she was most excited about. Of all the times she'd fantasized about this kiss, this moment, she couldn't have imagined the reality of it being so exquisite.

Ben's eyes lit up at her confidence. He pulled her face to his and slowly brushed his nose against hers. It didn't take long for his mouth to move toward hers. She parted her lips eagerly and felt the warm softness of his lips covering hers. In that moment, everything she had always felt for him was confirmed. She knew that it had been worth all of the time she had spent wanting him. She wasn't the fool she had always believed herself to be. It was as if every longing inside, everything that she had ever been ashamed to admit, was finally being revealed with her feelings for Ben. Finally, as his tongue glided over hers, she tasted pure elation, desperately needing to go on, but knowing that she needed to savor every moment.

He kissed her deeply, his hands pressing harder against her with each soft moan. He pulled his lips from hers to nip at her neck, leaving a trail of soft kisses up to her earlobe. Dylan tilted her head ever so lightly to give him access. Every part of her felt flushed, a fiery gale flooding through her from this one spot that he touched. How could such a simple touch cause such a reaction? She closed her eyes tight as she whimpered, a sound she didn't even recognize.

Ben returned his mouth to hers as his hands moved down her back to pull her shirt above her head. Dylan felt her arms lift into the air and she trusted his every move; he would guide her all the way. As her shirt hit the floor, she was surprised that she didn't feel exposed. It was right; she was his, and she would never feel self-conscious around him again. She leaned back and willed him to move his mouth to her chest. As if he were completely in tune with her every need, Ben began the slow descent from her neck to her chest, placing soft kisses all the way down. Thankful for the hands that held her in place, she felt herself shudder against him, an eruption that took over her entire body and reminded her that she was awake; she was *alive*.

She grasped at the bottom of his shirt; she needed to feel him against her, smooth and bare. Ben laughed against her skin and leaned back to help her. As his bare chest was revealed and pressed to hers, he smiled, a gleam in his eye.

Dylan moved her unsteady hands through his hair and felt a shiver rip through his body. Her fingers grazed over his back as she began to find her control. It seemed almost too much for Ben to take as he groaned into the soft curve of her shoulder and skimmed his hand over her breast. The intimacy between them formed a connection that she had never experienced before. She could never regret waiting for it. She was bound to him, now, believing in him completely, and free to show him how much she needed his steady hold.

He gently stood and kept her legs wrapped around his waist. He turned and slowly laid her down on his bed and moved above her, a hand on either side of her head. His breathing deepened as he moved his mouth back to hers and pressed his body down, aligning himself hard against her.

Dylan could feel his hand gently tug at her pants and the reality of it all came crashing down on her as she reminded herself to open her eyes; she wouldn't miss a single moment of this time with him. She would look into the eyes that were finally staring into hers, and she would push away the anxiety that threatened to consume her at any minute. She reminded herself that this was the man she had saved every part of herself for; he was finally there, making her feel wanted and *so needed*. She would give it all to him and she would be present, not cowering behind closed eyes.

As she lay there, bare, prepared, thrilled, and fervent, Ben stared down at her as she moved beneath him. With a shaky hand, she brushed the inside of his waistband, carefully dragging her fingertips along his hidden skin. She felt satisfied when he blushed and his teeth clamped down on his lower lip. *I'm the one making him lose control,* she reminded herself in astonishment. As if he could read her mind, the blush drained from Ben's face and he smiled as he helped her with the rest of his clothing. It didn't matter how inexperienced she was, he was going mad with every movement she made, and he was well aware that she knew it.

He moved back down to her, bringing their bodies together and preparing her for what was to come next. "There's no going back after this," he whispered breathlessly. "Are you sure?"

Dylan eagerly pulled him to her. "I don't even want to *look* back," she answered, her labored breath matching his. She had never been so sure of anything in her life.

He pressed his mouth to hers and slowly moved into her, mindful of the pain that she would feel. He pressed his forehead to hers as he sighed and caressed her face. She wrapped her fingers around his neck and inhaled sharply, exhaling into the air above them.

"Okay?" he asked, trembling, his breath held tight.

She managed a small murmur. "Yes."

He wrapped his hands in her hair and kissed the tip of her nose, her jaw, her ear, taking his time; every movement suffused with a gentleness she had never known he could possess. As he thrust deeper, his warm lips traveled from her neck to her breasts, creating a gratifying distraction that masked the small ache below.

This was her undoing, as the need for him to keep going flooded her entire body. The pain subsided and she felt herself pulse against him, her back arched, a sign for him to release what she was sure he was holding back for her comfort.

"My God, Dylan," he groaned against her skin. As he moved deeper, he let himself say things that he would never have said before. "I never knew it would feel like this," he admitted through a whisper.

"I did," she whispered back with such certainty that it was almost too much for him to take.

He raised his head slowly and silently willed her to look into his eyes. They beamed at one another, a genuine, blissful smile that neither could resist. As his pace quickened, he finally let go and gave in to his urges. She gave every ounce of herself to him and, as they came together, she knew that he was doing the same for her. She had wholeheartedly given everything that she had to Ben—the only man that she would ever love—on a level so profound and intimate that she would never have to wonder or fantasize again. *This* was now her reality and it was better than anything she had ever imagined.

CHAPTER SEVEN

Dylan couldn't sleep. She refused to miss any part of the moment she found herself in. She lay on her side, staring into Ben's beautiful eyes. She was seriously considering a life inside the walls of Ben's room. She would never leave if given the chance to stay forever.

Ben held her hand as it rested on the sheets. His thumb rubbed against hers, a small but gratifying movement. Her legs were intertwined with his beneath the blankets and their naked bodies were as close as could be. There was so much heat in that bed. They both feared losing even a fraction of it if they were to move apart.

Ben flashed a rare, peaceful smile. "What are you thinking about?" he asked gently.

Dylan smiled and touched his cheek, sighing as she thought long and hard. "Happiness," she finally answered.

"I don't believe I knew what that was until just now," he admitted, surprising them both.

"Thank you for not flaking," she whispered.

Ben sighed. He ran his hand through her hair and along her soft cheek, sending chills down her spine. He pulled her face to his and kissed her passionately. He moved his body closer and wrapped his arm over her hip.

She was confident, safe, and enthralled by every movement he made. Dylan moved onto her back and pulled him above her. She loved that he gave her that control. She enjoyed pulling him to her, the warmth of his skin, and the feeling of being beneath him.

They made love again and, just like the time before, Ben's eyes looked deeply into Dylan's. She wasn't sure what she enjoyed more, the love in his stare or the sensations from his touch. Either way, she couldn't imagine them ever coming to an end.

*   *   *

"Stay with me," Ben pleaded. He pressed Dylan against her car, almost forbidding her from opening the door. "You don't have to leave."

Dylan sighed. "You know I don't want to, but I have to. I promised Meredith."

"Meredith will understand."

"No, I assure you, she won't." Dylan giggled into his chest.

"The homeless don't need you. I need you," he said, kissing her over and over on every inch of exposed skin he could find.

"There's that holiday spirit of yours," Dylan teased. "Very festive."

Ben kissed her cheek, her ear, her neck, even her eye. He groaned as he inhaled her scent and found satisfaction in the fact that he could also smell himself in her hair.

"You're making this extremely difficult, Ben," Dylan almost scolded. "I promise I'll see you later."

"What am I going to do while you're gone?"

"Go hang out with Jonah," Dylan advised with a chuckle. "I'm sure my brothers are wondering where you've been."

"I don't know them, remember?" he teased. He was only half kidding, though. He would gladly give up all men named

Mathews if it meant Dylan would come back up to his bed. She was the only Mathews he needed.

"Are you still coming to the light show?" she asked, and kissed his nose. "Maybe your mom will come, too?"

Ben laughed. "No, she won't." He leaned in and kissed her mouth. "But I'll be there. We can hide and hold hands again," he said, and kissed her soft lips.

Dylan beamed. "You do remember."

He sighed again, ashamed that he had allowed her to go all these years not knowing how he really felt. "I remember everything," he whispered.

They kissed once more and he grudgingly moved away, releasing her to the outside world, a place he hated more than anything because it now possessed Dylan. He watched her drive away and the sudden emptiness consumed him.

It was a good time to find Jonah, like Dylan suggested.

* * *

What Charlie found so wonderful about Meredith was her massive heart and good nature. At first glance, of course, most people found themselves assuming that she was about as shallow as a puddle; there didn't appear to be more lurking beneath her surface. As materialistic as she could be, no one would ever be surprised that her father was a wealthy man, president of a major appliance manufacturer. And, yet, there was another layer to Meredith that ran deeper than most people knew. It was a facet that those close to her saw on a regular basis. She adored the people in her world and she would do anything and everything to make them happy. And it didn't stop with the people that she loved. She seemed to spread happiness everywhere she went, even the shelters and outreach programs she volunteered for. As prissy and spoiled as she was, Meredith would always give back.

Usually, she pulled Dylan along with her, spreading good cheer and doing good deeds. Normally, Dylan found the act enlightening and good for the soul. Today, however, she only thought of one thing: Ben.

"Why are you glowing, sister?" Meredith asked, while scooping holiday dinner onto an open plate. "You look unusually happy."

"I'm just in a good mood. Is that okay?" Dylan asked with a red face.

"No. I don't buy that." Meredith stared at her with inquisitive eyes. "Are you dating someone?"

"Why does everyone keep asking me that?" Dylan hissed.

"Because Charlie said you weren't interested in Michael or Ollie ... whatever you all call him. I could've told him that, but you look like you're giddy today." She pursed her lips and narrowed her eyes, before adding, "Too giddy. Were you with a man?"

"I don't know what you're talking about," Dylan lied, and spooned up some mashed potatoes. "Why are you all so interested in my love life?"

"Because we want you to have one," Meredith joked. "Although ... I think you do have one and you're keeping it a secret. I'm female and we tend to know these things, Dylan."

"Well, if I am dating someone and I haven't said anything yet, then I will when I'm ready, okay?" Dylan loved her secret love affair, but with the family she had, she was well aware they would not just let her live peacefully in private.

"Charlie said Hugh told him that you didn't sleep at home last night." Meredith's face was amused. "That means that you spent the night with someone."

"I'm twenty-two years old. I'm allowed to spend the night out." Dylan shook her head. "I need to get my own place."

"Cambridge, Massachusetts is a nice place to live," Meredith teased. "Will you be moving there?"

Dylan almost choked. She said nothing as she continued to spoon the potatoes onto each plate that passed by. She knew her face was red, but she tried to act oblivious, nonetheless.

"Uh-huh," Meredith said with a satisfied grin. "Got ya."

"I didn't say anything," Dylan shrieked. "You're assuming things."

"Charlie said Ben left early last night." She paused to stare at Dylan. "I haven't heard very good things about him when it comes to women. Are you sure you want to go down this path?"

"You don't know him, Meredith." Dylan always found it necessary to defend him, now more than ever. "Besides, you're wrong."

"I know your face is red and I know you both were nowhere to be found last night." She shrugged. "Your brothers would never suspect, but I'm new and my eyes are a bit more open."

The conversation ended only because Dylan knew she was busted and there was no point in continuing. She also knew that Meredith would never say anything to Charlie. No matter what, she still was her most trusted friend.

But the odds of them all letting this go were slim to none, Dylan knew. She wasn't too sure how much longer she would be able to get away from her brothers without their curiosity getting the better of them. It was only a matter of time before they began following her around.

Dylan wasn't granted her privacy in the family that she had. She would never butt into her brothers' lives the way they seemed to always be in hers. Even with Brandon and Jonah in California and Hugh in Washington, Dylan's life would never be her own.

* * *

Ben stepped through the garage door of the Mathews' house and smiled when he ran into Linda. "Hey Mom Two," he said, stealing a freshly baked cookie from the wax paper on the counter.

"Hello, Son Five," she replied, slapping his hand. "Those are for tonight."

Ben adored Linda's acceptance of him belonging to her family. She even included him in her Christmas list. It wasn't just a shirt or a CD of some sort. She would buy him thoughtful presents, even a shirt that matched the ones she bought her own sons. Each one of their wardrobes were a bit too similar because of Linda's endless need to treat them like a group of quintuplets. Eventually, they learned to alert one another of what they were wearing, just to avoid any matching mishaps.

"Where's Son Four?" Ben asked.

Linda licked homemade frosting from her thumb and raised her other hand to point out the window.

Ben walked out through the sliding glass door and sat down on the patio in back. "Hey," he called to Jonah, who was helping Brandon with the fireworks for the Christmas Eve show.

Jonah didn't look up at him. "Where the hell have you been?" he asked with laughter in his voice.

"I had some things to do," Ben replied casually.

"Who?" Jonah asked with a smirk.

Ben laughed uncomfortably, because he figured that if Jonah really knew who, he would be nauseated with himself for even asking that question. "No one," Ben answered, attempting to mask his amusement.

"Well, you've been MIA since last night. I just figured this was about a girl." Jonah dropped a cord of lights and headed over to Ben. "Are you coming over tonight?"

"Yeah," Ben answered. "I wouldn't miss it."

"I don't know where Dylan's been." Jonah sighed and looked around. "She took off from Ollie's last night."

"Yeah?" Ben asked as absentmindedly as he could. "Hmm."

"We invited Olerson tonight."

"Why are you assholes pushing Olerson on her?" Ben tried to conceal the jealous fit raging in his head, but his mouth was not doing so well at being discreet. "She doesn't like him. You guys need to get over it."

Ben could feel Jonah shift in discomfort. That was about all that Jonah needed to do to show his disapproval of Ben's occasional outbursts. It wasn't that Jonah didn't know how to deal with Ben's flare-ups. It was just that he chose his battles with Ben.

"I'm not pushing him on her," Jonah responded after a few uneasy moments. "I just think he's good for her."

"Well, she doesn't like him." Ben sighed, slightly embarrassed.

Jonah didn't reply, a signal of retreat. He stood up and left Ben alone again while he went back to being Brandon's assistant.

Ben looked around and remembered his life in the backyard he stood in. He almost laughed out loud when he remembered a time he could never forget. He was fourteen and Dylan put on a purple bikini, nearly killing him. However, as his mind dove further into the memory of that day, he frowned.

On her way to join the swimming boys, Dylan had bashfully snuck out of the sliding glass door with her mother behind her smiling proudly. Ben realized now that the bikini must have been Linda's idea, an attempt to make her only daughter more feminine.

Ben had stood on the diving board, ready to do a cannonball, but completely frozen in a state of jaw-dropping horror. He had never seen so much of Dylan and he truly didn't enjoy the show, given what it was doing to his body. Ben dove into the water and came up just along the edge of the pool to hide the overwhelming evidence of his appreciation.

"You look stupid," he'd yelled when Linda disappeared.

Dylan's face had broken with hurt as she teared-up. She'd looked down at her feet and let her once-proud shoulders fall. Ben had known even then that she was seeking his approval, but he couldn't let her know that she had won him over.

"Weed, put your other one on," Brandon had urged with sweetness in his voice. Always the overprotective brother, he'd added, "You're still too young for that."

"She'll never be ready for that," Ben had shouted. "She has to be a girl first."

"Mom said I look nice," Dylan had said quietly through quivering lips.

"She's your mom, Weed. She has to tell you that," Ben remembered urging, for his own sake, of course. She had looked too beautiful and much too perfect. "Go put your old one on and let's play water basketball." He'd thrown the wet ball at her face and laughed when it exploded with water spray, soaking her hair.

Dylan hadn't cried, though. She'd simply lifted the first thing she saw—a baseball—and thrown it back at him. Hard. Ben had dodged the flying ball and stared at her with shock in his eyes.

Dylan had run into the house and didn't return with a new suit on, or even at all. Ben had known she was hurt and, whether he'd admitted it to himself then or not, the guilt he'd felt that day was heavy. Still, he would not falter and admit why he was so desperate for her to *not* be in that bikini.

"Ben?" Jonah called for what must have been the tenth time. "Hello?"

Ben snapped back into the present and realized Jonah was standing in front of him. "Sorry. What?"

"You checked out for a minute, buddy."

"I'm back now." Ben laughed uncomfortably. "What do you need?"

Jonah shook his head and threw an extension cord to Ben. "Help," he answered sternly.

The atmosphere was a bit awkward. Ben truly feared the idea of his friends finding out about what he had done with their sister. He wouldn't object to them taking turns punching him. He had slept with his best friends' sister like a downright dog. He deserved a good beating.

He even found himself looking at them differently now. He almost wondered if he would have to choose between them all. He would choose Dylan. He would choose her over them, and that was what frightened him the most.

* * *

Traditionally, the entire neighborhood spread out in the street to enjoy the light display that erupted over the Mathews' home every Christmas Eve. Neighbors brought dishes to pass and sang songs of Christmas cheer to get the spirit going.

In the emptiness that loomed as a result of the boys' absence, Linda Mathews regularly contemplated moving into a smaller house or even a condo. When Christmas came around, however, Linda was reminded of why she could never leave her beloved home.

In the neighborhood the Mathews lived in, the friendly atmosphere persisted just as it had twenty years before. The two-story homes sat side-by-side. Some were similar and others had their own distinct personalities. It was a charming little community; no one would move away unless they absolutely had to.

The street in front of the Mathews' house began to fill as it did every year at this time. The women set up tables and food, while the men stood over Brandon, Charlie, Hugh, and Jonah to make sure they wouldn't blow themselves up. Some things never change.

The children of the subdivision had mostly grown up and allowed themselves to step back and embrace their childhood with memories of Christmases past and the innocent joy they'd felt while watching the sky burst with festive colors. It was a timeless tradition that no one would ever be ready to let go.

Dylan spotted Ben as he appeared at the side of her house. He was not quite out of the shadows and she was the only one that knew he was there, because she had been desperately watching for him to arrive. Ben motioned for her to come to him and she wasted no time obliging with a guilty grin. She walked around to the other side of the house discreetly and searched for him in her own back yard. Ben pulled at Dylan's hand and guided her through the dark. Together, they hopped over a concrete divider and found the darkest corner that they could locate on the other side.

As Ben ran his lips against the skin of her neck, Dylan smiled, out of breath and tingling from head to toe. "Mr. Raymond is the only person that doesn't come tonight and you choose his yard to do this in?"

Ben kissed Dylan's slender neck, and teased, "He'll be missing two shows then."

He leaned back and made it a point to clasp her hand in his, eyes lighting up from a sudden burst of gold in the sky. "Here we are again," he said with a warm smile.

Dylan's eyes fell to their joined hands as she smiled. "Here we are," she answered. "Now what?"

"Now I do what I should have done the last time that we were under these lights together," Ben said with the sincerity that she had come to know well.

As another burst of lights erupted above them, Dylan's heart quickened and Ben slowly moved to press his warm lips to hers. She grazed her tongue against his and deepened their kiss as a whimper escaped from her throat.

Ben pulled away, breathless, and teased, "Of course, I may not have been able to leave it at just a kiss back then, especially if you made that sound."

Dylan looked at him mischievously and licked her lips. "I hope you don't leave it at just a kiss now," she teased with a smile.

He pulled her against him and buried his face in her neck, nipping at her earlobe and skimming his warm tongue along her skin. "That would take a lot of strength," he admitted in her ear.

"I wish we could sleep together tonight," Dylan confessed, dizzily. She didn't even try to conceal her sounds of pleasure as Ben moved his mouth and body against her.

Ben pulled Dylan's dress up and stood between her legs. "Trust me. I'll make it to your room tonight," he whispered.

Dylan's toes practically curled. She had never felt such passion or need to be touched by someone. She was new to the world of sex, but she could never have imagined the lingering sensations that Ben was able to leave on parts of her body that he wasn't even touching. It was as if those parts were begging for his attention, asking for his lips and hands to feel their way over and satisfy her need.

"You're beautiful," he whispered, a genuine smile on his mischievous face. He gazed at her with passion, heat, and sincerity before pulling her to the ground and positioning himself above her body.

"Make love to me," she murmured, and undid the button to his pants.

The festive colors and booming noises from the gathering only yards away dissolved into mere background as Ben obliged and moved into Dylan. He was smiling down at her, the lights bursting above his head. With a groan, Ben increased his pace and pressed his mouth to hers. Her stomach fluttered as he pulled at her bottom lip with his teeth. She sighed, head spinning with need as she took him in. She couldn't resist him, nor could she think of a reason she would ever need to. She was convinced that she would ultimately drown in this new version of him.

Dylan closed her eyes and lost herself in the moment, in tune with each thrust, touch, and sound that he made. As another burst of gold erupted in the sky, they both cried out at the same time, their voices disguised by the sounds of the festivities nearby.

Ben collapsed onto Dylan and kissed her neck while he caught his breath. "Beautiful," he whispered into her ear.

Dylan gasped into the air as falling embers danced above them and smoke from the fireworks clouded the sky. She smiled as the sensations came again in an aftershock that was almost as good as the rush before.

Ben raised up so that he could look down at Dylan. "I don't want to move," he said, pushing his hands through her hair. He rubbed his nose to hers and sighed against her lips.

"We have tonight," Dylan reminded him with a grin.

"Yes, we do," he agreed with a smile of his own.

They got to their feet and kissed as Dylan fixed her dress. It was almost unbearable to pull away from Ben, knowing he would be stolen away by her brothers. She knew where he wanted to be, but she was beside herself knowing that she could never kiss or touch him out in the open.

"Wait," Ben said once more. He held her hand and slowly eased her back to him with a wayward look. "I'll see you later. You know the spot?"

Dylan laughed, unable to control her adoration. There was no sense in even attempting to hide her joy. "I think I know, but you should draw me a map just to be sure I know how to get to my bed."

"It's easy," he teased, drawing her closer. He guided her fingers to his chest and placed her palm over his heart. "We'll meet right here."

Dylan's breath came short as she stared at him, shocked. Who was this man?

"Right there, then," she whispered, and stood on her toes to press her mouth to his.

They separated after many moments of rushing back for another final kiss, making their ways back to the festivities around opposite sides of the house.

Dylan went first. She crept up onto the porch and positioned herself comfortably, alone and somewhat hidden, in an attempt to claim that she had been in that spot the entire time. She sighed as she looked up into the sky, smiling fondly at the sounds and lights of Christmas Eve.

Dylan watched as Ben joined the crowd of her brothers in the driveway. She laughed quietly each time that she caught him searching for her until his careful eyes finally found her on the porch. He smiled quickly and turned his head back in Charlie's direction as if to at least pretend to be interested in the activity there.

You love me, she thought as his eyes wandered discreetly back to hers.

When Dylan was twelve, she had painted Ben a picture for his birthday: two children, standing on a mountain and holding hands under a giant, red heart in the sky. When it had dried, she'd rolled it up and wrapped a silver bow around the paper. She'd nervously walked it over to the McKenna's house and laid it on the porch, all before running away.

He had never said a word about it. Never said a thank you or even a more Ben-appropriate comment about how awful it was. It was as if it never happened.

Dylan remembered crying on the very porch she sat on now. Carl had come, cradled her to him, and wiped the tears from her cheek.

"Boys are stupid," she recalled him saying. "They never know a good thing until they've run it over a few times."

Dylan had tried to breathe through her tears. "He hates me, Daddy."

Carl had shaken his head and pushed the wet strands of hair away from her tear-soaked face. "No, no. It's just the opposite. Ben likes you and that's why he goes the extra mile to show how much he doesn't. He's a stupid boy."

Carl had died six months later.

The red, green, and gold burst above her head, bringing her back to the present. She looked up and felt her father all around, as everyone did on this night, she suspected.

"I miss you, Daddy," she whispered into the sky.

"Hey," Michael said, stepping up onto the porch to join Dylan. "Why are you alone?"

"I'm just thinking of my dad, remembering him." Dylan rolled her eyes and sat forward in her chair. She could feel Ben's glare without looking up.

"Do you want some company?" he asked, sitting before an invitation was granted.

"Why aren't you over there with my brothers?"

"I wanted to talk to you about the way things were left yesterday." He seemed sad, which only irritated Dylan now. She had made her decision and he needed to respect it and settle for her friendship. "I don't want things to be weird and I'm scared you're going to quit," he admitted.

"I'm not going to quit, Michael." She laughed. "I need the money if I ever want to get out of my mother's house."

"That's good." He sighed and looked to the ground. "Are you going to tell your brothers about Ben?"

"There's nothing to tell." She could feel her defensiveness of Ben rising. "You should really mind your own business, you know?"

"You're right." Michael held up his hands. "I'm sorry."

Dylan stood up. "I'm going to go find my mom," she said, before he could stop her. She stepped off the porch and walked across the yard, leaving Michael staring after her.

Ben tried hard to mask the triumphant satisfaction he felt watching Dylan leave Olerson on the porch by himself. He couldn't believe Michael's determination and, much to his dismay, he was extremely threatened by his presence in Dylan's life.

Ben felt ownership over her, which was nothing new but maybe a bit more intense now that he had made love to her. When they were younger, he could remember feeling a bit jealous even of Dylan's family. If it were acceptable, he would have placed his stamp of ownership somewhere on her body, marking his territory like the dog he knew he was. Maybe then he could justify the rage he felt when someone even tried to speak with her.

He wondered if they were being too obvious in dodging each other. Dylan hadn't been much for explosives when they were younger, but he couldn't imagine her avoiding it the way she was tonight.

"Are you staying here tonight?" Charlie asked, yanking Ben's eyes away from Dylan. "My mom has, like, ten presents with your name on them under the tree."

Ben smirked. "I hadn't planned on it before, but I guess I'll stay. I should probably head home early in the morning for Ruth." He paused and laughed as he realized something. "She didn't even put up a tree."

"Does that surprise you?" Charlie asked, sounding perplexed. "Has she ever?"

"I guess not. I must have forgotten."

Charlie turned to grab Meredith as she passed. He nuzzled her hair and whispered something in her ear. He walked away as if Ben wasn't even there, wrapped up in his own little world with his wife-to-be.

Ben looked over at Dylan and felt almost pained that he wasn't allowed that same privilege. He would have given anything to be right next to her in that moment. He would hold her hand and nuzzle her hair, too.

He stood unaccompanied in the driveway and looked up at the bright show. He didn't want to speak or check out the girls that had developed into women while he was gone. No one could compare to Dylan.

Oh, the man he had become in only twenty-four hours! It was quite a change from the man he had been. It was a gooey feeling, full of sap and warm tingles that, sadly, he wished he could bathe in for the rest of his existence.

He was sure Jonah and Hugh knew something was up, and he wished he could release his feelings into the air with the fireworks so they would all know. Of course, that would mean certain death for him. The Mathews men were known to keep guns in the house.

The show ended and, one by one, the crowd drifted away, heading home to continue their own festivities alone. Ben retreated into the Mathews' home for the traditional cookie decorating in the kitchen.

They sat around the table as Linda set up the frosting and sprinkles in the center. None of them looked excited about this forced custom, but they wore their fake smiles as best as they could to appease their mother and her never-ending love of holiday rituals.

"Now, we each have six cookies to decorate, which will give us forty-eight." Linda smiled as she dug into the frosting and began to work.

"Here's two," Hugh teased. He set down the circular cookies that were decorated perversely, to no one's surprise.

"That's a nice rack," Jonah pointed out. "Put those on the naughty list."

"No boobs!" Linda scolded. "Take those apart right now."

Ben shook his head and laughed; he had been the one to first do that five years before. He remembered saying that they were Chrissy Turner's because he had just felt her up in the back yard. Linda smacked his head then, as she smacked Hugh's now.

"Why do we always have to have dirty cookies?" Linda asked, mystified. True, she had raised four boys, but she would never understand their perverse nature.

"Because you have dirty sons, Mom," Dylan answered, frosting obediently. Under one raised brow, she glanced at Ben, who wagged his eyebrows at her.

"I know the one son that isn't dirty," Meredith said, pointing to Charlie. "Right, baby?"

The entire group remained quiet; then the uncontrollable snickering began. Everyone except Meredith and Charlie erupted into howling laughter.

"Who do you think taught us?" Hugh got out through his laughter. "It wasn't her," he said, pointing to Linda, which caused everyone to laugh harder.

"Hey," Brandon said, slightly offended by the fact that he was the oldest of the group and not given any credit for being dirty.

"Oh, who are you kidding?" Linda said to Brandon through her giggling. "You were never as bad as this one."

"What about him?" Charlie asked, pointing to Ben. "He's the worst of us all!"

"Yeah, there's a long line behind this one, Meredith." Jonah put his hand on Ben's shoulder. "You should be happy you got that one. Charlie's only slightly offensive compared to this guy."

Dylan pursed her lips, but remained quiet as she pinched red sprinkles onto her cookie. Ben watched her face as it fell. He decided it was time to change the subject. "If we can't do boobs, can we at least do balls?"

"No!" Linda hissed back at Ben. "No body parts whatsoever. Only Christmas related cookies."

"Here, I'm done with mine," Dylan said. She laid out her six cookies and smiled proudly. In the center of each cookie was a letter. When she put them all together, the five cookies spelled DADDY, and the sixth had a red heart in the center.

The group stared at the cookies and, one by one, smiled at each other as they remembered their beloved missing husband and father, Carl Mathews.

It was as if he'd never missed a year of it, Ben realized. The only difference was that this time, Dylan's foot was on his knee under the table, something he couldn't have imagined allowing before—or, more importantly, something he could never have imagined how much he would enjoy. He would gladly do it again for all the years to come.

*   *   *

As Dylan's door opened and closed quickly, she smiled. She turned over in the dark and felt Ben's gentle hands pull her to him.

He rubbed his nose against hers, something she would never tire of. "Merry Christmas," he whispered, and kissed her fervidly.

Dylan sighed into him and thought that he couldn't be a more perfect gift if he had a Christmas bow wrapped around him. "Merry Christmas," she whispered back.

She felt his heart beating through his chest, perfectly in sync with hers. He pulled her arms above her head and held her hands in place as he kissed her neck and groaned against her skin. She wouldn't allow herself to wonder if this was too good to be true; it was too good to even care.

They melted into one another and made love quietly in her bed, something they had never done before, but had so desperately wanted.

*   *   *

Linda wrapped her loving arms around Ben as soon as he stepped in through the sliding glass door. "Merry Christmas, sweetie," she said, kissing him on the cheek.

It was quite a difference from the hour that he had just spent waiting for his own mother to crawl out of her bed, only to say nothing about it even being Christmas. He wasn't surprised, of course. He had placed her present—a necklace that he hadn't put much thought into—on the kitchen counter and headed over to the only people that had ever made him feel welcome.

Ben beamed as he pulled away and took a second to look at Linda. "Merry Christmas," he said.

"She made us wait for you," Jonah said, before sipping from his coffee. "And she wouldn't even let us sleep while we waited."

"It's Christmas," Linda reminded. "We don't sleep in on Christmas."

Dylan appeared from the kitchen and smiled at Ben, who couldn't help but light up with a smile of his own. It was as brief as they could manage without alerting the others to how happy they were at just the sight of one another. Fleeting glances would never be enough, Ben was beginning to understand. He thought about the way he had woken up just hours before, her naked body entangled with his, and shivered as chills raced up his spine.

"Can we do this, please?" Brandon asked through a yawn.

"I want to eat and go back to bed," Hugh whined.

"Meredith isn't here yet," Charlie reminded, and frowned as the rest of his brothers groaned impatiently.

"Oh, for crying out loud," their mother said, her exasperation apparent. "You sound like a bunch of babies."

Dylan rolled her eyes and fell back into the soft sofa behind her. She pulled her knees up and smiled at Ben as he took the open seat across from her. It was, he knew, a terrible idea to position himself directly in front of the person that he wasn't supposed to look at; but he figured this would be his gift to himself: a moment of not being so cautious.

Meredith graced them all with her presence about thirty minutes later. She didn't receive the same greeting that Ben had, but Charlie did his best to make her oblivious to the fact that his brothers had been growing more annoyed with each passing second.

Linda sat in Carl's old chair and drank coffee while she watched her family open their presents. There was a pile as tall as Brandon next to her, but it was tradition for her to open her gifts last. "I wish you wouldn't spend your money on me," she would always say, and Ben felt his heart warm with familiarity as he heard her say it this time. It was as if he had not missed a single year.

After Brandon, Charlie, Hugh, Jonah, and Ben all opened the same shirt in different colors, they laughed at one another.

"Hell yeah," Jonah exclaimed when he opened Ben's gift to him: two tickets to the Diamondbacks' season opener. "Is this other ticket for you?"

Ben smirked. "You running short on women?"

"Hah," Jonah responded. "I wasn't sure if you were trying to ask me out."

"Nice," Brandon interrupted. He held a set of monogrammed Australian beer glasses into the air and smiled with appreciation. "Thanks, Ben."

"Thanks, man," Charlie said, as he stared down at the new pitching wedge from Ben. "This is pretty bad ass."

Hugh grinned as he opened his gift from Ben, his skin stretching over his cheeks like a child with a new toy. "A subscription to *Playboy*."

Suddenly, the room quieted with a sharp "*tisk*" sound from Linda. With a red face, Ben met her glare with an innocent expression. "What?" he asked, laughing. "He'll read the articles."

"I'm sure," Linda answered, her lips in a tight line as if stifling a smile.

"Readers are leaders, Mom," Hugh reminded without looking up from his present.

Ben got to his feet and crossed the room to hand Dylan a present wrapped in thick, silver paper. "For you," he said as he knelt to place it in her hands. He quickly winked at her, secretly enjoying the fact that he had caught her off guard.

Dylan moved the other presents that she had received from her thoughtful mother and brothers—clothes, paints, brushes, sketchpads, and a book on Van Gogh—and gently opened the gift. Ben watched her discreetly. He loved the careful way she pulled back the paper and undid the wrapping. She was wary, full of anticipation, and only he could tell. It was this dynamic between them that he adored the most. Only he could read her every expression like a book, and only she could read him just the same.

Ben watched as Dylan bit her bottom lip and attempted to hide her amusement when she figured out what he had given her: a hot pink football. She looked up to meet his eyes and flashed him the most beautiful smile he had ever seen, leaving him nearly breathless.

Somehow, Ben was able to pull his eyes from Dylan's and take a quick glance around the room to make sure that no one had caught their moment. When he landed on Meredith's suspicious look, he knew it hadn't gone entirely unnoticed. He lingered there for a moment, trying to read her expression, until he was forced to focus on Linda, who had begun to open her gifts.

"Wow," Linda said, holding up the framed painting that Dylan had done for her. It was an exact replica of a photo from Carl and Linda's wedding day. As Linda stared at the colorful image, a single tear traveled down her cheek. "Honey," she said, "this is absolutely gorgeous. Thank you."

Dylan smiled, her chin quivering and her green eyes sparkling with tears. "You're welcome," she managed to say. Ben watched her carefully and felt a pang in his chest when he realized that he couldn't wrap her up in his embrace, run his hands through her hair, and kiss her temple. When her eyes finally met his, all he could do was flash her a tender smile—a smile that would tell her how it killed him to see those tears in her eyes.

"Oh, a day at the spa!" Linda gasped, pulling Ben's attention back to her. "Thank you, Ben!"

Ben chuckled and nodded. "Full package for the hardest working mom I know," he said with a wink.

"A massage, manicure and pedicure, facial, oh, and hair, too!" Linda announced excitedly. "What do you guys think about highlights?"

"Is it time for breakfast?" Hugh asked, ignoring his mother.

"I'm starving," Jonah said with a grimace. "Let's eat."

Ben smiled at Linda, who was still soaring from thinking about her spa day, and said, "Definitely get some highlights."

Ben looked over at Dylan and felt himself blush when he caught her appreciative look. "Thank you," she mouthed, and stood to join her family at the breakfast table.

Ben rapidly stood to walk next to her and inconspicuously ran the tip of his finger along the palm of her hand. He had to remove it too quickly for his liking, but he felt himself flood with an easy understanding that he would eventually be free to have his hands on her later that night.

* * *

Later, as his room grew dark with the setting sun, Ben warmed at the sight of Dylan entering his bedroom. He sat on his bed as she straddled his lap and pushed at his chest, urging him to lie back.

"It's time for *your* present," she said playfully.

CHAPTER EIGHT

December thirtieth was always the day that Linda wanted the Christmas décor and lights taken down. Despite her love for the holidays, and her moody sons' protests, she wanted her house back to normal immediately because she thought that entering a new year with old holiday decorations still up was not only tacky, but bad luck.

Jonah stood on the ladder and pulled down each light that hung from the eaves of his mother's home. Ben stood just below him, carefully wrapping each cord into a neat circle, knowing Linda would make him fix it if the wrap was less than perfect.

Jonah looked down at Ben. "So, you hate Olerson, right?"

"I'm not a fan," Ben confirmed cautiously. "Why?"

"You don't like the guy, but you want to go to his bar for New Year's Eve?"

"I like his bar." Ben looked up at Jonah. "Did you have something else in mind?"

Jonah shook his head and continued to pull the lights. "No, I guess not."

"Then what's the problem?" Ben asked, attempting not to sound like Dylan had anything to do with his plans.

"No problem."

"Good."

"My sister is working. Did you know that?" Jonah didn't look down this time.

"Oh?" Ben felt his face flush. That color had seemed to grace his cheeks more and more in the past few days. He felt alive when his skin lit up at the mention of his Dylan. It was quite sappy and a tad embarrassing, but he loved it.

"Well, she'll be happy to hang out with us, I suppose." Jonah turned to hand Ben more of the strand.

"Sure." Ben tried to act nonchalant about her. He couldn't figure out why he found it so difficult to do now, when he had been doing it his entire life.

Jonah climbed down the ladder and lifted an eyebrow at Ben. "You've checked your watch, like, twenty times in the last half hour."

"Yeah?" Ben stopped shaking his impatient leg. "So?"

"You got somewhere to be?"

"Uh, I have to help my mom with some things in a bit," Ben lied terribly. Dylan would be at his house soon and he needed to leave.

"Right," Jonah replied, shaking his head.

Jonah didn't buy his story, but Ben knew he'd never call him on it. Jonah's laidback nature made being his friend easy. He knew when he was welcome to information and he didn't care enough to badger someone when he realized he wasn't.

Why couldn't he tell his best friend that he was with the girl of his dreams? He would look even guiltier for not telling Jonah about his relationship with Dylan. Wouldn't all her brothers find out soon enough? What would be the difference between then and now, anyway?

"Jonah," Ben began.

Jonah looked at Ben. "What?"

Ben stared. He thought about how to get this out. He wondered if Dylan would be angry with him if he told Jonah without her consent. He couldn't bear that.

"What's wrong with you?" Jonah waited. "Are you okay?"

"Nope," Ben answered unintentionally.

Where was his wit, his quick thinking? It was all spiraling down into oblivion with his need to be near Dylan. His façade was cracking and Jonah was sure to see right through it soon enough.

He stuttered, which was even more unlike him, not to mention a bit humiliating. "N-nothing. Never mind."

"Okay," Jonah nodded and went back to his work.

Ben's discomfort dissipated when Hugh ran around the house and leapt up to the patio beside them. He was out of breath from laughing, howling like a child. He hunched over and held an empty bucket between his knees, a bottle of whipped cream dangling loosely from his free hand.

Brandon ran around the corner soon after, carrying a large, plastic candy cane from the lawn and looking a bit angry. He was soaked from head to toe and had whipped cream all over his face.

"That might be the funniest thing I've ever seen," Jonah said.

Ben laughed in agreement. "The giant candy cane may be the best part."

They watched in amusement as Brandon chased Hugh all over the yard and tried to catch him for retaliation. He never dropped the candy cane, which only added to Ben and Jonah's entertainment.

* * *

Ben stepped through the back door of his mother's home. He wasn't alarmed when he found her sitting on the couch, staring at a wall with an empty glass in one hand and her divorce papers in the other.

Ben thought about running back the way he came, but he knew this was his only time to be alone with Dylan. He couldn't abandon a chance to hold her and make love to her all day.

He looked into his mother's glazed-over eyes. She looked sad and maybe even a bit irate this time. Vodka made her angry.

She would never have that look without her drink of choice to back it up.

"You're home again," she said, glaring at Ben.

"I'm expecting company." Ben began to clean the kitchen despite the fact that he intended to keep Dylan in his bedroom. He needed something to do while he had the inevitable conversation with his doped-up mother.

"You never rush home to me," she slurred. She picked up a bottle of vodka and poured more into her glass. "Typical."

"Typical?" Ben wasn't in the mood to fight with her, but, then again, was he ever? "Look what you want me to rush home to, Mom."

She drank from her glass. Her hands shook almost violently. Ben remembered only vaguely a time when those hands were comforting to him. He had been a small child and had fallen down. He had wanted those hands then. It killed him to despise them now, but this wasn't even the same woman who had comforted him. She was gone, along with those hands, and now this depressed, rotten woman had taken her place.

"You shouldn't drink with those pills," Ben warned. He knew it did no good, but he felt obligated to remind her anyway.

"You shouldn't try to be like your father so much." A tear dropped from her eye and rolled down her cheek. "He's not a hero."

"I don't need any heroes," Ben reminded.

"That's right," she closed her eyes and sighed. "You're your own hero."

"I had terrible parents. One must improvise in that kind of situation. Go upstairs please. You're embarrassing." Ben drummed his fingers on the counter. "Please, Mom."

Ruth stood up and moved slowly to the stairs. She walked past him without even glancing his way, which only relieved Ben more. This meant she would go pass out in her bed, buying him enough time to be with Dylan until morning.

When her door finally closed, Ben could hear the sound of glass shattering against her wall. Then muffled sobs echoed down the stairs. He rolled his eyes and hoped that she would pass out before Dylan arrived.

* * *

Dylan climbed the steps to Ben's room and was instantly greeted with a kiss when she opened his door. Together, they leaned against the wall and wasted no time as they chatted away and undressed each other. Over the past week of their new physical relationship, they had learned how to multitask brilliantly.

Ben was not very good at hiding his need to have his hands on Dylan when she was in front of him. His drinking had become very rare, because he knew he would not be able to hold back from kissing or touching her in front of his friends if he was drunk. He could not believe how obsessed he had become with her. He wondered if she knew how badly he needed her. He had not dared to tell her, but did he really need to? He suspected that she had always known.

"What took you so long?" Ben asked between kisses. "I thought I was going to die waiting."

Dylan laughed at his impatience. They had just made love that morning. "I had to help Meredith pick out her veil."

"I really don't like her," Ben teased in his hot, husky voice. He lifted Dylan's skirt and removed her underwear quickly.

Dylan's shirt opened easily. Her planning no longer revolved around what matched or smelled clean. It now weighed heavily toward what was easiest for Ben to remove.

He was very adamant about having her naked. He wouldn't admit this to her yet, but once he even considered suggesting they join a nudist colony just so she would never have to get dressed again. The only downside to that would be the other men that would see her. His jealous side would not handle that well.

Ben felt around to her back in search of the clasp to her bra.

"No, no," she whispered. "It's in the front."

Ben smiled. "You clever, brilliant girl," he said, and moved his hand to her front.

He unhooked her bra and opened it wide. He moved his mouth to her neck and entered her at the same time. They groaned together, Dylan pulling Ben's hair as he was overwhelmed with pleasure.

Ben made sure that they were in sync at all times, even making sure that he came when she came. He wanted to be as connected to Dylan as possible, so he could feel what she felt; he even kept their noises of gratification in harmony. The more synchronized they were, the more alive he felt.

After, they lay in his bed, naked and entwined. Ben could feel Dylan's heartbeat against his side as her head rested on his chest. They made no attempt to cover up and, if Ben had his way, they would lie like that forever.

"I heard Hugh ask Jonah where you've been," Dylan said.

Ben sighed. "I probably should spend more time with those guys," he admitted. "I'm sure they know I've been spending time with someone. They just don't know who."

"We can't tell them," Dylan warned. "Not yet."

Ben ran his fingers through her hair and smelled the curled locks. He wondered if this was something the Mathews men could handle or, more importantly, trust. It was highly likely that their first reaction would be to accuse him of only wanting one thing from Dylan. They all knew what a pig he could be, so they would have every right to be worried.

"I'm always up for a little sneaking around, but I'm ready for this to be out now," he admitted. "You have no idea how close I came to telling Jonah today."

"They'll be mad, Ben." Dylan scowled as she lifted her head from his chest. "We don't even know what this is, so we don't have much to tell them, anyway."

Ben laughed, and joked, "I can tell them all the dirty things I do to you." He rolled to his side and brushed her cheek with the back of his hand. "They'd never believe the truth."

"Which is?"

Ben couldn't say he worshiped her, though it was clearly the case. He smiled and moved his face closer. He rubbed his nose against hers and said nothing; his actions spoke so loud he didn't need to.

*   *   *

"Are you almost finished?" Ben asked with a dramatic sigh. His impatience amused and gratified Dylan. She loved to tease him. The idea of him finding it unbearable not to be able to touch her only made her want to toy with him more.

"You can't rush art," Dylan answered with a smirk.

"What will you call this one?"

Dylan lifted one eyebrow and glared at him. She was fully aware that the look she gave him would only drive him closer to the edge of madness. He seemed so very turned on by her snippiness.

"How about *Impatient Man*?" she teased.

"I like *Desperate Man*," Ben suggested. "You can't sit on my bed naked and expect me to look at you like this."

"Why not?" She feigned confusion.

"Because it's just not right, that's why."

"After all those times we lay in my bed while I was denied any sort of physical interaction, you can't sit here for an hour so I can sketch you?" Dylan shook her head in mock disgust. "I love your double standard."

"Is this your revenge, then?"

"Yes," she answered quickly.

Dylan took her time with each line. She enjoyed painting more than anything—next to her newest hobby with Ben, of course—but sketching was definitely her next love. It was easy to sketch him, if only because she did it so often.

Ben loved the way she bit her lip as she sketched. Her eyes were somehow lighter with the glow from the bright white paper reflected in them. How could someone as perfect and lovely as Dylan be described as an ordinary human being? She had to be something else.

Ben grinned. "I'll let you have your vengeance for today."

"Only today? You have twenty years of payback, at least," Dylan warned.

"As long as I get to enjoy you after the retribution, I suppose I can handle this part," Ben said. He raised his eyebrows and grinned mischievously. "I never claimed to be anything more than a childish pervert."

Dylan looked at him with a brazen smile. She ripped the top page from her sketchpad and got to her knees to crawl over to Ben, who welcomed her into his arms and kissed her mouth tenderly.

"Does this mean I'm forgiven for playing hard to get for the last two decades?" he asked quietly.

Dylan shook her head and smiled. "No. It just means I'm finished with my drawing."

Ben took it from her hands and looked at the perfect drawing of his face. She had drawn him with a genuine smile. He looked as happy as he felt in that sketch and it was all because of her. This was how she saw him because this was how she made him.

"Perfect," he whispered. He looked down at her as she lay against his chest, smiling back at him. "You're perfect."

Dylan took the drawing from his hands and placed it on his nightstand. "I'm only perfect when you look at me," she whispered. She reached up and kissed his mouth, sighing into his lips and rubbing his cheek.

"Will you kiss me at midnight tomorrow?" he asked, grazing her lips with his. "I feel it very necessary to do other things to you, but I'll hold back until your brothers aren't watching."

Dylan smiled and closed her eyes. She allowed the feeling of his lips to take over, the sensation reaching all the way down to her toes. She settled into his safe arms and melted to his chest.

Ben didn't take his mouth from hers as he used one hand to turn off his light and cover them with a blanket. They wouldn't go to sleep just yet, but he loved feeling like they were in their own little world, cloaked in darkness, locked into each other, as if the universe revolved around only them.

* * *

Ben hurried to get ready. Taking a nap had been a bad decision, he realized now, in his race to look good. Being with Dylan left him no time to sleep, what with the constant love-making at night—not that he could ever consider that a problem.

He was unusually dressed up for being away from school and work, but, considering that it was New Year's Eve, he figured a tie would be a nice addition to his ensemble. After checking the mirror once more, he rushed down the stairs and attempted to make a quick dash to the back door.

"Benjamin," his mother called in a more sober voice. "Wait a minute, please."

Foiled, he thought. He stepped into the family room and leaned against the wall. He was always alarmed by the sight of her. Not because he didn't expect her appearance, but because she eerily reminded him of someone who was terminally ill.

"What is it?" he asked impatiently.

"I'm sorry about yesterday," she said in a shaky voice. "I let this divorce get the best of me and that wasn't something I wanted to do in front of you."

Ben wasn't sure if he was more irritated by the fact that she was attempting to have a heart-to-heart when Jonah was waiting for him outside or because she was pretending that she had never behaved that way before. What "best" part of herself was she referring to?

"It's fine," he answered shortly. "Goodnight."

"Benjamin, wait." She patted the seat next to her and smiled. "Please?"

Ben sighed heavily, but sat down beside her anyway. "Can you make this fast?"

"I figured out who your visitor has been this past week." She shook her head and smiled. "Dylan Mathews is a very pretty, very nice girl."

Ben thought nothing of his mother's findings only because he had never tried to hide it from her. He figured there wasn't anyone she could really tell, anyway. She wasn't very fond of

Linda because she was jealous of her for being a better mother to Ben than she had been.

"She's very innocent, no?" Her eyes narrowed at Ben.

He laughed to himself, knowing that if Dylan had been innocent before, that part of her was long gone now. "I suppose she can be. Why?"

"Do you love her?"

"It's a bit early for that, Mom." Ben sat back against his seat. "It's only been a week."

She smiled tiredly. "Benjamin, it's been your whole life."

"Okay, what's your point?" he snapped, miffed at the surprising insight she'd had into his life when she had always seemed to only watch from afar.

"You should leave her alone." She crossed her arms and looked away as a tear rolled over her pale skin. "You're only going to hurt that girl."

Ben stood up. "I'm not my father."

Ruth looked up into his eyes. "Oh, yes, you are."

"Is that all you wanted?" Ben asked, trying not to choke on his mother's hurtful words. "May I leave now?"

Ruth nodded and smiled through her streaming tears. "You can't help it. I love you just the same."

"Have a good night," Ben said. He headed for the door and, before he could open it, Ruth called out once more.

"If you love her, you'll take my advice. Let someone else love her so that she never has to feel the way I feel now."

Ben spun around to face her. "You feel this way because you never tried to heal. Your victim rights expired a long time ago, Ruth."

She smiled sweetly. "I love you, Benjamin. However, I feel nothing but pity for the girl that you *love*."

Ben rushed out of the house, unable to hear another torturous word. He knew that she was ill, but he had never imagined she was capable of hating him so much.

He jumped into Jonah's car and slammed the door.

Jonah jumped. "Whoa, take it easy on the car."

"Shut up," Ben snapped. "Just drive."

Jonah knew that this was the side of Ben he didn't need to agitate. "Right," he said obligingly, under his breath, and he drove off into the night.

"She's so goddamn sick in the head," Ben growled. "When is she going to stop it with this shit?"

"Is your mom giving you grief again?" Jonah asked, though he already knew. "C'mon, man. You can't let her get to you like that. Actually," he said with a puzzled look, "you usually don't. What did she say this time?"

Ben knew he couldn't divulge his mother's comments without revealing his secret. He slowly calmed as Dylan's face flashed into his mind. His pounding chest slowed when he remembered he was on his way to see her, his Dylan.

"Ben?" Jonah's voice awakened him.

"It's not important," Ben sighed. "Sorry about your door."

"You're so damn psycho," Jonah said with a chuckle. "Talk about a flip."

Ben laughed. "It was the door slamming. It must've helped."

"I guess so." Jonah shook his head and continued to drive.

* * *

Dylan stepped into Ollie's and sighed dramatically at the thought of her approaching night. New Year's Eve was always a reunion of sorts for everyone who grew up in Phoenix. The year before, Dylan had made over four hundred dollars. She was even able to sneak out at one, quite wasted herself due to Michael's lack of rules on that particular evening.

This year, she wanted nothing more than to be alone with Ben, despite the amount of money she knew she was capable of making. She thought of nothing but pressing her lips to his as the New Year came.

In honor of the holiday, she decided to ditch her regular jeans and T-shirt and go with something short and sparkly. She was pretty sure it would positively affect her tips and she was absolutely convinced Ben would go mad watching her all night, which would guarantee an interesting end to her evening when she was finally alone with him.

She smiled to herself as she began to set up her bar and prepare for the celebrating patrons to arrive. She felt giddy.

"Where's your hat?" Michael asked from behind her.

"I'm not wearing that thing again."

Michael laughed. "You have no idea how adorable you looked last year." He looked her up and down with widened eyes. "This is nice too, though."

I didn't wear it for you! She wished she could say something to put an end to his flattering comments once and for all.

"Are your brothers coming in tonight?" Michael asked, ignoring Dylan's eye roll.

"Yep," Dylan answered without looking at him. "They should be here soon."

"Ben, too?"

Dylan turned and glared at Michael with one hand on her hip. "Yes."

Michael's hands came up defensively. "I was just wondering."

Dylan groaned angrily. "Michael, let's make a deal. You stop saying Ben's name in my presence, and we'll stay friends, okay?"

Michael's head snapped back in astonishment. He looked more surprised than hurt by her deal. He stepped closer to Dylan and narrowed his eyes while he chewed on his lower lip.

Dylan retreated only partly. "I like working for you, but your backhanded questions about Ben need to stop."

Michael's shoulders sank. "You're right. Truce?"

Dylan poured two shots and handed one to Michael. "Thank you," she said, clinking his glass with hers to say cheers to the New Year. It was a peace offering that she knew she wouldn't regret. Hopefully, their date was behind them, including the dreadful kiss.

The night carried on as any holiday does in a bar. Dylan was quite pleased with herself for choosing the outfit she did. Unlike the year before, she felt equally matched in looks with a lot of the other women. She felt feminine and pretty, feelings she had been sure only Ben could inspire in her.

"Oh, bartender?" Ben called, slightly taunting. "More shots please."

Dylan floated over to him. "What would you like?" she asked flirtatiously.

Ben leaned forward and looked around. His eyes met hers as he smiled mischievously. "You," he said in a whisper.

"You have me," Dylan sighed.

"I don't have you now," he said with a hint of disappointment. "I definitely don't have you in that tiny, sparkly thing you call a dress."

Dylan laughed. She thought long and hard about pulling him over the bar by his tie. Would anyone really even notice? She looked around and realized that not a single person was watching them. No one suspected their secret. No one knew what they did when they were alone.

Dylan stared at Ben seductively. "It's almost midnight," she warned.

Ben's lips curved. "I know." He raised his eyebrows and leaned forward. "They're not going to even notice."

Dylan scanned the room and watched as each of her oblivious brothers concentrated on everything in the room but her and Ben. She finished setting out all of the champagne flutes and shots along the bar and walked around to stand beside Ben.

Michael stood on the bar and called out to everyone as they gathered up close. "Let the countdown begin!" he yelled. "Grab a drink!"

Dylan passed out the champagne and took her place beside Ben with a shot glass of her own. They stood in front of each other, pressed against the bar, smiling as if no one else was around.

Dylan's stomach felt fizzy, and she shook with excitement. Ben's smile was so genuine and warm. He seemed to see only her in that moment. She didn't care who was around and she knew they wouldn't even notice her and Ben as they all kissed each other.

The countdown began with ten. The group smiled and yelled out numbers as the clock gradually made its way to midnight. Dylan thought it was slower this year, only because she was mad with impatience.

Ben's lips were on hers before the crowd could even make it to two. Dylan's arms wrapped around his neck while she stood up on her toes and moved into him. His tongue slid into her mouth and, in that moment, it was just the two of them there in that room. There was no sound or movement around them. They were alone in their world and she wanted so badly to stay there forever.

They were forced apart too suddenly for their liking; it was almost painful to walk away. They had to keep going around the group for the traditional New Year's greeting. However, they didn't break apart unsatisfied. They had snuck in their midnight kiss and they were very aware that there would be more to come when they were finally alone.

As Meredith hugged her, she whispered into Dylan's ear. "No one else noticed that, but I certainly did."

Dylan smiled, knowing she was caught. "I don't know what you mean," she lied unconvincingly.

"By the way he looks at you, I would never imagine him to be what I've been told," Meredith whispered again. "He doesn't look like a womanizer."

Dylan looked at Ben and smiled. "That's because he's not."

* * *

Ben climbed the stairs to Dylan's room in the dark. He had made this trip so often that he didn't even need the wall or railing to guide him. If his shadow were permanently cast against the wall, it would always lead to that same room. It would grow a size every year, charting his progression to manhood by the path to Dylan's bed.

He slowly opened her door and gently closed it behind him. He was sure she would be asleep because it had taken Jonah forever to pass out. He had impatiently thought about punching him to knock him out cold, if he had gone to sleep any later. He made a promise to himself afterward to make sure he never allowed Jonah to mix an energy drink with his vodka again.

The moon glowed through Dylan's window and seemed to light her up as if she were in a fairytale. She was so naturally flawless.

He removed his shirt and pants before crawling into her bed. He moved closer to her warmth and felt the thrill of just holding her against him. He brushed her long hair from her moonlit face and kissed her forehead.

Dylan stirred and opened her tired eyes. She smiled. "What took you so long?"

"Your brother wouldn't shut up."

"I missed you," she whispered.

Ben's heart slammed inside his chest. He felt his feelings spiral out of control, and knew that she truly was the only one for him. He was proud that she belonged to him and he couldn't wait to tell it to anyone that would listen.

"I missed you, too," he replied, nearly choking with surprise. He couldn't remember a single time in his life that he had ever uttered those words. Ben only said things to please people when he wanted them to leave him alone. This was genuine.

Dylan snuggled to his chest and kissed his collarbone. Her warmth enveloped him as she wrapped her leg around his waist. She was his and he was hers. There were no barriers with Dylan. She had knocked them all down the minute he pressed his lips to hers.

He wanted to whisper that he loved her, but he couldn't find the words without crying. He thought it would be foolish of him to say something like that in tears. That would surely make her run.

Come with me, he thought. *Don't make me be without you.*

She could live with him in Cambridge. Her job clearly allowed that. It was easier for her to come to him. He couldn't leave school, though he would if she asked him to. She never would, though. Did that make him selfish?

Ben imagined a life with Dylan. They could have a small, one-bedroom apartment. She could paint masterpieces on the walls and he would watch every stroke. They could brush their teeth together, sleep together every night, make food together—naked, of course. They would never wear clothes unless they had company.

He rubbed his nose to hers. He kissed her lips, her neck, and her forehead. He nearly cried when she put her hands to his cheeks and looked at him like he was her everything. Her expression mirrored his and he could tell that she knew what he was feeling then.

"Ben," she whispered, "I never want to be without you again."

His heart burst with feelings, as if he were released from all the walls he had spent so many years building. He had always known it; he only belonged to Dylan.

CHAPTER

NINE

Dylan smiled when the sunlight touched her face. She moved and nuzzled into Ben's perfect arms. She buried her cheek into his bare chest and sighed as his hands moved into her hair.

She looked up at his face and saw that his eyes were still closed. "You're smiling," she said pointedly.

Ben grinned, keeping his eyes shut. "No, I'm not."

"You're dimples are showing," she teased.

"I don't have dimples," he said, squeezing his lips together to keep his absurd expression in check.

"You're a liar."

"That's my story and I'm sticking to it."

"Whatever," Dylan replied with a giggle.

Ben stretched and turned into her arms. He pulled her closer and kissed her gently.

"Do you think they'll notice if we stay in here all day?" Dylan whispered. "Maybe everyone will forget we exist."

"Possibly," Ben answered before kissing her neck.

Dylan pulled back and stared into his eyes. "What will happen when you leave next week?"

It was a fair question, Ben knew. He sighed. "I wanted to talk to you about that, but not now." He sat up and rubbed his hands over his face.

"When, then?"

Ben groaned and looked down at Dylan's suspicious face. "I'm not flaking. Stop looking at me like that."

Dylan said nothing as she stared back at him. She contemplated an explosion in her room that could launch him over the houses and through his roof, where he would land in his own bedroom and out of her life.

Oh God, he's flaking.

"This isn't a control thing, Dylan," he said as if he were inside her brain. "It's a timing thing, and I want it to be right."

"You've planned this discussion, then?" Dylan asked, crossing her arms.

"I haven't planned one moment of this, actually." He laughed and pulled her to his lap. "I'm all messed up. This was the last thing I expected."

Dylan pouted with his arms around her. She tried not to laugh at his open-hearted comments, but they were too adorable. Through her giggle, she asked, "So when does this discussion take place?"

Ben pursed his lips and smiled bashfully. "Tonight. Over dinner."

"Dinner?" Dylan's heart rate accelerated. "Out in front of people?"

"Well, maybe somewhere that won't involve people we know."

They leaned into a kiss. She wrapped her arms around his neck and pulled him closer, a wordless acceptance of his dinner invitation.

Ben stood up and got dressed quickly. "I gotta get out of here, like now. We're getting a bit careless. I want people to know, but not to find out when we're naked in your bed. Brandon would murder me before I could even explain."

"Thanks for that vivid picture of Brandon finding us naked. Yuck," Dylan said, and tiptoed across the room. She cracked the door and peeked out, scanning the shadowy hallway. "Their doors are all closed."

Ben stretched and yawned. "They're all hung-over."

"I'm sure we won't be seeing any of them until later."

Ben wrapped his arms around Dylan's waist and pulled her back to him. She loved the feeling of her skin against his. "Still, I should get going," he said to her with regret.

"I know, I know. This is the last way they should find out about us."

"What will you do while I'm gone?" Ben asked with a hint of sadness. He swiped a stray hair from her face, tracing her cheek with his fingertip.

Dylan slid from his lap and curled up into the fetal position on her bed. "Sleep," she said with a relaxed smile. "Goodnight."

Ben leaned down and kissed her forehead, her cheek, and then her lips. "Sleep," he whispered sweetly. "I'll see you later."

She watched in agony as Ben once again slipped from her morning, leaving her alone in bed. She closed her eyes and felt peace about their relationship.

She had never been to Massachusetts before. She'd seen snow, but never lived in it, nor had she ever expected to want to. But she knew he wanted her to go back with him and she knew what her answer would be.

She would happily follow Ben around the world.

* * *

Ben had a new spring in his step. He practically skipped through the yards as he walked back to his mother's house in the early morning hours.

He waved to Mr. Raymond, flashing a genuine smile and ignoring his angry neighbor's yells for being on his lawn. Normally, he would have flipped him off, but not today. It was different today.

He wanted so badly to tell Ruth what he had found in Dylan. He wished that she could know that it wasn't too late for her to have that, too.

It would be a tragedy if there weren't someone out there for everyone. Dylan was clearly made for him, created for him, and put here for him to love and need. Why couldn't everyone have that? What would be the point if they didn't?

Ben strutted through his mother's back door and ignored the usual darkness of his childhood home. The curtains were all drawn, the black drapes a constant barrier to the sun for as long as he could remember. Today, that meant nothing.

"Mom?" he called from the bottom of the stairs.

When he got no answer, Ben made his way up to the landing and turned his head up to her room. Her door was closed and no light was shining through from the other side.

"Mom?" he called again. He took the last few steps slowly as he kept his eyes focused on her door.

He pressed his ear to the wood that separated them. He listened. There was nothing: none of the usual weeping or movement of any kind.

He wanted to talk to her, to finally welcome a conversation. He hadn't felt her friendship or that motherly connection in so long—too long. He was ready to feel that with her. He was ready to allow her in for once, to share what he discovered.

Ben slowly turned the brass knob to her door and stuck his head through the opening. "Ruth?" he whispered.

He stepped through the door and stopped when he saw her in bed. Her back was to him and she still wore the same white pajamas from the night before. Her hair was down and a few strands covered her face. A bit of sun had managed to creep through the slats of the blinds. The beam of light just grazed the rim of the empty glass in her hand, creating a tiny sparkle just above her fingers.

"Didn't I tell you to stop drinking with those pills?" he asked loudly.

Ben froze when he noticed her blue skin. He drew in a quick breath and held it when he saw the empty prescription bottles spread out over her floral comforter. He couldn't make his feet move as he watched for her still back to give some sort of indication of breath.

Knowing there would not be an answer, he called out to her again. "Mom," he said, his voice cracking on the word.

His chin quivered, but it was his anger he was trying to suppress. He chewed on the inside of his cheek and stared at his mother's lifeless body. He couldn't be surprised and he couldn't find it in him to be sad. He just stood.

You stupid woman.

"Very weak, Ruth," he whispered, and left the room.

* * *

Dylan sighed and threw the covers off. It had been almost two weeks since she had been able to sleep peacefully and now, just when she was able to successfully drift off, loud sirens tore through the back of her subdivision as if every square inch of it were on fire.

"Ugh!" Dylan groaned as she kicked the sheets from her legs. She pulled her pillow from her head and sat up quickly. "You have got to be kidding me!"

Without warning, her door flew open and Jonah's face appeared through the opening. "Is Ben in here?" he asked urgently.

Dylan pulled the sheets to her body, and screeched, "No! Get out Jonah!"

"Those ambulances are at his house!" he yelled, and slammed the door.

Dylan jumped to her feet and grabbed whatever clothing she could find. She dressed frantically, attempting to block out the horrible images that flashed in her brain: Ben tripping down the stairs; Ben getting hit by a car; Ben having an aneurism; a heart attack; Mr. Raymond finally shooting him for trespassing on his lawn . . .

Doors opened and closed in the hallway just outside her room. The panicked sounds of her brothers stampeding through the house and Linda's fearful voice echoed up to Dylan's room as she raced to get ready.

By the time Dylan made it to the sliding glass door, her family was already through the first yard and on their way to Ruth's. Dylan sprinted after them with tears in her eyes.

She caught up and ran on Charlie's heels. She ran with speed and she ran without thought. If she let her mind go, it would only lead her to the worst of conclusions. Even the slightest thought that Ben may be hurt was too much for her to stomach.

As they crossed the final yard, a lot filled with only gravel and a short palm tree, Ben's slouched body came into view. He sat on his porch with his arms resting on his bent knees. He seemed to stare into space as the firefighters and paramedics moved all around him.

A police officer stood over him and quickly scrawled over a notepad in his hand while he nodded slowly, almost mechanically.

"Ben," Jonah called.

He leapt over the soil that, years before, was covered in beautiful flowers. Now it was overgrown with weeds.

Ben's exhausted eyes focused on Jonah as he slowly lifted his head. There was no sign of tears, though. Ben seemed to cry in other, less obvious ways, as Dylan had learned over the years.

"What happened, Ben?" Linda carefully asked, as she wrapped her arm around his back. "Is it your mother?"

"She's dead," he whispered without feeling.

Linda gasped. "How?"

Ben opened his eyes and stared at Dylan, who was wordless in the corner. She stood speechless with guilt, relief, sadness, and shock—every emotion manageable. She wondered if the relief she felt that it was Ruth and not Ben made her as horrible as she suspected.

Linda stood and approached the police officer who had been diligently taking notes off to the side. She spoke to him in a low voice.

Dylan and Ben stared at each other. Dylan wanted nothing more than to comfort him. Just as she did the night he got into a fight, she wanted to clean his wounds and hold him. This wound was not so easily healed, though. This was something she couldn't make better with a wet cloth and a kiss.

"She's not a victim," he announced, shaking his head.

"You can still be upset," Charlie said, placing his hand on Ben's shoulder.

Ben shrugged it off and put his hands on top of his head. He turned his back on everyone and faced the front door. His broad shoulders moved up and down as if he was trying to gain control over raging emotions.

Dylan felt helpless as she watched Ben's usual walls shoot up around him. She wondered if she should reach out and comfort him. Would he even allow that?

"Ben, come home with us," Linda pleaded in her subtle, but demanding way. "The officer says he's done with you for now."

Ben shook his head. "I need to make calls, tell everyone."

"C'mon, man. You can do all that at our house," Hugh said. "You don't need to be here."

"I don't want to be with anyone," Ben snapped. He took a deep breath. "I just need a minute."

Brandon grabbed Hugh's shoulder and eased him away. "Let's give him some breathing room, guys."

Linda wrapped her arms around Ben's tense body. "We're here when you need us."

One by one, the Mathews family departed, unknowingly leaving Dylan behind as they went. She watched for them to disappear before turning to him and searching for something to say.

"Will you be all right?" she asked quietly. The stupidity of that question only hit her after it came out of her mouth. She wanted to slap her own face for even allowing it to escape.

Ben hissed a sarcastic sound. Disgusted, he shook his head and turned his back on Dylan.

"Stupid question." She put her arms around his waist and rested her face against his back. "What can I do?"

"You can leave me alone."

"Please don't shut me out, Ben."

Ben sighed deeply. "Then don't force me to, Dylan."

"Let me be here for you."

He turned to face her with his cold glare, the old callous expression she knew all too well. As his eyes narrowed at her, Dylan felt his need to be alone. He truly didn't want her there.

"Mr. McKenna?" a police officer said as he approached. "I think we're about finished here. The coroner took your mother's body to the morgue. Do you have any questions?"

Ben looked at the officer blankly. "Can you tell when she— when she did it?" It was almost unbearable for Dylan to hear the struggle in his voice.

"We can't be too sure, but the coroner said so far it looks as if it was only a few hours ago."

Ben looked down. "Right," he said quietly.

The officer left, leaving the two of them standing on his porch alone.

"Please go, Dylan," Ben demanded. "I don't want you here."

Dylan almost took a step back from his blatant disregard. He had just lost his mother in the worst of ways and now she would be his escape. She would take his anger and verbal abuse if it made him feel better. She was willing to be there in any way he wanted, no matter the pain it caused her.

When Dylan didn't respond or move, Ben growled with anger. "Dylan, go!" he snapped loudly. "I don't want to do this to you, but I need you to leave. *Please.*"

Dylan's chin quivered. "Okay," she obliged through a painful lump in her throat. "When you're ready, I'm here."

Ben turned his back on her once more, walked into his mother's house, and slammed the door.

Dylan walked slowly, arms crossed, at a loss for words and wanting more than anything for Ben to need her. She felt selfish and heartbroken. Her emotions raged.

She stepped through the back door of her home and found her family gathered around the kitchen table. Linda spoke on the phone as the Mathews boys sat in silence.

"Who's she talking to?" Dylan asked Hugh.

"She's setting up an appointment at the funeral home that we—" he stammered. "You know. The one we took Dad to."

Dylan nodded, understanding his struggle to get his sentence out.

Linda hung up the phone and buried her face into her hands. "Oh boy," she said with a sigh. "This is going to be difficult."

Charlie took a deep breath. He looked down at his folded hands and pounded them against the table. "How could she do this to him? How could she push for him to come home after five years and then kill herself, knowing he would find her?"

"He seemed like he was changing. He seemed ... I don't know ... happier," Brandon said.

Dylan closed her eyes, forcing a single tear down her cheek. Her family didn't know that they had fallen in love. They didn't know they had planned to discuss their future that evening.

Jonah stared at Dylan with concern, curiosity, and possibly even pity. He didn't take his eyes off of her, saying, "We'll take care of the stress for him. We'll make sure all the planning is handled while he gets his head straight."

"It's no use, Jonah. He's already doing it," Hugh said. "He's already pushing everyone out."

"Just let him be!" Jonah snapped. "Not everyone needs a fucking hug."

"Well I know one thing," Linda said, "we'll deal with it like a family, damn it. You boys are not going to let this be a reason for you to fight, so you can knock that off right now."

"I'm sorry," Jonah said quietly. "I just know how he works, and he needs space."

"Ben is a part of this family and we'll give him whatever he needs," Linda announced. Her eyes welled with tears. She shook her head angrily and smacked her hands to the table. "Damn that woman! Even in death she's a shitty mother!"

In unison, the Mathews children gasped for air and looked at their mother in shock. It was very rare that she lost her temper like that. Her protective feelings for Ben took over in that instant and she cried, something she had vowed never to do in front of her children.

Brandon held his mother's hand. "Mom, he'll be okay."

Linda sank deeper into her hands. "No, he won't. This is going to be what sends him straight over the edge."

Dylan couldn't hear another word. She nearly flipped her chair as she stood up and ran for her room, sobbing harder with each step she took. It was unbearable to hear Linda's prediction for Ben's grim future, because she knew that version didn't involve her.

* * *

"I'm sorry to hear that, son," Warren McKenna said, over the phone. "I will pay for the funeral. Put all the expenses on my card."

Ben could hear his father's new family in the background. He could hear laughter and dishes clanging together. Was he actually doing *dishes* with them?

"Don't worry about the cost of anything," Warren said, as if Ben ever had before. Money was never a worry for Ben. He couldn't even recall looking at a price tag in his lifetime. Why would he worry about it now, for his mother's funeral?

"Make sure she gets the best, son."

"You're not coming, then." Ben said, already knowing the answer.

"I just think it's best that I stay away."

Ben cleared his throat, concealing his pain. He swallowed hard and shoved it all back down to his gut, where it would fuel his anger. He bit his lip and held his teeth there on his skin. The physical pain took away the mental agony. He'd rather bleed than feel emotion.

"You understand," Warren said.

"Yes," Ben said, and hung up.

Ben looked around his mother's kitchen. It was plain and white. It was clean and always unused. It was cold. It might as well have been a tin can. He gritted his teeth and stared at the empty house he was supposed to call home.

He picked up the metal stool that sat in front of the black, granite counter. He lifted it up by the seat and, in one powerful motion, smashed it into the sliding door in front of him, shattering the glass. He lifted the stool again and rammed it into the white tile floor again, and again, until the stool was twisted and broken, until all the air in his chest was gone and he could no longer scream.

*   *   *

The room was practically empty. The funeral director pointed to two suit-clad men and motioned for them to remove any vacant seats to make it look less bare.

Ben sat in the front row beside his aunt, his mother's older, and very absent, sister. He sat still. He could almost have been stone if it weren't for his color, Dylan observed.

The Mathews family sat in the row behind him. Linda had planned the funeral herself, all the way down to the selection of flowers and music. She'd let Ben call the numbers he found in his mother's address book. Only half the people he contacted showed up, a clear indication of Ruth's nonexistent life.

The minister spoke quietly. Dylan wondered what he could really say to make sense of it all. A sad, lonely woman took her life in such a way that she managed to give her only child one last smack in the face. She had always blamed him for being his father's son and, eventually, she had found a way to make him pay.

Ben stared at his mother's closed casket. He'd asked for it to be shut and hadn't felt the need to explain why. Dylan thought it was one more thing in his life that he would bottle up and shut away.

Dylan watched the back of Ben's head. She resisted the desire to reach out and touch the soft hair above his collar. That was her favorite spot to touch when they kissed. She would run her fingers around to his neck, just at the nape, and hold them there, gently stroking as she pulled him closer to her.

No one said anything about Ben's father. Nothing was said about how Ruth killed herself— she could just as soon have died of a heart attack or in a car crash. There were no recent pictures;

it was quite possible that none existed. The funeral was just as Ruth had lived her life, if you can call it living.

Ben stood when it was over. He didn't smile as he shook hands and nodded at the mourners that felt sorry for him. He did not look sad; he did not look angry. His face was cold and unfeeling. He was simply there discharging his duty as her son. It was one final way to appease her before he said goodbye and never thought of her again.

Dylan and her family waited for everyone to leave. The Mathews boys stood all the same, blank expressions and hands stuffed into their pockets. They looked awkward, but handsome in their suits. It was a bizarre moment to think of this, but Dylan couldn't help but take note of all their similarities. They could have been quadruplets.

Ben approached them reluctantly. He watched the floor as he walked, avoiding any and all eye contact. It was likely the first time that her brothers had witnessed signs of weakness in Ben. He was always so confident and sure. Now, he seemed fragile as a child beneath his hardened expression.

"It was a nice service," Brandon spoke first. He put his hand on Ben's shoulder. "Are you coming home with us?"

Ben shook his head.

"We'll leave you alone," Jonah said, patting Ben's arm. He turned to his family. "Let's go."

The group dispersed, patting him on the back as they walked out the door. They knew he didn't want to speak, but found other ways to tell him they were there. Linda hugged him quickly and scooted away before he could see her cry.

Dylan stood in front of him, debating to say anything at all. She chewed on her bottom lip and felt the moist traces of nervousness in her palms as she squeezed the strap of her handbag. He felt like a stranger.

Ben finally looked up and met her eyes. His were tired, angry, full of hate and fear. His eyebrows fell as he narrowed his eyes and gritted his teeth. She knew he didn't want to hear any words of wisdom that she had about the loss of a parent. *This is hardly the same*, she could already imagine him saying. He looked prepared to lash out with venom if she were to compare the two, so she didn't. What he needed was silence; she knew this well. She said nothing, but felt a kiss on the cheek would be okay for now. She leaned in slowly and pressed her lips to his skin, allowing her fingers to stroke the back of his neck, fulfilling her earlier longing. When she pulled away, his eyes were closed and he looked pained.

"I'll be waiting for you," she whispered, and walked away.

CHAPTER

TEN

On Monday, Jonah stepped through the broken door of Ben's mother's home. As he walked across the kitchen floor, he crushed shards of glass. He wasn't surprised by all the destruction, and he was positive the mess had been there for days.

Jonah figured he had been passive about Ben's space for long enough. It had been three days since the funeral, giving him ample time to freak out and get his head together. It was now time to step in and take control the only way he knew how: guy talk and beer.

The glass crunched beneath his feet and he silently thanked himself for wearing shoes. He pretended not to notice, though. He acted as if it was a completely normal thing to step on broken glass.

Ben was leaning against the counter, thumbing through the newspaper. He didn't look up at Jonah, but he knew he was there. "Be careful," he warned.

"Thanks," Jonah said with a smirk.

Ben looked up and checked behind Jonah. "You didn't bring the rest of them?" he asked sarcastically.

"No, I'm alone."

"They finally gave up, did they? I was thinking of getting a dog to keep them from driving by every day," he said coldly.

"I guess." Jonah didn't want to argue. He knew that if he defended his family, Ben would tell him to leave. "You feel like hanging out tonight?"

"What'd you have in mind?" Ben asked, raising an eyebrow. "Cookie decorating with your mom?"

Jonah shrugged, ignoring Ben's spiteful comments. "We could grab a few beers."

"With everyone else?" he asked, as if it were a test.

Jonah smiled and nodded. "If that's what you want. Boys night out?"

Ben sighed and crossed his arms. "I could use that."

Jonah thought about grabbing a broom and cleaning up the broken glass. He stopped when he realized that if Ben hadn't done it already then there was a reason. He was discreet in scanning the room, knowing Ben would be watching for his reaction to the disaster around them. A stool was missing, he noticed, then he found it in a nearly unrecognizable twist of metal by the battered front door. It was quite clear that his friend had had one serious meltdown and took it out on the house and all his mother's belongings.

He met Ben's cautious glance, and laughed when he couldn't think of anything to say. "Well," he said, looking around, "it looks like you had a good time."

For the first time in days, Ben smiled.

* * *

Dylan's eyes filled with tears on a regular basis these days. She slept alone, woke up alone, and couldn't find it in her heart to be angry at Ben for abandoning her. She would leave the room whenever the painful subject of him came up, never explaining why.

Her only solace, the only place she felt half human, was behind the bar at Ollie's. She worked long hours and was on her third closing shift in a row. Dylan knew she wouldn't sleep even if she were home, so she felt as though the tips she earned would at the very least make up for the bags under her eyes.

When she got home from work this time, however, her bed was not empty. Ben sat on the edge of the mattress with his head hung low and his shirt in his hands.

He looked up at her, his empty eyes bloodshot. "I didn't know you were closing tonight," he murmured.

Elated, Dylan floated across the room. She sat next to him and rubbed the nape of his neck. She leaned her head to his, and whispered, "I wouldn't have if I knew you were here."

Ben chuckled. "I just got here."

She could smell the alcohol on his breath. "I see," she said, sitting back. "You went out with my brothers, then?"

Ben nodded drunkenly. He leaned into her lap and nuzzled his face into her stomach. "You smell good," he slurred, his voice muffled by her shirt.

"I'm sure I don't. I've been working all night."

Ben slid his hands inside her shirt and felt for her bra. He unhooked it from the back and grabbed at her breast in the front. She didn't stop him. Part of her wanted his hands on her. Maybe it would feel the same as before and their lives could just go on as if they hadn't skipped a beat.

She ran her fingers through his hair as he groped her drunkenly. She knew this wasn't a display of affection. She was well aware that his heart was nowhere near this, but, with pathetic desperation, she hoped he would remember a time when it was.

Dylan leaned back and allowed him to fall on top of her. He kissed her; it was a kiss she didn't recognize, rough and messy. He wasn't gentle or patient as he forced his tongue into her mouth and grinded against her. He seemed to not even be in his own head.

"Ben," Dylan said with her hands on his chest. She pushed his heavy body up. "Ben, stop."

He abruptly sat up, leaning on his hands. He seemed to snap out of it as he stared down at her. He looked surprised, like he had forgotten who he was with. Still befuddled, he leaned his head back down and nuzzled her neck and hair. He relaxed into her arms and sighed, sending a gust of hot air against her skin.

"Sleep," she whispered with tears in her eyes. "Just sleep."

Ben passed out quickly. Naturally, his hand remained resting on her breast. His jeans and shoes were still on. He felt like dead weight on top of her, but she didn't mind. He was there and that was all that mattered.

* * *

Ben managed to sneak out of Dylan's grasp quietly enough. He had been awake for some time, standing over the bed and staring down at her peaceful face. He forced himself to walk away, knowing he shouldn't have been there to begin with.

As he moved down the stairs, he tried to walk as quickly as possible. The chances of Jonah and his brothers being awake so early in the morning were very slim, but Linda was sure to be up and lurking somewhere in the house. When he stepped into the empty kitchen, he sighed in relief, knowing that, from there, he could say he had been in Jonah's room. He reached the sliding glass door and opened it slowly, ready for his quick escape.

"You know," a voice said from behind him, "they may not see it, but I do."

Ben turned to face Meredith, who stood in the laundry room with a shoebox in one hand and a wedding planner in the other. She had obviously just come in from the garage, and had paused to fix him with a disapproving glare.

"See what?" Ben asked, rolling his eyes. He didn't really care for her to elaborate, but he figured she would.

She stepped closer to him. She placed her belongings down on the table and rested her hands on her hips. "What you're doing to Dylan. You do know what you're doing, right?"

"I'm sure you'll tell me."

"Absolutely." She grinned sarcastically and continued. "Because I don't care about you like everyone else in this house does. I care about Dylan."

"Could you get to the point?"

"Gladly."

Ben raised his eyebrows and waited for her to continue, pitying Charlie for being stuck with her forever.

"For a minute there, I thought they were wrong about you, but I see now that I was the one who was wrong. You obviously can't handle love." Meredith moved closer and spoke quietly. "You're only going to hurt her, Ben. I know you don't want that."

He nodded slowly. His gut turned, knowing she was right. His mother had been right; he was poison to anyone that loved him. More importantly, he was lethal to anyone that he loved in return.

"If you care about her, or her family, you'll let her go."

"Don't talk to me about this family. Who the hell are you, anyway? You've been here for what, ten seconds?" he asked sharply. He stopped himself from going on, keeping his respect for Charlie in the back of his mind.

Meredith smiled and rolled her eyes. "Ben, I couldn't care less if you don't like me. I don't really like you, to be honest. I want you to think about Dylan. You know I'm right."

"Thanks for the chat," he said, and slipped out the door.

Meredith watched him leave and was well aware of the line she had crossed. The love that Charlie and his family had for Ben ran deep in very different ways for all of them. The boys loved him like a brother, Linda as a son. They didn't understand how deep it went for Dylan, though. Sure they teased her, but that just made sense. They didn't really know the extent of it, and they surely wouldn't support it now. In Meredith's mind, she was protecting them all, including Ben.

* * *

Michael watched sympathetically as Dylan poured shots and wiped the sweat from her brow with the back of her hand. She was slammed and exhausted, but there was no way she would admit defeat during an NBA rush. Countless orders came in, one after another. Dylan raced around robotically, as if her mind was on nothing else. She was a machine.

As she stood at the register, closing out her cash tabs, Michael came to her from behind and placed two hands on her small shoulders. "Take a break, Dylan," he instructed gently.

"I don't need a break," Dylan answered with a fake smile.

"Yes, you do. Everyone needs a break." Michael's lips pursed. "That's not a request. Go outside and get some air."

Dylan threw her bar towel at his chest and pushed past him. She walked through the kitchen and swung the back door open. As she walked outside, she kicked a bucket over and collapsed onto an orange crate that was sitting just outside the back entrance to the bar.

She wanted to scream. She wanted to punch someone. She wanted Ben to appear, and not to slip out while she was sleeping. Why didn't he want her? When her father died, Ben was what she wanted. Ben was all she *needed*. She had cried into his lap and couldn't have felt better with his hands stroking her hair.

She cried into her hands. She sobbed and shook as she tried to catch her breath. It was so unlike her to weep uncontrollably. It made her feel so weak.

A hand rubbed her shoulder. Dylan looked up and met Michael's compassionate eyes. He half smiled as he continued to stroke her shoulder.

"I don't know what's going on, Dylan," he began gently, "but I'm here if you want to talk."

Without thinking, Dylan stood up and fell into his chest. She sobbed, soaking his shirt. She let her arms fall limp at her sides as Michael held her there, resting his chin on her head and swaying gently.

"Dylan," he whispered as he stroked her long hair. "Shhh, don't cry."

Dylan continued to sob into Michael and, for a moment, pretended his arms were Ben's. His chest didn't feel like Ben's chest, and his scent was off, but his hold would do for now. She couldn't help it; he was the one who was there.

Michael placed both hands on her cheeks and just about buried his face in her hair, inhaling deeply. He smelled her hair in the familiar way that Ben always did. He rested his chin back on her head and whispered, "Everything will be okay."

Suddenly, Dylan didn't feel okay. She realized this might be too comfortable for Michael and decided to pull away. "I'm sorry," she said through a shaky breath. "I don't know what came over me."

Michael laughed and hung onto her waist. "It's all right. You seem to have needed a friendly hug."

"Yes, a *friend* would be nice."

"May I ask what happened?" he asked, his hands still on her.

Dylan shook her head and stepped out of his hold. She put her hand on the doorknob and opened it slightly. "It's nothing," she insisted, and stepped inside.

It was something, though. Something she couldn't say out loud. She was counting down the days until Ben left, and he was still treating her as if the last several weeks hadn't happened. She was plagued with the sickening feeling that he was going to leave without her.

They went back to their busy night and worked side by side. Dylan felt a release she couldn't describe. She chalked it up to just needing a hug and thought nothing more of it from there.

Michael and Dylan worked well together at the bar. When they really got into a groove, it almost looked rehearsed the way she would go under as he went over. He would grab a bottle from a high place he was sure she couldn't reach before she even asked for it. He worked one end of the bar and she the other. They were always in sync as they moved up and down the rail.

The game ended and only a few patrons remained. Michael and Dylan cleaned up from their rush and decided to reward themselves with a shot while they took a breather.

Dylan hopped up and sat on the end of the bar. She folded her legs and popped open a beer to chase her shot.

"You feeling a bit better?" Michael asked.

Dylan shook her head and looked down. "Only when I don't think."

"This must be why I've been seeing so much of you, then?"

Dylan took a refreshing drink from her bottle. "I suppose," she answered. "Work keeps my mind on other things."

"How's Ben doing?"

"Like you care," Dylan teased.

Michael's hands went up in defense and he stepped closer to her. "Hey, I don't like the guy, but it sucks what happened to him."

Dylan could see that he meant it. "Yes, it does suck," she agreed with her head down.

She wondered if this conversation and the hug from before was a betrayal. She had stopped it the minute she understood what the embrace meant to Michael. It would always mean more for him.

"Speak of the devil," Michael said, almost cringing as he pointed to the door.

The train of Mathews, followed by Ben, stumbled in. To no surprise, they were drunk and followed by a group of unfamiliar girls. Ben, with his arm around a blonde, stared hard as he walked over to the bar where Dylan was sitting. His glassy eyes narrowed at Michael, who was standing way too close to Dylan in that moment.

"What's this?" Dylan asked, eyeing her new enemy.

"Grab us a beer?" he slurred. "*Please*."

Michael quickly set two bottles in front of him. "These are on me," he said sternly. He patted Dylan's back gently, attempting to calm her anger at Ben and his new friend.

Ben squinted and smirked. "Well, thanks, Ollie!" he said with such sarcasm that anyone was sure to pick up on it.

Charlie managed to get Michael's attention from the other end of the bar, leaving Dylan alone with Ben and his blonde. It was an unfortunate position, and she desperately wanted out of it.

"Weed," Ben began drunkenly, "this is Angela."

"Veronica," the blonde corrected with her hand out. "I'm Veronica."

Ben didn't seem to care about his mistake. "Whatever," he said with a callous chuckle.

Dylan, disregarding the girl's hand in front of her, shook her head and stared at Ben. "What are you doing?"

"I'm enjoying Angela's company," Ben replied.

"I said my name is Veronica," the girl whined.

"Yes, yes. And I said *whatever*," he replied with his hands on her cheeks. He moved closer to Veronica's face and, in a final blow to Dylan, he rubbed his nose to hers.

Dylan hopped down from the bar and headed over to Michael and her brothers. She pushed past Ben with his idiot blonde and tried desperately to hold in her inevitable tears.

Dylan stepped into the circle of intoxicated men and Michael. "I'm going home," she yelled over the drunken banter.

Michael stepped out of the absentminded crowd and moved closer to her. He placed his hand on her back and whispered in her ear, "Are you going to be okay?"

Before Dylan could move, or even answer, Ben's arm was reaching over her and his fist was crashing its way into Michael's jaw. The fight ended quickly, with Ben's arms locked in Charlie and Jonah's grips. They pulled him back as he tried to break free.

"Get him out of here!" Michael hollered and pointed to the door. He didn't hit him back and Dylan seriously wondered why. If they had been anywhere else, she was sure it would have been a full-on brawl by now.

Hugh shook his head in disbelief. "Ben, what the hell?"

"He's upset about his mother," Brandon said. "I'm sorry, Michael."

"It's fine," Michael said with a towel full of ice pressed to his face. "He needs to go, though."

"No, he knows what this is about," Ben growled. "It's not about my mother, you asshole."

Michael snapped. "What's it about then, Ben?" He waved his hands around the group. "Tell your friends what it's about."

Ben shrugged off Jonah's and Charlie's hold. He pointed his finger and almost fell into a stool. "You touch her again, and I'll kill you."

"Her?" Hugh asked, confused. "Her who?"

"I'm right here," Michael urged with open arms. "Dylan's got you all figured out, anyway. She'll come to me on her own. It's only a matter of time."

Ben lunged again, enraged. This time, Brandon was ready and caught him on his way to Michael. With quite a scuffle, he pushed him out the door and into the night air.

Dylan glared at Michael. This was not the way she wanted her brothers to find out. Michael was the sober one, the responsible one. No matter how badly Ben behaved, Michael shouldn't have antagonized him.

Michael sighed regrettably. "Dylan, I'm sorry," he said. "He just pushes, you know?"

"I quit," she said, and walked out the door.

Charlie, Hugh, and Jonah followed, drunk and dumfounded at what had just taken place before them. It was clear from their expressions that they were replaying everything in their minds.

Dylan stepped outside and followed Brandon as he dragged Ben down the sidewalk. When she caught up to them, Ben was finally released and slammed up against a brick wall.

"You want to explain this?" Brandon asked, angrily. "Are you really this stupid, Dylan? How could you even think getting involved with him was a good idea?"

"Just go get them," Dylan answered, pointing behind her.

"I'm not done with you," Brandon warned, and stormed away.

Dylan felt as if she was in trouble, which only irritated her more. Brandon, out of them all, felt that he was her father sometimes, which she felt was stupid seeing as how he was only six years older than her.

"You're screwing Ollie now?" Ben asked with a belligerent snarl. "I knew it."

"You should go," Dylan said, pulling at his hand. "Let me get you a cab."

"No, wait," he said, and pulled her to him. He made no attempt at discretion and held her like they had been in a normal relationship for years. "I miss you," he whispered drunkenly.

Dylan nodded with tears in her eyes. She was hurt and sad, though, mostly confused by his behavior. "Why don't we talk about it tomorrow?"

"You can come to my house." He laughed carelessly. "We know for a fact no one's there, don't we?"

"Ben, you're falling apart," Dylan whispered compassionately. "You have to try and get a grip on this."

"You can't fix me," he whispered. "You should give up."

The Mathews brothers caught up to them. They all stood quietly, knowing the secret that Ben and Dylan had been hiding for weeks. They looked on in confusion, waiting for an explanation to come and knowing they wouldn't be getting one.

"C'mon, man," Jonah said, pulling at Ben's arm. "Let's get out of here."

Ben yanked his arm from Jonah. He leaned in closer to Dylan's face, and said, "You should run back in there. Your boyfriend's waiting." He turned and walked away, stumbling into the wall as he headed down the sidewalk, and finally disappeared.

Jonah turned and looked at Dylan with a torn expression. He looked in Ben's direction and then at his sister, whom he felt probably needed him the most just then. It was an awful place for him to be in.

"Jonah, he'll only talk to you," Brandon shouted, and pointed down the sidewalk. "We'll take care of her. You and Hugh go get Ben."

They ignored Dylan when she shouted, "I don't need to be taken care of!"

Jonah and Hugh raced to catch up to Ben. Dylan wanted them all to go so she wouldn't be bombarded by anyone's questions.

"Weed?" Charlie asked, breathless and confused. "You and Ben?"

Dylan spun around, tears running down her cheeks. "My name is *not* Weed!" she screamed, and stormed off into the night.

CHAPTER ELEVEN

They say that everyone dies alone. When Carl Mathews left, he took a piece of the world with him. The house, the land, all that he touched in his life, seemed less after he was gone.

On his deathbed at home, exactly where he wanted to be, he asked his family members to come to him, one by one. They'd taken turns, Brandon first, then the rest by age. Each child had left the room in tears, but smiling. He'd sent them each away with something from his heart; it was something they would keep with them forever.

It was clear that he had passed the torch to Brandon, declaring him the man of the house and protector of his baby sister, a job Brandon committed to with all that he had in him. He had always watched over her, but now, more than ever, he felt he needed to do so in his father's honor.

Each one of the boys had been given a job and told something that Carl would have wanted to teach them someday. He'd sat with them all and joked, making each of them laugh through their tears as they left the room and sent the next person in.

At last, when Dylan's turn arrived, she walked into his room and wasted no time getting into the bed and nestling into his safe, fragile arms. She knew time was wearing thin in moments like that one.

"You have a button nose," Carl whispered as he gently poked the tip. "You make buttons beautiful."

Dylan stared at her dying father, unaware that she was crying. In all of her thirteen years, this was the moment that had made her feel more alive than ever. Call it growing up, or having an epiphany, perhaps. She liked to think of it as the day her father transitioned into an angel. She almost felt pride at being able to witness it. Despite the pain his absence caused, she knew he would never really be that far because she watched him leave.

Carl had been weak, but his heart was bigger than ever; it was open and ready. His pale face looked peaceful in the luminous sunshine. The dust particles dancing through the stream of gold added a spiritual feel to the room. Dylan was young, but even then she had been so blessed with an eye for creativity that even her father's deathbed seemed beautiful.

It had been obvious what was approaching. His eyes were red; his hair was gone. He weighed less than Dylan, she was sure. He looked ninety years old, so much older than the forty-five-year-old superhero he had been only five months before.

"Does it hurt?" she'd asked innocently.

Carl shook his head and pointed to Dylan's heart. "This hurts worse. I hear it breaking."

"Will you ever come back?"

"I'll never leave," he'd said. "You just won't see me anymore. I can't leave you, you know?"

"Can I talk to you?"

Carl leaned forward weakly and kissed his daughter's forehead. "Always," he answered.

"Where will you be?"

Carl sighed as he kept his lips to his baby's hair. "Everywhere you are." He pulled away and smiled, before adding, "Where I can watch you with health in my heart."

Dylan imagined him floating above her. In all the things she'd learn from her parents and church, she had never truly understood the idea of being watched by people she herself could not see. But now, she had found that she was willing to believe anything if it meant her father could still exist beyond his untimely and completely unjust death.

"Now, I want you to remember something for me," he'd instructed.

Dylan smiled through her tears. "Anything."

"Someday you're going to fall in love. Someday you're going to fail. Someday you're going to be broken. You have to keep the fight inside you—the fight that I love about you—the fight that makes you Dylan."

She'd nodded, sending more tears down her wet cheeks and onto her soaked shirt.

"Promise me you'll remember how wonderful you are. Promise me you'll allow yourself to be beautiful, inside and out."

"I promise."

"That's my girl." Carl ran his hands through her hair and pulled her against his chest. "And when you fall in love, you'll know that he's the one because you'll feel it in your soul. You'll know when to surrender to it, and you'll know when to let it go."

Even then, Dylan had pictured Ben.

"And if he breaks your heart, I've instructed your brothers to kill him," he teased. There was some truth to that, though, and Dylan wasn't surprised.

Nothing else had been said between the two of them. Nothing else needed to be done. They quietly watched the sun as it disappeared into the sky and was replaced by an orange moon.

The entire Mathews family had stayed in the room with Carl that night, Linda and Dylan in the bed with him and the boys spread out in chairs and on the floor.

Ben had mostly stayed away, leaving Carl a note earlier in the day. No one else ever saw it because Carl did exactly what Ben had requested: he'd shredded it to pieces and thrown it away.

Carl Mathews died the next morning. It was quiet, expected, and the most difficult thing that any of them would ever go through. He left them with laughter in their hearts. He left them with peace in their souls. He left them knowing that they would survive without him as long as they stuck together.

* * *

"I don't know what to say," Linda said with a sigh. She looked out the window and sipped from her coffee. "Should we have expected this?"

In the Mathews family, as Carl had instructed them years before, they would all band together when predicaments were exposed. The boys filled Linda in on the new developments, hoping for direction. They could discuss it as a family, even if there weren't any answers to be found. In this instance, no one was even sure of the questions to ask.

"It all makes sense, though, you know?" Hugh said. "He's been nowhere to be found and she hasn't even been coming home at night. Oh, God, I can't even wrap my head around it."

"Why her, though?" Brandon asked angrily. "Out of all the girls Ben could have, why her?"

"Are you saying she's not good enough for him?" Charlie asked with an eyebrow raised. "She's the best he'd ever get."

"I didn't say *he* was too good for her, dumbass. I'm asking why he would choose to make our little sister one of his castaways." Brandon seemed to get more agitated as he spoke. "You really think he didn't use her?"

"Oh, man, that sucks," Hugh groaned. He placed his forehead on the table. "I can't even think of it."

"I don't think he used her," Charlie said. "I think there really was something there and he lost it when his mother did what she did. I think it makes sense for them to be together."

"Don't defend him!" Brandon shouted.

"Do we have to kick his ass now? I mean, is that even okay to do?" Hugh held his turning stomach. "This is Ben. I can't fight Ben."

"No one's fighting Ben!" Charlie's voice was slowly rising. He stood and looked at Brandon. "Let's just see how it plays out. Give it a chance before you go all crazy big brother on him."

Brandon stood, too. "We're seeing how it plays out right now. He's leaving my little sister brokenhearted. Where the hell are your loyalties anyway?"

"With *our* little sister, of course, but—God—this is *Ben* we're talking about. He might as well have our last name!" Charlie looked at Linda. "Mom?"

"Beating up Ben won't make anyone feel better. I think we should just leave it alone," Linda answered. She was torn and it showed in her sad expression. "I've heard he may be getting ready to put Ruth's house on the market."

"See?" Brandon said. "He's gone. He's leaving her."

Jonah sat, arms crossed, chewing on his lower lip. For the entire morning he had said nothing. One thing was clear to them all: he was ridiculously lost over the whole thing.

He stood in the middle of the conversation and slowly walked to the other side of the room as if he hadn't listened to a bit of their bickering. His hands were shoved deep into his pockets as he hid in the corner.

No one in that room felt the way he did. Ben was his best friend and Dylan was his twin. He thought, *Let them be together if they want.* But he knew better than anyone that Ben was going to break Dylan's heart. Selfishly, the only thing he questioned was where that left him, stuck between his best friend and his twin sister.

He had to hear Ben out. He needed to know where his head was, how he felt. He hated to ask such invasive questions. After all this silence on the matter, though, he deserved to get answers.

"Where are you going?" Brandon asked as Jonah headed for the door. "We're in the middle of a discussion."

Jonah said nothing. He only walked out the back door and made his way through the yards.

* * *

Jonah's face looked somewhat different, Ben noticed. At first, he questioned whether he was dreaming; it was difficult to tell the difference these days. Life was more of a blur than anything lately.

"You up?" Jonah asked. He sat straddling a chair, holding a glass of water in one hand and aspirin in the other.

Ben sat up and pressed his hand to his throbbing head. "Hell," he mumbled.

"It gets worse," Jonah snapped.

"I don't want a lecture."

Jonah stood furiously, knocking the chair to the ground and startling Ben. "Maybe that's exactly what you need, you piece of shit!"

Ben stared up at him, resigned. He'd known it was only a matter of time before this moment came and, as the previous night played over again in his head, he knew this conversation was only fair.

"Do yourself a favor and just shut up, Ben."

A foreign look of rage was on Jonah's face, and Ben tried to grasp the fact that he was on the receiving end of his fury. He must have wanted to unleash this all on him the night before, but Ben had been incoherent from beer and whiskey. Now, here Jonah was, having stewed all night, and ready to explode. It was strange, looking up at his best friend's angry face.

Ben sighed, long and heavy. "All right, get it over with. Tell me what an ass I am." If there was ever someone who could get away with speaking to Ben this way, it would be Jonah. Ben knew that he owed Jonah a lot after all the trouble he'd caused the night before. Jonah had a right to be heard.

"You honestly think this is about what you did last night?"

"Isn't it?" Ben half-laughed awkwardly, feeling a bit nervous as this new version of Jonah stood over him with clenched fists. *Would he really punch me?* "I got wasted and punched Olerson. Sorry, man."

"I don't care about what you did at Ollie's. That was just another bar brawl to add to the list." Jonah stood his ground, refusing to sit again. He seemed as though he was trying to keep his cool, but it didn't look as if he would win that battle.

Yes. Yes, he would definitely hit me. Ben shook his head, then turned and looked at nothing, suddenly remembering the reason he punched Michael. *Oh shit.*

"I don't ask a lot of you. I never have. I don't know how serious it was—if there was anything at all, that is." Jonah looked down and shook his head. "I've kept my opinions to myself because I hoped this was actually something different for you, but I can't just let you do this to her. I should have stopped it."

"Oh. That." Ben's throat burned. *Of course that.* "You knew the whole time, then?"

"All the times you went up to her room in the middle of the night? How could I not?" Jonah stared and waited. He waited for Ben to gasp, jump, implode—something!

"I don't know what to say," Ben said in a cowardly whisper. "I didn't realize you knew."

"Say that you're sorry for hurting my sister. Say that you'll go over there and fix it. Say something that will make me not want to punch you—say anything."

"I can't fix this, Jonah." Ben looked down. "I wish I could."

"Why her, anyway?" Jonah growled in frustration as he turned and headed for the door. "You shouldn't have come back. You should have left her alone."

"I know," Ben replied quietly. "That's why I'm leaving today."

Jonah laughed sarcastically. "And, let me guess, you have no plans of coming over and telling her to her face."

Ben shook his head. His chest stung as he allowed his next words to come out. "I am who I am, though, right?"

"You really are a selfish bastard, Ben." Jonah brought his fist to his mouth, attempting to calm his rampant nerves. "Don't come back. Leave her alone. And, you know what, you can leave me alone, too."

Jonah left, slamming the door behind him.

Ben watched his brother leave in a rage. It was less than what he knew he deserved. He was doing them all a favor that they would never thank him for. As lonely as life would be without the Mathews, he didn't deserve any of them.

*   *   *

Dylan could hear the chatter from downstairs, and she knew without listening what the conversation was about. It was just another invasion of her life that they all helped themselves to on a regular basis. Why did they always feel it so necessary to invade her privacy?

She reluctantly made her way downstairs. If it weren't for the list of supplies she needed to get for her class, she would have stayed in bed all day, just to avoid them all. She hadn't been sure if she would even finish out the term. That's how certain she had been that she would be leaving with Ben. She had put the task off for long enough, now, and her class was getting ready to resume after its holiday break. The chore couldn't be ignored any longer.

She rounded the corner and flinched, prepared for the worst. Her brothers and Linda stopped speaking and stared at her sympathetically. It was obvious what they thought. Brandon was enraged. The rest of them looked torn and confused. Dylan wanted to scream. They were turning it into their problem.

"Morning," she said, biting her lip and avoiding an outburst that was sure to make her day worse. She had neither the strength nor the patience to defend herself today.

"Hi, honey," Linda said in a fake, cheery voice. "Would you like coffee?"

Dylan shook her head. She stared, confused and suspicious. They looked at her through careful eyes, gawking as if she were a time bomb. They looked frightened but thoughtful.

"Hey, Wee—I mean—*Dylan*," Jonah began, "we thought you should know—"

Dylan put her hand up to quiet him. "You don't get to say," she said sternly, assuming there would be an opinion following his words. She wanted to be clear that nothing they believed would matter to her.

"Ben's leaving," he continued. "He's leaving right now."

Without a moment's thought, Dylan ran out the back door. She sprinted through the yards and over the gravel. She nearly stumbled over a small cactus, forgetting it had been there as long as she could remember. She was clumsy, unfocussed, but, most of all, she was determined to get to him. How could he leave her like this?

She cleared the final yard and came to the edge of the curb right across from Ben's house, stopping with a near screeching halt. The scrapes on the bottoms of her feet only reminded her too late that she was barefoot. She was in her pajamas and still hadn't brushed her teeth. She felt ridiculous.

She couldn't make her feet move another step. She stared at Ben's house. Unbelievably, it managed to appear even more depressing than before. When Dylan would pass the home on her way out of the subdivision, she would smile, and think, *There's Ruth's house.* On occasion, she would look up toward Ben's window and smile, hoping for his return. Only, now Ruth was gone and, very soon, Ben's room would be empty again.

She thought of Ben packing his bag, ignoring his mother's closed bedroom door. She imagined the house demolished. She knew that he had probably destroyed anything within reach. That was always Ben: polite destruction.

She had no idea what she was even going to say to him this time. She hadn't thought of a greeting as she ran. She was always so careful with her words with Ben; she handled him fragilely out of fear that he would point out her stupidity. The last few weeks with him had made her feel the roles were reversed, but now they had come full circle and she was almost dizzy from the abrupt change their relationship had taken.

A yellow cab sat in the drive and Ben slowly walked out the front door. He looked sad, alone, angry, tired. She stared as he set the alarm and walked down the stone path that ran to the waiting taxi. She watched, debating whether to call out to him.

Screw it, she thought. He owed her a goodbye. "Ben!"

He stopped walking and froze. His shoulders lifted and then fell as he sighed. He was in the middle of a fast getaway and she was ruining it now. "What?" he asked without looking.

"You could at least look at me."

He turned slowly, raised his hands, and asked, "Happy? I'm looking at you."

"No," Dylan answered. She stepped down and walked closer to him. She walked like she was going into battle—and, in a way, she was. "What are you doing? You don't want this."

"You have no idea what I want," he said. He straightened his black leather bag on his shoulder and turned toward the taxi. His wall of arrogance seemed taller and much thicker than usual.

Dylan stepped after him. "I'm just going to follow you. I'll get into that cab if I have to."

"Why are you making this so hard, Dylan?" Ben snapped uncaringly.

"You really don't know?" Dylan felt a tear fall down her cheek. "Because I love you, Ben," she whispered.

Ben's jaw tightened. "Well, I'm sorry for that. I didn't mean for that to happen."

"You're sorry?"

"Don't do that," he ordered and ran his hand through his hair. "Don't be such a girl."

"What?" she asked, pained. "I *am* a girl."

"I know you're a girl," he grumbled. "Just go back to your house. This conversation isn't going anywhere. It's stupid."

"Ben, let me help you. We can work this out together." She stepped closer, pleading almost. "What happened to your mom—"

Ben snapped. "What *happened* to my mom?" he asked incredulously. "What *happened* to her was this: while I was off fucking my best friend's sister, she shoved pills down her throat and died."

That was her undoing. Dylan's chest stung, her throat burned. She launched herself at him without thought, and shoved him hard in the chest. She slammed her fists against him, one after the other, until all the energy drained from her. She was breathless, animalistic, and completely devastated.

Ben remained unfazed by it all. "Feel better?" he asked when she was done. "That's what you wanted, right? The truth?"

There was nothing she could say to make it stop, to change his mind. He was going to do this. He was going to leave. She was sure he would never come back this time.

She backed away slowly while she attempted to catch her breath. She gasped at the painful emptiness that he was able to leave behind. She was shaken to the core but, as her father had told her years before, she knew it was time to let love go. There was nothing more she could do.

Ben didn't look at her a second time. He carelessly walked away and got into his cab. As it drove away, passing Dylan as it went, he refused to look at what he was leaving behind. He wouldn't even give her one last glance.

"You got a clinger not taking the hint?" the driver asked Ben as they sped away. "Sometimes you have to just hit 'em hard."

"Something like that," Ben replied quietly.

"Well, it looks like she got it now, though, right? I mean, you demolished her back there."

"I did her a favor."

"I don't think she thanks you," the driver said with a chuckle.

Ben turned his face and looked out the window. He watched in agony as his neighborhood grew smaller and smaller behind him. "She will," he whispered, while barely holding on to a falling tear.

CHAPTER TWELVE

Dylan spotted Meredith's impatient face in the doorway of her classroom. Her cheeks were rosy, a sure sign she was feeling the pre-wedding stress a bit more as the big event approached. It seemed as if every day there was some new emergency that only Dylan could help her solve.

Dylan saw through Meredith's helpless act, though. The wedding was a convenient way to distract her from frequent thoughts of Ben, and Dylan was positive that Charlie asked Meredith to be an even bigger pain than before. They all treated her like an explosive, all her bottled up feelings primed to go off at any moment.

Meredith lifted her arm and pointed to her tiny watch. She mouthed the words *wrap it up*, and made an expression of urgency.

Dylan nodded to Meredith and rolled her eyes as she turned her back. She still had five minutes left. It was her future sister in-law that needed to check the time, not her. She continued to wander around the room, checking over shoulders and nodding at every line, every angle. She hardly ever shook her head. In her mind, art was art. Each artist had her own voice, her own magic.

She would only assist with blocks to creativity, or if she felt more personality or feeling could be expressed in the work. Dylan made her art with feeling.

As Dylan ended her class, she hollered instructions she hoped were heard as the students fled the room. She remembered a time when they hung on every word she uttered. But, to be fair, even she was bored of her monotonous voice these days.

"Okay. So, we have a final fitting tonight and I need you to help me with the flowers tomorrow," Meredith rambled as they walked through the parking lot. "You're good with that stuff."

"Flowers?" Dylan laughed. "I didn't know that was my thing."

"It's art, right?"

Dylan shot Meredith a puzzled look. "Yeah, if I'm a florist."

"You know what I mean, Dylan." She waved her hand in annoyance. "You're creative."

"Whatever."

The drive to Maria's Bridal was a slow one in the evening rush. Life was back to normal after the holidays, everyone settling into the familiar habits of their lives. Rush hour traffic lost any festivity it might have had, and road rage had returned.

Dylan tried to blend in. She smiled her most convincing smiles and even added a fake laugh once in a while. No one close to her bought into her charade, but none of them dared tell her to get over it. She was trying to heal and that was all they asked of her.

"Did you decide who you want to be paired up with yet?" Meredith asked as she navigated around a curve. "Is Michael definitely out?"

Dylan glared at her. Meredith didn't have to look back to know that her expression was not a friendly one. "Okay, I'll take that as a yes," Meredith answered.

Dylan shook her head and sighed. "It's your wedding, Meredith. Do whatever you want."

The girls walked through the double doors of the bridal shop and almost instantly Meredith's face was all business. She was ready to get into her dress and be the princess she was meant to be.

"Hello," one of the women addressed them. She sounded as prissy as she looked, Dylan thought. "The gown is ready for you!"

"Perfect," Meredith beamed. "What about the bridesmaids' dresses? I have one of them with me. I don't really know if this one eats, though, so you may need to take it in a bit."

"I believe we have them ready." The woman looked Dylan up and down. "You must be the size six in the back. I surely hope you don't get any smaller or we'll be using a flower girl's gown instead." She chuckled as she pranced to the back.

Dylan nodded and plopped herself down into a comfy-looking circular chair. She wasn't prepared to play dress up today, and she certainly wasn't in the mood for any eating tips from anyone. She was pretty sure she hadn't shaved her legs since the last time she was with Ben. That was definitely going to pull a snide comment from Meredith, something Dylan despised.

Meredith oohed and ahhed at her wedding dress as they pulled it from the garment bag and displayed it with a twirl. She sipped champagne and looked like she had done this her whole life.

"Dylan, isn't it beautiful?" Meredith shrieked. "I could look at it all day!"

Dylan smiled and chuckled. She had seen this dress too many times to keep track of. She had helped Meredith decide on it only the month before. It was a dress. It was a big, poofy, white dress.

Like a pro, Dylan stood on a stool as she held the dress up in the air and dropped it down over Meredith's head. She fastened satin buttons until her fingers were sore. She lifted the back of the gown, led Meredith up to the mirrors, and fluffed out the long, sparkly train until it spread out beautifully.

"Wow," she whispered, realizing that she truly was in awe of her future sister in-law. "Charlie is going to cry."

"I know, right?" Meredith practically screamed. "Everyone should have a wedding dress. I'm a princess!"

Dylan gathered up Meredith's hair and pinned her veil into the bunched locks. She spread out the jeweled tulle, and pulled it all the way down.

"There," Dylan said with genuine sweetness.

The girls stared at Meredith's reflection for what seemed like hours. If Dylan had been much for crying in public, she was sure she would be a blubbering mess. The result of all the shopping, fitting, champagne-sipping, and veil-searching was right in front of her. It was a lovely feeling.

"Okay," Meredith began, as Dylan carefully lifted the gown from her body, "let's see if your anorexic butt swims in that tiny dress."

Dylan shot Meredith a scowl that Meredith pretended not to see. Dylan knew she had lost a bit of weight and she was well aware that the dress was going to be a tad big.

She pulled the light pink gown from the hanger and carelessly flung it over the dressing room door. The form-fitting strapless dress was the one Dylan had fallen in love with at a time when she enjoyed the way she felt in it.

As she slipped into the long gown, it only confirmed what everyone thought. She most definitely had lost some weight. She zipped the dress and realized she looked like a twelve-year-old boy in it. Her curves—the few she'd had before—had disappeared with Ben. She felt ugly for the first time in her life.

"It's too big," she yelled from the fitting room.

"Well, may I see it?" Meredith barked. "We have to know how much to take in, Dylan."

Dylan sighed deeply. "Fine, but keep your comments to yourself." She opened the door and stepped up to the mirrors.

Meredith stood next to the seamstress. They didn't have to say anything; it was obvious what they were thinking by the frowns on their faces. Of course, they voiced their opinions anyway.

"Dylan," Meredith whispered, "you have to eat."

"I am eating!" Dylan snapped. "I just don't have much of an appetite."

"How do I fix this?" the seamstress asked sharply. "Suppose I do and she just keeps losing the weight? The beading on this dress will make multiple alterations very difficult."

"Then we'll wait until just before the wedding," Dylan suggested. "A week before."

"Oh yes, that would be easy," the seamstress said sarcastically.

"I'll pay more," Dylan offered a bit more sternly.

"You could eat, you know?" Meredith shot. "It would be lovely if you could try that."

"I should eat, yes, I know!" Dylan blasted back. "I should smile, laugh, get over it, and—God help me—I should do this all for your wedding and this stupid dress! I'm sorry that I can't move on for you, Meredith. Really, I am. It must be really putting you out, my heartbreak and all."

Without another word, Dylan turned and stomped to the fitting room. She unzipped the dress and shook it from her feet, refusing to be courteous in hanging it back up. "Do whatever you have to do," she yelled. "I don't care."

She didn't want to carry on this way; she didn't mean to. She just didn't know how to force happiness on herself. She didn't know how to make herself eat, smile, laugh, pretend Ben didn't exist, that she hadn't felt something for him and been completely connected with him.

She watched her reflection as a tear formed in the corner of her eye and escaped, rolling down her cheek and dropping from her jaw to her collarbone. She didn't even feel human anymore. She moved through life in a blur, praying each day would bring some sort of light at the end of the desolate tunnel she found herself in.

She picked up her clothes and dressed without care. She had become a slob. She dressed funny, she had bags under her eyes, and she looked like a skeleton. If someone didn't know she was brokenhearted, they'd probably think she was a crackhead.

Dylan slowly stepped out of the fitting room and barely looked at Meredith, who still looked shaken. She picked up her bag and headed for the door. She didn't care to apologize for snapping. She could only take so much, and she wasn't about to be ganged up on by her brother's wife-to-be and some seamstress with lipstick all over her teeth.

The drive home was silent. Meredith didn't even consider coming into the house as she dropped Dylan off. Dylan didn't bother reminding Meredith that her car was back in Scottsdale, at her work. She wanted to be as far away from her as possible. She knew she wouldn't survive being in the car with Meredith for another minute. She would find a ride tomorrow.

* * *

Linda sat alone at the kitchen table, sipping from a mug filled with hot tea. She sat there a lot these days, looking out the window and thinking of her divided children. Brandon, Hugh, and Jonah wouldn't even speak to Charlie, who seemed to stand firmly in Ben's defense.

She wondered what her husband would have done with this situation. She knew he enjoyed Ben as much as the rest of them. When Carl had tinkered with the car, garbage disposal, plumbing, and anything else he could get his hands on, the boys had surrounded him and absorbed everything that came out of his mouth as if they were the most fascinating things anyone had ever said. Carl had always given Ben a turn, encouraging his participation as much as his own biological sons. Carl had loved Ben and Ben loved him.

Still, Linda knew that Dylan had been Carl's heart and soul. He couldn't love his daughter more, and this was what he had always feared. He knew that one day she would get her heart broken, but what would he have done if he knew that the heartless monster who did it was Ben? Would he feel as bitter as Brandon, Hugh, and Jonah? Or would he feel as torn as Charlie and herself? Not even Linda knew the answer.

Ben did not return calls, text messages, or even emails. She knew that it wasn't because he didn't care. She loved him maternally and would always see the good in him, despite the fact that he left her only daughter in shambles. He needed space and time and she would be there when he needed her. Of course, she would never allow Brandon, Hugh, or Jonah to know that she felt that way. They might disown *her* if they knew she still hoped for Ben's return.

Dylan's heartbreak was obvious, especially in their empty house. Charlie raced around, preparing for the wedding and working to pay the extra bills. They never saw him. It was as if he didn't even live there. The other boys had all gone back to their lives in California and Washington. The Mathews home had become a very depressing place to live, Linda noticed.

She raised her brow and beamed at Dylan as she stepped in from the garage. "Hey, honey!"

Dylan wore her fakest smile and Linda had come to know it well. "Hello."

"How was the fitting?"

"Meredith is mad at me," Dylan said as she whirled past her mother. "My dress is too big."

"Can't they just take it in?" Linda asked, knowing it wasn't really about the dress. She herself had noticed Dylan's dramatic weight loss and feared for her as the rest of them did.

"One would think that, right?" Dylan answered, walking up the stairs and closing her bedroom door, ending any and all conversation.

"Great talk," Linda muttered with frustration.

Upstairs, Dylan pulled her clothes off and sank onto the bed. She threw the pillow that she had placed in Ben's spot across the room. She had latched onto it every night since the last day she saw his face; the day he destroyed her.

"Pathetic," she whispered, and closed her eyes.

This was not the person she was raised to be. If her father could see her now: skinny, ugly, pale, pathetic ... she was stronger than this and it was time for her to remember that.

"Tomorrow," she promised herself aloud, "tomorrow will be better. I *will* make it better."

* * *

Ben listened to his voicemails with rolling eyes and clenched teeth. He allowed his inbox to fill completely before he forced himself to listen to them. Most of the time, his phone was off. He only turned it on when his use of it didn't involve anyone important on the other end.

The tenth and final message that Charlie left that week played in Ben's ear. He felt it would be less disrespectful if he at least listened to the whole thing. He had no intention of returning the call, though.

"Hey, man. It's Charlie ... again. I just wanted to let you know that Meredith and I still want you at the wedding. Well, maybe not so much her, but I do." Charlie paused and sighed loudly. "C'mon, Ben, you're more of a brother to me than my other brothers right now. Prove them wrong and show them that you give a shit about something. Anyway, the invite is still open. If you show up, cool. If not, you owe me sixty-five bucks for your plate." He chuckled to himself, before adding, "Just kidding. Call me."

Ben erased the message and sank to his cold mattress. He felt guilty, but not so much that he was willing to admit it out loud. Charlie would give up soon enough. Not much kept Charlie Mathews' attention.

He rolled his eyes at each random message from another insignificant girl, asking where he'd been and when they could get together. He cringed at the message from his mother's sister, who suddenly cared about being a part of his life. He chuckled at the message from Linda, asking if he wanted her to send the shirt he had mistakenly left behind at her house. He knew that it was only an excuse to call.

The final message was from his realtor, saying she had successfully had the damage to the house fixed up and cleaned. Ruth's home was now ready for sale. *Finally*, he thought. He was more than ready to get that house—and all it held inside—as far behind him as possible. He couldn't seem to muster up a single fond feeling when he thought of his mother's cold home.

Ben slumped back against his pillow and pushed play on his remote. *Breakfast at Tiffany's* was a movie that Dylan had enjoyed for as long as he could remember. She had tried to make him watch it one night and he truly attempted to, but, somehow, in their entangled position on his bed, they had decided that making love was a better plan.

He found himself smiling as he watched this crazy woman avoid love at all costs. He didn't find the film to be as great as Dylan made it out to be. He did, however, feel that much closer to her, like a part of her was in his television, or maybe even his bed. He smiled again, imagining Jonah catching him as he watched this ancient chick-flick. How could he ever defend his masculinity then?

He pushed pause and shut off the TV when a knock at the door reminded him where he was. He had been doing that a lot lately, it seemed. He drifted in and out, forgetting that he wasn't in Phoenix anymore, and then suddenly being reminded that he was back in his cold apartment in Cambridge.

Ben opened the door, not at all surprised by the guest that stood in his hallway.

"Professor Tanner," he said quickly. "Come in."

The professor stepped in with his arms folded behind his back. His thick, red scarf dusted with snow was an indication to Ben that he had walked a great distance to pay this visit, so it was probably important.

"Ben, how are you?" Professor Tanner asked, removing his coat and gloves. He kept his scarf on for some reason. "I just spoke with your father."

"Oh?" Ben asked, not surprised. He knew his father would be using his connections to make sure his mother's death didn't cause any setbacks in school. It was only a matter of time. Professor Tanner was a well-respected man who could make things happen or not happen. More importantly, he was Warren McKenna's closest friend. Needless to say, Ben had expected this visit.

"Why didn't you say anything about your mother?"

"What is there to say?" he asked carelessly. "What could be done about it?"

Professor Tanner narrowed his eyes as he studied Ben's expression. "You're a strong young man, Ben. I like the drive in you. I believe it will take you as far as you want to go—all the way perhaps." He paused to place his hand on Ben's shoulder. "I'm not sure anyone is as strong as you're trying to be, though."

"I'm not sure what you mean, sir."

"I can pull some strings and request that your internship be put on hold at Weis and Carter. Just until the fall, when you're a bit more focused."

Ben felt enraged, but kept it in his gut where it belonged when speaking to his criminal law professor. "Sir?" he asked, confused. Weis and Carter was Ben's dream. It was the largest law firm in the country; law students referred to it as the Holy Grail. He had fought hard to be chosen for the internship, and he wasn't about to let it go now.

"Son, this is your only shot with the big boys. If you screw this up, you'll never get a chance to do it again."

"I understand that, sir. That's why I believe it would be a mistake to postpone the position now. I need to direct this anger somewhere and I think—I know—that this is the best thing I can do right now."

Professor Tanner frowned.

"Sir, if I bow out now, how will I ever make it when I actually have to fight a case in the middle of another life crisis? I'm always going to have problems. I work best this way."

The professor stuck his finger in the air. "This is your *one* chance, Ben. Don't blow it."

"I won't let you down," Ben reassured. "So, I can keep the internship then?"

Professor Tanner pursed his lips. He nodded once and put his hand on Ben's shoulder. "If I see you slip in the slightest, and believe me there will be people watching, I'll pull you from it without a moment's hesitation."

"Yes, sir," Ben said with a quick nod. "I won't let you down."

When the door closed and Professor Tanner was gone, Ben exhaled his rage. He found counting to ten was a helpful habit when dealing with people who could crush his future in their hands. Kissing ass was another one of his many talents. He despised doing it, but he would do it in desperate times.

The part about the conversation that angered him the most, though it didn't surprise him, was that his father had felt the need to make the call in the first place. His father, whom he had not heard from since his mother killed herself, only wanted to make sure that Ben's meltdowns didn't embarrass him.

Ben flopped back down on his bed and pushed play once more. Audrey Hepburn's face reappeared on the screen, warming Ben's heart and slightly embarrassing him even more. He felt ridiculous, weak, and sappy. He contemplated putting on a good porno just to reassert his manliness but he couldn't bring himself to do it.

He missed Dylan.

CHAPTER
THIRTEEN

On a Tuesday in March, Dylan walked across a busy intersection in Phoenix. Of all the times she had been on that street, she had never realized the lofts above the stores. As she walked, her eyes stayed focused on the open windows above a retail store that she had never been in. She jumped when a car barely missed her, and then waved it away when the driver laid on the horn in anger. She decided to look straight ahead until she made it to safety.

She loved this area of Phoenix. It gave her a lingering pleasant feeling each time she passed through it on her way to the school. When she had noticed the ad that morning, she'd thought of it as speaking directly to her. She might hate it and decide against her idea, but she owed it to herself to at least look.

She opened the door that was tucked between two stores, and took the stairs up to the second floor. "Two-thirty-two," she whispered, scanning a ripped piece of paper that she had jotted the address on.

Dylan stepped through the open door and smiled instantly. It was just how she had imagined: open and spacious, bright with the sun that streamed through the numerous windows. She looked down at the hardwood floors and realized they were brand-new, like the ad in the paper claimed.

"Ms. Mathews?" a soft voice said.

Dylan beamed her most professional of smiles. "Dorothy?"

The small, fair-haired woman approached with her hand extended and her dealing face on. She was very properly dressed in business attire, and even had a briefcase to complete her look. Her heels made a clicking noise against the floor as she walked, and it looked as though she moved cautiously to avoid scuffing the hardwood.

"So," Dorothy began, spinning around and gazing at the high ceiling, "it's nice, isn't it?"

Dylan looked at the windows and the open space that surrounded her. She couldn't have cared less about the ceiling. She nodded delicately, waiting to hear the price before she got too excited.

But as she looked around the loft, it was hard to ignore the twirls of elation her stomach was doing.

"You're an artist?" Dorothy asked, looking at Dylan as if she were about to break out into a *Grateful Dead* tune. "Full time?"

Dylan laughed. "Struggling artist, you might say." She never quite knew exactly when one earned that title. What if someone asked her what she did for a living? Did she have to sell her first piece before she could actually claim she was an artist? Should she say she's a teacher and just leave it at that? It was almost like acting, she thought. When could someone really say that they were in the profession of acting? When they had their first major role?

"Well, for the price, I suppose this studio would suit you." Dorothy looked worried now that Dylan had used the word "struggling." "There's plenty of space to put a bed here as well. It has all the commodities: kitchenette, bathroom, and dining area. The closets are small, but you could always stick an armoire in the corner there for extra storage."

Dylan nodded along as Dorothy went on. She loved the openness of the room. No matter what, it was far more privacy than she had ever had before, and that alone was cause for celebration.

She already had a space for everything in her head. She imagined her easel set up in front of the window. She had always dreamed of her very own studio. She wanted nothing more than to wake up in the middle of the night with a vision and stumble to her canvas where she could instantly feel creative release without putting on pants or brushing her hair. She just couldn't do that in her family's home.

"So?" Dorothy asked.

"How much?" Dylan asked with her arms crossed. "The ad offered a good deal."

"The landlord is asking seven hundred a month. That includes water and gas." Dorothy smiled.

"If you can get him to go down to six hundred, I'll take it," Dylan answered quickly.

Dorothy pulled out her cell phone and turned her back, as if that prevented Dylan from hearing. She spoke in a low voice and laughed a bit with the person on the other end. Her tone of voice changed; it sounded like she was sucking up like a pro.

She ended the call and slipped the phone back into her purse. "We have a deal," she said with a grin. "When would you like to move in?"

Suddenly, Dylan's heart thumped. The surreal moment had caught up to her and she knew the next step would be facing her mother. How could she even begin that conversation?

"I—I'll call you," Dylan stammered. "I have to give notice to ... my ..." *What should I call my own mother without sounding like an adolescent?* "... other landlord first."

"All right. When would you like to get the ball rolling?"

"Ball?" Dylan asked stupidly.

"When would you like to sign the lease, dear?" Dorothy asked, seeming taken aback by Dylan's sudden awkwardness. "You're sure this is what you want?"

"Positive," Dylan replied quickly. "I'm ready to sign a lease now, in fact. I just need to give notice."

"Okay. Well, we'll have to run a credit check. How about we meet with the landlord this weekend, and you can sign the lease then and get to know him a bit. He's a very nice man."

"That's just fine." Dylan felt giddy all of the sudden. "Call me and let me know when and where after my credit checks out."

Dylan left and practically skipped through traffic again. She was even more absentminded than ever. Just the thought of being on her own, in a quaint little studio apartment, gave her joy that she hadn't felt in over two months. She felt her life changing and welcomed it happily.

* * *

Heavy snow had been beating down on the east coast for days. Classes wouldn't be canceled, which pleased Ben because he found himself in a coma of sadness when he wasn't able to work and walk among humans. He would watch the news every day, crossing his fingers that school would go on and save him from another viewing of *Breakfast at Tiffany's*.

Ben walked along a snow-covered path that ran through campus. This was the long way to class, and seemed to be the last part of campus that was ever shoveled. He didn't care that he was walking through two feet of snow. He had been avoiding people as much as he could since his return to Cambridge.

His breath blew into the bitter air as he walked. He was cold, which surprised him. The winter weather hadn't really bothered him before, and now he found that the crisp cold was a bit painful as it whipped at his face. Unexpectedly, he had gotten used to the desert weather in only a few weeks.

Ben gave a quick nod to each familiar face he passed. If they looked like they wanted him to stop, he pretended he was in a hurry, giving an apologetic glance and a shrug of the shoulders while he raced by them.

As usual, he thought of Dylan as he walked. He thought of her smile, her laugh, her gentle touch, her lighthearted sense of humor, her angelic nature, and, of course, he couldn't help but think of her legs. Who wouldn't think of her legs? He laughed to himself. This was it, he thought. He would never have that again. He had found the best part of himself in her and, like that, it was gone. He had been a fool to believe he could have it, anyway.

He wondered if she had moved on. Someone would find her soon enough. She was too perfect to pass up. For the first time, he didn't feel enraged when he thought of her with someone else. He wanted her happy, even if he couldn't be the one to make that happen. He just wanted her to smile for the rest of her life. He would only feel peace if he knew that were possible.

"Ben!" He ignored a female voice that he recognized. "Ben, I know you hear me!" she called again.

He contemplated a quick sprint through the quad, but he knew it was too late. There was just no escaping this girl. She was about as close to a stalker as someone could be without officially giving them the title.

"Hey," she said in a breathless voice. She had seriously chased after him. "When did you get back?"

"Hey," he said, without answering her question. She would only nag him if he told her he'd been back for over two months. She had called him at least every day since his return. He simply had no interest in her and the pestering way she tended to scold him the few times she had been able to catch him before his trip to Arizona.

"I've been calling you, Ben."

"I've been busy," he said, still walking.

She caught up to him and began to walk alongside him. "Have you started your internship? I still can't believe you got it. How's your mother?"

Ben paused for only one step, allowing her to move ahead of him. He hated that she walked so close to him, as if they were a couple strolling to class together. He took another step and kept space between them this time.

"That was two questions too many," he answered quickly. She had never even met his mother, another sign of her weird, stalker-like behavior.

Ignoring his comment, she went on. "You know, the last time we were together, you made me feel really slutty. You just vanished."

Ben laughed. "Maybe that's because it was the *only* time we were together." They had met in a bar and slept together only a few hours later. He had snuck away from her crazy wrestling hold in the middle of the night and avoided her from then on. It was no different than any other girl he slept with. This one simply refused to take the hint as easily.

"So this is the blow off, then?"

"It's something, I suppose." He was almost out of breath. He hoped she didn't have to go as far as he did, but, then again, she seemed to be there only because she was looking for him. He had taken this way every day since he'd been back, and this was his first time running into her. It didn't seem to be an accident.

"I don't want to be your girlfriend, Ben."

He laughed again. That was not even a possibility, and he could hardly keep a straight face at the fact that she felt he worried about what she wanted from him.

She stopped him with a hand on his chest and shot him what seemed to be an attempt at a seductive grin. "I think we're on the same page is all I'm saying."

Ben stepped away from her hand. He narrowed his eyes. "I promise you, no one is on my page. If you were even near my page, you wouldn't have found me today. "

"I just want to have a little fun." She winked at him, which he found tacky. This girl seriously lacked common sense.

"I have to go," Ben said coldly. "I'm late."

She stepped aside, and said, "Call me."

"Right," he said, and continued off to class.

He couldn't even remember this girl's name, if he had ever knew it to begin with. Chances were that he'd never even asked.

He raced into the room as the professor was closing the door. In this class, if you didn't make it in before she shut the door, you didn't make it in, period. However, Professor Gray seemed to like Ben, because she always seemed to slow it down when she saw him running. Of course there was also that small detail that she had once interned under his father, so that helped.

"Mr. McKenna, just in time," Professor Gray said with a smile. "Lucky."

Ben smiled and sat down in the third row. He was out of breath, irritated from his run-in with the one-nighter, and freezing from the harsh cold outside. He had to put his game face on, however. Professor Gray was another one of those people who held his life in the palm of her hand. Ben was pretty sure she wanted to sleep with him, which he didn't mind. She was surprisingly hot for a woman twenty-eight years older than him. He'd do it. He chuckled to himself at the very thought.

"Are you ready for Weis and Carter?" Professor Gray asked, running her finger along the edge of Ben's desk. "I've heard they have high expectations for you—due to your name, of course. Do you think you can handle that sort of pressure?"

"I can handle anything," Ben answered quickly and proudly. He didn't want to sound smug, but he knew this would be a breeze for him. This was going to secure his future.

"Let's hope so." She pursed her lips in an awkward smile that was meant only for Ben, and walked over to her desk. This was the same way she began with him every day. Naturally, he found it completely amusing.

This was when Ben could take his mind off of Dylan and forget that he was in a hideous state of depression. He could focus, work, and find the drive that he was known for. Being with her had made him discover just how weak he could be. This was the place he belonged.

* * *

Linda cleaned to music. She loved to clean, which even she found odd. She called it free time. For Mother's Day, years back, her children had pitched in and arranged for a cleaning lady to come once a week. They had decided to let her go when Dylan came home to find Linda cleaning and the cleaning lady enjoying a sandwich at the table.

Dylan walked in to find her mother dancing with a feather duster in her hand and earphones in her ears. She sang to the shrine of Carl's pictures on the mantel. She pointed and bellowed loudly as she wiped the frames, thinking she was the only one in the house. Many times Dylan had caught her doing this. Linda never seemed to mind when she finally realized she had an audience.

Linda looked like she was in a wonderful mood, so Dylan thought it was a good time to give her the news that was sure to upset her. Maybe if she started out happy, then she wouldn't be so upset about Dylan moving out.

When Linda looked Dylan's way, Dylan smiled and waved to get her mother's attention.

Linda pulled the earphones from her ears and finished the tune without the music to guide her. She moved up the step and took Dylan's hands in hers and began to sway them both back and forth, dancing and singing to her embarrassed daughter, who refused to sing along.

"You're a brat," Linda teased. "You should always want to dance with your mother."

"Gross," was all Dylan could say at the thought.

Linda picked up a wicker basket and began to fold the clean clothes that were inside.

"I need to talk to you, Mom," Dylan began bravely. "Do you have a minute?"

Linda's eyes turned suspicious as she studied Dylan's face. "Oh, Lord." She took the seat behind her without looking. "You're pregnant."

"What? No!" Dylan laughed. "I'm not pregnant, Mom."

Linda placed her hand against her chest and sighed. "Whew," she said dramatically. "I think babies are lovely, but not when my baby is having them."

"Why would you even think that?"

"I found condoms in your bedroom," Linda admitted shamefully. "I just figured—I don't know. I'm sorry. I wasn't snooping. I was getting laundry. I'm happy you chose to be safe, though."

"Please stop." Dylan's face lit up like a tomato. She shook her head and tried to push back the nausea she felt rising. "Really? You found condoms, so your first thought was that I'm pregnant?"

"I know. That doesn't make any sense, does it?" Linda smiled and shrugged, embarrassed. "I'm sorry. Now that we have that out of the way, I think I can handle anything. What is it?"

Still stunned, Dylan let the words flop out of her mouth. "I found a studio apartment in Phoenix and I'm moving out."

Linda's mouth fell open. "I take that back. I'd rather you were pregnant."

Dylan rolled her eyes. "Mom."

Linda put her hand up and closed her eyes. "Wait just a minute," she demanded. "You what?"

"It's perfect for me," Dylan continued. "It's open and captures the light just the right way. I went and looked at it today and now I just have to meet the land—"

"Wait just a damn minute, young lady," Linda interrupted. "You've been walking through this house like a ghost, nearly giving me a heart attack from stress and worry, and now, just like that, you're moving into a studio?"

Dylan shrugged and then nodded.

"Absolutely not!" Linda shrieked with her hands in the air.

"Mom, you really don't have a choice in this. I'm an adult."

"Oh really, Miss Maturity?" Linda laughed sarcastically. "So grown up, aren't we? You were such an adult while sneaking around with your brother's best friend."

Dylan stood up. "I'm going to go upstairs and leave you to yourself. Maybe you should calm down and think it through before we continue."

Linda crossed her arms and turned her face to the window. She closed her eyes, avoiding the tears Dylan could see accumulating.

"No matter what, Mom, I am doing this." Feeling guilty but certain, Dylan placed her hand on Linda's shoulder. "You're going to have to accept it sooner or later. I'd like for it to be sooner so we can enjoy the next few weeks together instead of being angry with one another."

As Dylan walked to the stairs, she was stopped by the sound of Linda's voice. "Dylan, wait."

"Yes?" she said with a triumphant smile. She walked back into the kitchen and stared at her mother's wet face. It was always a shock to see Linda cry. It seemed like, lately, Dylan had seen it more than ever before. She used to see her mother as an invincible pillar of strength. It was nice to see the human side of her once in a while.

"I don't want to be alone," she said, sobbing. "The boys are gone and Charlie is getting married in two months; you were my last lifeline."

Dylan collapsed into the chair across from Linda with a sigh. She noticed that Linda didn't mention her father's absence, which made Dylan respect her so much more. Anyone else would surely use that as leverage, but not Linda. She played fair.

"Mom, I *do* want to be alone, though. I want my own space, for once." She looked at Linda's puzzled face and figured she should elaborate. "All my life, everyone has had a hand in what I do and how I do it. And, now, even my relationships are up for discussion."

Linda frowned. "We just knew you were hurting, that's all."

"Ugh," Dylan groaned. "Don't you get it, though, Mom? I don't want that. I want to hurt on my own and deal with it my own way. If I need any of you—and, believe me, sometimes I will—I'll ask for your help. I want it to be my choice, though."

Linda stared. She had stopped crying—for now at least—and she looked more confused than anything. It wasn't her fault. She thought of her family as a team, and she just didn't see the way they all relentlessly smothered Dylan.

"I'm always going to need you, Mom. I just want to be able to decide for myself when it is that I ask for your help."

Linda pursed her lips. Little by little, understanding began to make its way into her expression. She fidgeted with a placemat on the table for a few seconds and then stood up.

"All right, then," she said with a sigh. "I guess my baby is leaving."

Dylan smiled and stood with her arms open. She moved closer and wrapped her mother up in a warm hug. "I love you, Mom," she whispered.

"Oh, baby, you could never know how much I love you," Linda said, and made no attempt to hide that she was inhaling her daughter's sweet, familiar scent. It was a known movement to Dylan. Her mother would always reminisce about when she was a baby and her soft hair would rub against Linda's cheek as she held her. It was something she never seemed to tire of, even twenty-two years later.

Linda pulled back, and warned, "You know your brothers are going to install a state of the art security system, right?"

Dylan laughed and nodded. "They're nothing if not suffocating."

"Well, I suppose we have to go shopping now. You need a lot of stuff: dishes, furniture, new bedding, and cute frames and decorations. I'm buying, so let's go."

They spent the rest of the day shopping, went to dinner, and ended the night with a chick-flick on the couch. Dylan slept in Linda's bed with her and, for the first time in a long time, she remembered how much she needed her mother.

CHAPTER FOURTEEN

On a surprisingly chilly Monday morning, Meredith stepped into her apartment full of boxes and sighed at the disorganization that had taken over her life. After the wedding, she and Charlie planned to move into a new house just one neighborhood east of Linda's.

She was a traditional girl, she liked to think, only willing to live with Charlie after they were husband and wife. Charlie fought hard against this, claiming they had sex more than most couples that lived together. In his mind, what was the difference? But Meredith wanted that guarantee from him. She wasn't giving in until she had his last name.

Charlie was already there, and she could hear him pleading for Ben to call him in the kitchen. This was one of many messages she had heard him leave Ben, although they were not all the same. Some were lighthearted, happy, and full of jokes. Others were eager, angry, and flat out rude. Most of the time, he just asked for a return call that Meredith knew he wouldn't get.

Charlie hung up the phone as Meredith rounded the corner. He squinted as he smiled at her. He was so handsome, sweet, and strong. He had a way that no man had ever had with her before.

"Ben again?" Meredith asked coldly. She was so tired of Ben's ghostly presence in her life. He wasn't there, physically, but he sure seemed to be a pain despite his absence.

"Yes," Charlie answered in a sigh. "I wish he would just call me back."

"Maybe you should give up," Meredith replied. "He obviously doesn't want to speak to you."

Meredith thumbed through the mail that had come, but remained well aware of the angry eyes fixed on her. She knew how callous she seemed about everything except the wedding. Even to Dylan, Meredith's attitude reeked of *Get over it.* So what? If this was the only time in her life that she would be allowed to be selfish, then so be it.

It was true, she rolled her eyes in disgust at even the mention of Ben's name. And, yes, she couldn't hear another word about Ben McKenna and his totally undeserved place in all things Mathews. It was enough to drive her insane! The fact that Charlie insisted on holding a spot open for Ben at the reception caused an endless throb inside her head that seemed to pound with the word *Ben* over and over again.

This was her time, damn it!

"You don't know him," Charlie snapped. "You don't know what he's thinking."

"Do you, Charlie?" she shot back, beyond fed up.

"I think I do more than you," Charlie answered sharply. "Ben's different from you or me. He doesn't work like everybody else, you know?"

"Maybe you want to believe that, but I don't know, Charlie. I think he may just be a selfish jerk." She said it carelessly as she flipped through her mail and smiled at an RSVP that had come. "This may just be his way of saying 'I don't care about you Mathews people anymore.' He clearly wants to be left alone."

Charlie stood so quickly it startled her. He was her gentle giant most of the time, so it was clear she had crossed a line. The chair he had been sitting on flipped back and fell to the linoleum floor behind him.

"Careful with the chair, Charlie Bear," she warned patiently. "We're tapped out from the wedding and I'm not about to ask my father to buy us new chairs. How could I even explain a temper tantrum?"

"What the hell, Meredith?" he asked, nearly shouting. "Ben is my brother."

"No, Charlie. Ben is not your *brother*." She stood her ground with her hands on her hips, completely tired of this subject, but needing to go on with the low blows to make a point. "Brandon, Hugh, and Jonah are your brothers. Dylan is your sister. You do remember Dylan, right?"

"I know things you just couldn't, Meredith." He sighed and set the abused chair upright again. "I think—no, I know—that everything will work out. That's why I want him to come to the wedding. If he sees Dylan, maybe he'll realize he made a mistake. Maybe my brothers will speak to him again."

"Charlie, he's trying to avoid her. He doesn't want to see her!" she snapped in annoyance. "He knows she's better off without him!"

"How could you know that?" he asked, confused. "You don't even know him."

"Because," she began, ignoring the danger signs that flashed through her brain, "I'm the one who told him to leave and he agreed. He knew I was right. He knew Dylan was better off without him."

Charlie's eyes filled with angry bewilderment. It was almost as if she had punched him in the gut with that admission. She might as well have. He looked dizzy with betrayal.

She wanted to grab her words and pull them back. She should never have said that, she knew. She had only wanted to prove her point, but her ego had gotten the best of her. She waited for Charlie to react, which was all she could do at that point.

"Why would you do that?" he finally asked. "What right did you have?"

"He was hurting her, Charlie. He was being so selfish."

"Meredith, the only thing Ben's ever heard his entire life is how bad he is. His mother always told him that people were better off without him. He was told every day that he was just like his father. And—God—his father was no better. He always found a way to remind Ben of how worthless he was. He drilled it into Ben's head that it was weak to care about people. You told him what he was afraid of. You only reminded him, Meredith."

"Oh," Meredith answered in a whisper. "I didn't know that."

"Like I said, you don't know him. He wasn't pushing anyone away because he didn't care. He was afraid Dylan would end up like his own mother." Charlie's eyes watered. "How would you feel if your mother did what Ben's did? Guilty? Angry?"

"Probably both." She felt lower than scum. She couldn't even look at Charlie, knowing she had screwed up. Ben wasn't family by blood, but Charlie drew no lines when it came to him, and he expected the same from Meredith.

"Ben doesn't handle emotion well. He never has because the right people never showed it to him." Charlie grabbed his keys from the counter and headed for the door. "Ben is my brother, Meredith. I'm sure of that. You, on the other hand, I'm not so sure of right now."

"Where are you going?" Meredith asked in fear. He had never walked out on her before and here he was leaving in anger over someone else, telling her she really wasn't at the top of his list. "Charlie?"

"I can't believe how cruel you were, Meredith," he said with his hand on the doorknob. "You're the one who's selfish. You said those things to him because you're jealous of him. I'm certain of that. I'm not sure I even know you."

"You can't just leave, Charlie. We have to work this out."

Charlie's lips pursed. "I don't know that we can." He said nothing else before stepping outside and letting the door close behind him.

Meredith stood in disbelief on the other side. She still held the RSVP that had come in the mail. She sank into the chair behind her and wondered if that had really just happened. Did her life really take such a drastic turn in a mere fifteen minutes? She still had her shoes on. Her cheeks hadn't even warmed from the unusual chill in the air outside. How had it come to this?

*　*　*

Dylan packed another box and set it on top of the tower of three she had placed by her door. Her room was just about empty, and it was sad to think of what she was leaving behind. She had spent so much time wishing to escape these walls that she hadn't stopped to think of what she would miss as she was shoving it all into cardboard.

She stared at her bed and thought of Ben and the last night they were happy. He had looked at her with such love in his eyes; she had been sure he was going to say that he loved her. He never had, though. At the time, she hadn't thought he needed to. There had been so much there that she thought she recognized. Though she had never had it before, she only thought she knew it then. Sadly, there was no line between fantasy and reality for her. She had betrayed herself and stupidly believed that the real Ben would be the Ben in her head. He had turned out to be the opposite: the Ben everyone else knew.

She promised to never regret the time she spent with him, though. She secretly wanted to remember every time he touched her, made love to her, and dazzled her with his charm and magnetism. He was talented, she had to admit. He certainly knew what he was doing.

She crumbled when she imagined him back at Harvard without a care in the world. He probably never gave her a second thought while he plundered through girl after random girl, filling their heads with lies and promises to call. Did he even give them that the next morning? Did he even ask for their numbers? She knew the answer.

She quickly wiped a falling tear and shook her head to will the rest away. She had made a deal with herself to begin the healing process. She wanted to eat, laugh, and feel somewhat normal again. She wanted to feel peace when she thought of Ben and his wondrous ability to shrug off love. The first step to that—she thought, anyway—was no more tears.

"Hello?" she heard Charlie call from downstairs. "Dylan?"

"Up here!" she yelled. "In my room!"

Charlie's feet thumped up each step and Dylan knew her mother would kill him for leaving his boots on in the house. He never usually left them on, a sign his head was elsewhere.

"Hi," Dylan said, as Charlie opened her door. "Mom won't like those," she warned, pointing to his dusty work boots.

Charlie looked disturbed. "Oh shit," he said, looking down. "I forgot." He hunched over and untied the dirty laces, before clumsily toeing off each one, and then falling to Dylan's mattress.

"What's wrong?" Dylan asked, seeing the anguish in her brother's face.

Charlie sighed and clenched his jaw. "I think the wedding's off."

"What?" Dylan was catapulted to her feet in surprise. "Why?"

"It's a long story," he said, rubbing his temples. "I just realized I don't know her like I thought. That's all."

"That's all?" Dylan shook her head. "Charlie, you may need to come up with something better than that."

"Maybe everyone was right before. Maybe she's not the one for me."

"I don't recall anyone telling you she wasn't right for you," Dylan reminded. "I remember people saying not to rush into things, but nothing about Meredith being the wrong girl."

Charlie growled in frustration as he continued to massage the sides of his head. "I don't know what I'm saying," he said. "I just don't know if I can trust her anymore."

Dylan returned back to her place on the floor. She couldn't be sure if what she was hearing was right, but she didn't want to get too crazy over it, knowing Charlie processed things at his own pace. She wrapped her arms around her knees and stared at her brother through narrowed eyes. He was visibly upset and it was clear this was not what he wanted. "Care to elaborate, Charlie?" she asked carefully.

Charlie's eyes turned sad as he met his sister's gaze. He shook his head slowly, and said, "Sorry, but no." He knew Dylan would only be angry at them both for even discussing Ben. He preferred only her presence as support, anyway.

"Well, if you're not going to tell me anything, then start helping." She threw a pile of clothes at him, demanding, "Fold these *neatly*. Do it like Mom would, not the lazy boy way, and then place them in there." She pointed to an empty box at his feet.

Charlie chuckled, but moved quickly. "Geez. Sometimes I wonder who's worse, you or Mom."

"I learned from the best," Dylan agreed. She supervised Charlie's first fold, and then smiled proudly when he held it up for her approval.

"If I find any of your underwear in here, I'm done," Charlie said. Just the thought had him reconsidering his decision to fold instead of telling the story. "I mean it."

"Like I'd give you *that* pile," Dylan hissed childishly. "Seriously."

"Well, I'm just saying."

Charlie smiled as he watched his baby sister. He hadn't taken the time to notice how grown up she was. True, she was only three years younger than him, and Jonah's twin for that matter, though he didn't think of Jonah as a helpless child, something he couldn't explain. Like his other brothers, he had never thought of Dylan as an adult before. And now, here she was, packing and preparing for her own home and her own life.

"Stop looking at me like that, ya dope," Dylan said, catching him out of the corner of her eye. "I'm only moving out of Mom's house. You're looking at me like I'm moving to Mars."

Charlie said nothing in his defense. He didn't have to say it out loud; their little girl was growing up. He and his brothers had all taken their father's request to the limit, and now it was time for them to let her go. Maybe they should have done it years before. But that would only have meant they were admitting that she didn't need them anymore. Charlie couldn't speak for the rest of them, but he was indeed proud of the woman before him and, for the first time, even despite the way Ben hurt her, he knew that she would be okay without his hovering. He would make no promises to completely stop the hovering, though. It was a DNA thing.

Dylan tossed a sock at Charlie's face. "Hey," she yelled, "speak, help, or leave. You're creeping me out."

"Hah," Charlie said, amused by this tiny girl who could level him with a sock. He looked back down and continued to fold random pieces of clothing and *gently* stuff them into the open box at his feet. He could feel her glancing at him with each article of clothing. "When did you get so anal?" he asked through laughter when her silent glares had become too much pressure for him.

"Where did you learn to fold?" she snapped back.

"I never fold. I toss on the floor, shove in a drawer, and throw back if I don't know where the hamper is." He grinned. "If it smells good, I know it's wearable."

"And that right there is why you need a wife," Dylan teased, laughing. "Christ. You better not let this one get away, Charlie. You need her. For the sake of hygiene, go get her."

Charlie laughed and shook his head. "I have to go. Thanks for the talk, though."

"Umm, you're welcome?" Dylan didn't feel like she did anything but yell about his folding. "Any time," she said sarcastically.

Charlie stuffed his feet back into his boots and kissed Dylan on the top of her head. "Bye," he said quickly.

"Where are you going?" she asked, practically dizzy from his abrupt movements.

"I have to call someone," he said as he bolted from her room.

He said nothing else. He raced down the stairs, out the garage door and, in only a matter of minutes, Dylan was listening to the sound of his truck revving up and pulling away.

She hoped he was going to make up with Meredith, something she should do as well. It had been nearly a month since the dress-fitting blunder, and the two still hadn't spoken.

Dylan wanted to pretend that she was a completely stubborn person, maybe a little like Ben, but she couldn't hold out for long. Meredith was her friend and she needed to make it right with her. However, she'd let Charlie go first. She had packing to do.

* * *

In the evening, Dylan heard the door to the garage open and close. Assuming it was Charlie, she stayed on the couch and continued to sketch a picture of her father.

There was a quiet whimper, and Dylan was puzzled at the fragile, feminine sound, knowing then it wasn't Charlie.

"Mom?" Dylan called out. "Is that you?"

"It's me," Meredith answered in a shaky voice, showing her blotchy face at the same time.

"Oh, Meredith!" Dylan gasped at the sight of her.

Meredith was a wreck. Her eyes were nearly swollen shut from crying so hard; her hair was stringy and uncombed. She wore sweatpants and a jacket, which shocked Dylan more than anything else. No one had ever seen Meredith looking like this.

Dylan stood and hurried over to her friend. "Sit," she instructed, with her hands on Meredith's shoulders.

"Oh, Dylan!" she sobbed and threw her head to Dylan's chest. "I'm so awful!"

"No. Don't say that," Dylan whispered.

"I am!" she cried. "If you knew what I'd done, you would think so, too."

"Where's Charlie?" Dylan hated being the shoulder. How awkward. She hated the sniffling and crying—not to mention the wet spot that she could already feel forming on her sleeve. As if the wetness weren't bad enough, she realized too late that the small chunk of charcoal she had been sketching with was still in her hand and was now mashed between her chest and Meredith's. Odds were, if she ever made it out of Meredith's grasp, there was going to be a large black smudge on them both.

Meredith shrugged, but kept her face jammed into Dylan's arms. "He won't talk to me. He won't even text me back." She lifted her chin and sobbed. "He left me!"

Dylan snapped her head back. "What? I was sure he was leaving to make up with you this afternoon. He left as fast as he arrived. I thought maybe he had come to his senses."

"He was here?" Meredith took a few sobbing breaths.

Dylan nodded. "This afternoon."

"He must not have told you why he's so angry with me."

"No. He didn't seem to want to."

Meredith collapsed into the chair behind her. "You're going to hate me, too."

"Meredith, no one hates you. I'm sure it's not that bad, whatever you've done."

"I'm the one that told Ben to leave you alone because he wasn't good enough for you!" she blurted. She covered her mouth with her hands and more tears streaked down her already wet cheeks. She uncovered her mouth, and added, "Charlie said I'm just jealous of Ben and—I don't know—I think he's right. I was jealous of him. He doesn't even have to work for his place in your family and I always feel so left out. Now look: my fiancé wants to end it with me for *him*." She took in a long, shaky breath. "I am so jealous of him."

Teetering on the edge of fury, Dylan drew in a deep breath through her nose. "I see," she answered in a quiet, controlled voice.

"I'm so sorry, Dylan!" She threw her face into her hands and cried even harder, if that was possible.

Dylan sat silent for a good amount of time. She watched Meredith's guilt-stricken breakdown and contemplated all of her options. Of course, her first instinct was to scream with clenched fists and tell Meredith what a nosy bitch she was. She wanted to tell her about Ben's childhood, his parents, and all the people in his life who had told him he could never be good enough. She was sure by the way they were acting, however, that Charlie had already done that and now didn't seem like the time to go round two on Meredith. It would be tantamount to kicking an injured animal.

Meredith looked up from her wet hands and stared at Dylan. She got to her feet and took a few dramatic breaths. "I'll leave you alone," she said. "I shouldn't even have come here. I really don't even know what I'm doing."

Dylan stared at the vulnerable mess of Meredith in front of her. She let out a deep, resigned sigh. "You're not the reason he left, Meredith."

"I'm not?" she asked with a doleful expression.

Dylan shook her head. "Ben does what Ben wants. He left on his own. I'm sure he had his mind made up way before you got ahold of him."

"But I told him—I told him he would be doing everyone a favor. I—I told him he didn't know how to love and that you deserved better than someone like him. I told him he didn't even deserve your family."

Dylan laughed, picturing it. "All very true things," she agreed. "Still, Ben wouldn't have left unless he absolutely wanted to. I fell for his garbage and it's my own fault. I knew how he was, Meredith. You didn't run Ben off. No one can do that."

"Will you tell Charlie that?" she asked with a quivering chin.

"I'll handle Charlie," Dylan answered with a nod. "He's just being stupid. It's not over."

"How can you be sure?" Meredith asked, still looking completely baffled at Dylan's response. "I mean, he is so mad at me."

"I'll think of something."

"I'm really sorry, Dylan. I'm sorry for everything." She sat back down. "I was so mean at the fitting. I shouldn't have been so selfish."

"It's okay." Dylan sat next to her and patted her leg. "I'm sorry for yelling at you and ruining your moment."

"I know how you feel now. If Charlie doesn't forgive me, I don't know what I'm going to do." She looked Dylan up and down and, in a less theatrical voice, she said, "By the way, you look kinda healthy since the last time I saw you."

Dylan beamed. "I took your not-so-subtle advice," she said, nudging Meredith with her arm. "And Charlie *is* going to forgive you."

Meredith left soon after. She left somewhat calmer, but still entirely saddened over Charlie's behavior. Dylan knew there was no getting through to him, even if she were to try, so she did the only thing she could think of: she called her brothers.

After speaking to Brandon, and leaving messages for Jonah and Hugh, she leaned back against the couch and felt as though she had done her part in the Charlie-Meredith saga. She knew her brothers would step in. They had their own thoughts about the wedding, but who didn't? Still, even Brandon admitted that Charlie would be making a huge mistake if he backed out over something so petty, a mistake he would surely regret when the dust Ben left behind settled.

Dylan stared at the sketch of her dad she had been working on before Meredith blew through the room and turned her quiet evening upside down. "I'm sad," she whispered to the black and white face, as if it were truly her father. A tear fell from her eye and landed on the paper, creating a small, wet blot over his penciled cheek.

"No. No crying," she reminded herself aloud. "When am I going to be okay?" she asked the drawing, wishing that it would answer her.

Once again, the door to the garage opened and closed. This time, by the clumsy stampeding, it was clear that Charlie was back. She wanted to feel sorry for herself, but she couldn't do that with everyone hounding her. She wanted to morbidly speak to a piece of paper, pretending it was her father. She certainly did not want to solve another couple's issues.

"Charlie?" she called.

"Yeah," he answered, poking his face around the corner.

"Get your ass over to Meredith's."

"Did you tell Brandon?"

"Yep."

"Thanks. I needed that phone call," he said sarcastically.

Dylan shot him a fierce look. "What a stupid fight, Charlie. Don't call off your wedding over *Ben*."

"It's not about Ben," Charlie snapped. "It's about her hoity-toity attitude. She thinks she's better than everyone."

Dylan jumped to her feet. "Yep, that's right. The charity-organizing, homeless-feeding, selfless saint really thinks she's better than everyone! Or, maybe—just maybe—she really was trying to help me."

Charlie looked baffled. "You know what she did?"

"I do. I do not, however, feel it's something you are allowed to use in your moment of cold feet!" she lashed out.

From his silence, Dylan guessed that Charlie knew she was right. He was only being stubborn. For whatever reason, the Mathews men were stubborn mules when it came to women. Dylan blamed it on Linda's coddling.

Charlie's face disappeared back into the laundry room.

The garage door opened and closed again. Dylan suspected at first that Charlie had left in a fit over her reprimand; however, it was clear as she rounded the wall, that this wasn't the case. It was Meredith and, now, in a surprising turn of events, Charlie and Meredith were in a tight hug, making up. They didn't even have to speak. They just seemed to fall into a hug at the sight of one another.

Dylan rolled her eyes and headed upstairs for bed. That was enough drama for one day.

CHAPTER
FIFTEEN

Get out, get out, get out, get out, Ben chanted silently while the girl talked about things he didn't care to hear.

Ben watched impatiently as Nicole got dressed in front of his bed. Like him, she was an intern at Weis and Carter. At the welcome party the night before, after six Jack-and-Cokes too many, it had seemed like a good idea to bring her home. Now, the following morning, he was ready for her to begin the walk of shame out of his apartment.

When he had first opened his bloodshot eyes, he had forgotten she was there. However, as soon as he flipped over and smelled the ashtray stench in her hair, it hit him like bricks. As if that wasn't bad enough, there was the death grip she held him in, with her legs practically locking his body into place. These girls and the grips of death that they called cuddling!

He tried to be as loud as possible, moving around and yawning with a loud yell. She finally woke up, but she seemed to only want to clamp onto him tighter, which Ben found completely bothersome.

He didn't want to be rude, if only because he was about to work with this person on a day-to-day basis and didn't feel like

dealing with any bitchy animosity from her. Finally, after ten or
so hints that he needed to get up, she got up and began to get
dressed. It was the first time he ever politely shooed a girl out of
his bed—polite in a Ben sort-of-way, that is.

Nicole crawled down on the mattress and kissed Ben's
cheek. She had been going for his mouth, but he turned his head
at the last minute. It was another tip-off he threw her way.

"Last night was great," she whispered, not taking the hint.
"What are you doing later?"

Ben moved awkwardly as he tried to escape from the pinned
position she held him in. "I have a lot of work to do," he lied.

Point taken, Nicole rolled her eyes and sat up to finish
dressing. She seemed fully aware that he was giving her the blow
off now, thank God. He hoped she noticed that he was somewhat
gracious about it, at least.

"Well, you've definitely lived up to all I've heard," she said in
a not-so-nice voice. "Your morning after was a bit more polite
than I remember anyone saying, though. My mistake for thinking
. . ." she trailed off as if she had stopped herself at the very last
minute.

Ben sat there, puzzled, and then it hit him. For a moment,
she must have misread his careful politeness as the possibility
that he actually liked her. Thankfully, she had realized that her
assumptions were completely wrong.

"Why do you have a finger painting taped to the back wall of
your closet?" she asked sneeringly, letting out a snobby giggle.
She was obviously embarrassed by his brush-off and now being
spiteful at the artist's expense. "Do you, like, have a little sister or
something?"

Ben looked just behind Nicole and felt nothing but a
stinging pain in his chest at the sight of Dylan's painting. On his
thirteenth birthday, he had watched from his window as she
placed it on his porch, and then ran away. He'd never said a word
about it. He had carried it with him from then until now, though,
always hanging it up in hiding places so that no one but him
would see it. He had known even then that the two kids holding
hands on a mountain, placed just under a bright red heart in the

sky, were he and Dylan. And, even then, it had touched him the way it touched him now.

Nicole must have noticed the look in his eyes because she retreated quickly. "I mean, it's cute and all. Who's it supposed to be?"

Ben stood and glared at her as he closed the doors to the closet. Normally he kept them shut, but he had obviously not been in his right mind the night before and forgotten all about it. The closet was a personal space. It was an invasion of privacy to have someone staring into it.

"Ben, I'm sorry. I didn't mean to offend you." She sat down to put her boots on. "It's good of you to have it hanging. You obviously don't want to hurt the poor thing's feelings. That means you have feelings yourself, which is surprising, really."

"Would you shut the hell up?" he snapped. "Just stop talking and get out of here."

She stood up and shot him a dazed expression. "Is it really that bad, what I said?"

"It was pretty shitty," Ben replied. "I don't care. Just leave."

"I didn't know you'd be so upset about a finger painting a ten-year-old did. God."

"Actually, it's not a finger painting. It's a painting that a very talented artist did when she was twelve. Her work is shown in New York galleries now, as a matter of fact." Ben growled in frustration. He was saying too much in defense of Dylan. "Just leave. Please."

"Ah, I understand now," she said with a smile. "I'm sorry, Ben. I won't say another word about it." She was being respectful now, but Ben was still annoyed.

"You understand nothing." Ben held his bedroom door open. "Bye now."

Nicole grabbed her jacket. "Well, it was fun last night. I'd love to say the same for this morning, but I can't."

Ben laughed. "I can't even say that I remember last night. You obviously didn't do much for me."

"Nice. That's real nice," she hissed, and threw his front door open. As she stepped into the hallway, she nearly ran into an unfamiliar man with an amused smile. His arm was raised as he prepared to knock on the door she opened angrily.

"Excuse me," Nicole said, pushing past him with tears in her eyes.

Ben sighed at the unexpected visitor. "What a morning," he groaned. "Hello, Dad."

Warren turned and looked down the hallway. He smiled, as he said, "You have a lovely way with women, Benjamin."

"She's just the end result of a drunken night."

"You should never allow the ones you don't plan on calling to follow you home, remember?"

"My mistake," Ben chuckled. His father was always full of advice. "What are you doing here?"

Warren looked around Ben's apartment as if he'd never seen it before. "You live better than I did when I was attending college, that's for sure. What a time in my life, though."

"Yes. You've told me."

Warren sat down on the couch. He looked around and then continued to recall his glory days. "I was poor and working my tail off, scooping ice cream during the day and cleaning campus classrooms at night. I didn't mind the work, though. It was that much more rewarding, knowing I accomplished it on my own. I vowed that my own child wouldn't have to work like I did." He pointed his finger as if to remind Ben what child he was speaking of. "You're very lucky, son."

"Yes. Thank you." Ben rolled his eyes as he turned his back on his father. He never told a story without sticking a jab at Ben.

"I didn't know I was supplying such a habit," Warren said, pointing to the liquor bottles in the kitchen. "You have yourself a full bar back there. Top shelf, even. It's a wonder you even meet the young ladies that run from your apartment in tears. You don't need to leave."

Ben sighed deeply. "The bottles aren't empty. I like a little variety. You should see the beer in my fridge."

"Benjamin, don't be so defensive. I have a right to comment on the items my son purchases with my credit card."

"Dad, I don't have time for this back and forth thing. To what do I owe this great pleasure?" He drummed his fingers on the counter. "Would you like a drink?"

"Scotch. Neat," Warren answered.

Ben smirked as he grabbed the Johnnie Walker. The man would ridicule everyone, but when it came to him, the guy who asked for scotch at nine in the morning, there was no room for judgment. Ben had meant water, or possibly juice if he had any. He poured the liquor into a glass and walked it over to his father.

"Thank you," Warren said, and sipped in his usual way, pompous and snobby. He lifted the glass and swirled his drink around. Ben wasn't sure why he did that, nor did he care.

Ben sat down across from his father and smiled as he stared at him, waiting to hear the reason for his unannounced visit. There was no way he was there under any sentimental circumstances. Ben watched as Warren looked around, just trying to find something he could scold Ben about.

Warren picked up a picture of Jonah and Ben on Spring Break in Cancun two years before. It was one of two photographs that Ben had framed and displayed in his bare apartment. Naturally, the other picture on exhibit was of him with his arm around Kendra Wilkinson. As his good luck would have it, he'd happened to walk right into a Playboy shoot on a night out in Chicago. He simply had to frame the evidence.

"Ah, Jonah," Warren said, avoiding the conversation he meant to have. "How is he?"

"Good," Ben lied. He hadn't heard from Jonah since he last saw him in Phoenix. He hadn't seemed good then. He'd looked close to punching Ben in the face, actually. "He's really good."

"That family has always been good to you, son."

"Sure."

"Son?"

"Dad?"

"Son." Warren paused while his eyes trailed to a random area of the room. He sipped from his glass again, and then he let Ben have it. "Jackie and I were married three weeks ago."

"You *what?*" Ben asked.

"I'm in the process of adopting her children. She has two lovely daughters; you have sisters now."

Ben wondered who in their right mind would marry that man and, more than anything, he wondered who the hell would allow him to be a father to their children. He was a lousy father to his own biological son. Odds were he'd be just as neglectful to them, too.

"How old is Jackie?" Ben asked before he thought. "I mean, you had her sign a pre-nup, right?"

Warren looked a bit insulted. "She's thirty-eight," he said too quickly, causing Ben to automatically subtract five years from his father's claim. "Why do you ask?"

"Where did you meet her?"

"She was the paralegal under Bob Dawson. Why?"

Ben smirked. "Was?"

"She doesn't have to work anymore." Warren sipped from his glass. It was obvious to him where Ben was going with his questions.

Ben nodded. He didn't have much to say. He wasn't surprised his father had found a plaything. He could only imagine what this Jackie person looked like. She was probably hot as hell in a trashy way, with her boobs hanging out of low-cut, slutty shirts. Knowing Bob Dawson, she probably wore tight skirts that showed her ass when she bent over to dig through file cabinets that were purposefully placed too low to reach.

Still, no matter how much fun Warren had with her, Ben hoped his father wasn't blinded by his own stupidity. He certainly hadn't expected him to get married, especially since he'd done such a horrible job with it the first time.

"If you're wondering about money, Benjamin, I've had your trust fund set aside since you were born. No one but you will ever get that."

Ben rolled his eyes. After he graduated, he wouldn't need his father's assistance ever again. He chewed on the inside of his mouth and tried to narrow in on what it was that had him so angry. Was he jealous?

"You need to meet her, son. She's a good person. She'll make a terrific mother."

That struck an unfamiliar nerve. Ben's mouth moved quickly as he leapt to his feet. "I had a mother. Have you forgotten her already?"

Warren looked into his glass and sighed. "No. No, I certainly have not."

"Oh, be honest. There's no one here to impress," Ben said sharply. "You forgot her a long time ago. Tell me, Dad, was it a relief to you knowing she was dead, eliminating your time in divorce court? You must have been happy when she shoved those pills in her mouth."

Warren stood angrily and backhanded Ben in the mouth. It wasn't the first time he used his hands to silence Ben. But it may have been his last.

Ben barely flinched. He smiled, an expression that was sure to irritate his father more. He wiped the blood from his lip and laughed. "Oh, there you are, Dad. Welcome. For a minute, there, I thought you'd sent an imposter in your place."

"Whether you choose to believe this or not, I grieved for your mother. It broke my heart when she did what she did."

"Maybe if you had been there, I could have seen this so-called grief. I suppose it's one of those *had to see it to believe it* things. I'm positive a night with Jackie took it all away, though."

"Damn you!" Warren cocked his fist back again.

Ben grabbed his hand and held it tight this time. "Damn *you!*" he shouted back. He threw Warren's fist away and stepped close enough to look deep into Warren's shocked eyes. He took deep breaths, inhaling and exhaling heavily. His shoulders rose and fell as he clenched his fist and latched onto his father's shirt.

Warren cowered. For the first time in his entire life, Ben had the upper hand with the man before him.

"You sad, wretched old man, you're as selfish and pathetic as they come." He shook Warren's shirt as he snarled into his face. "Get the hell out of my apartment. Go make your new family as miserable as you made my mother and me."

Warren's eyes were round with surprise. Ben had never spoken to him that way before. He looked into his son's raging eyes and wondered if they were wet with tears of fury or sadness. He didn't ask.

Ben walked to his door and opened it wide. "Get out of here. Don't come back."

Warren nodded as he adjusted his shirt. "You just kick everyone out of that lonely life of yours, don't you?"

"I learned from the best, sir." Ben's jaw tightened. His heavy breathing slowed somewhat, but it was still out of control. "Go," he said, jerking his head toward the door.

Warren stepped out into the hallway. He turned and, for a brief second, his eyes were sad, revealing a rare spark of humanity. "I didn't do everything right. But you and your mother never wanted for anything. I always provided."

"We needed you, not your damn money!" Ben yelled, and slammed the door in his father's face.

Ben sat back on his couch. He had always imagined that one day he'd stand up to Warren, and he'd always thought he'd congratulate himself after the big event. He had never considered he might feel the guilt that he felt now. He didn't feel any sense of accomplishment. He felt anger. He finished his father's scotch and stood to get himself another one. This was it. He was becoming his father. He *was* his father.

His voicemail alert light was red, he noticed. Against his better judgment, he put it on speakerphone and played the message that had been marked urgent. He knew it would be nothing good. His motions were robotic and he did it all without thinking.

"Hey man. It's Charlie. Listen, I just left my sister. I know you don't want to hear this, but—I don't know—I just think you should. She's different, you know? She's getting her own place and moving on. Meredith told me what she said to you. I freaked out on her and I may have called off my wedding. I don't know. Anyway, Dylan's fine, Ben. I thought maybe you were waiting to hear that before you showed your face around us again. It's just not as bad as you think. Everyone can get over this if you give them a chance, is all I'm saying. Hopefully we see you at the wedding," he laughed nervously, "if I even have one. Later."

What the hell did that even mean? *She's moving on.* Why was Charlie rubbing his face in it? Why wouldn't the world allow him to forget her?

Ben pressed the delete key. He slammed the last of the scotch, emptying the nearly full bottle, and threw his coat on. He stomped out of his apartment and went to the first bar he could find. He could have stayed home and gotten stinking drunk on his own. Not even he could explain why he left. It was one of those moments where his brain was screaming at him to stop, but his legs kept going.

He walked into the campus pub and sat down along the rail. The bartender could already see that Ben was in some kind of rage. He groaned in irritation and made his way over. He had seen him in there before, and he was well aware of Ben's quick temper and callous personality. He had just opened for the day and was not ready to begin it like this.

"Son?" he began carefully, "what would you like?"

"I'm not your fucking son," Ben snapped. "Get me a whisky. I don't care how it comes."

The bartender narrowed his eyes at Ben. "Sure," he answered as he poured Ben a shot. "We should probably just keep it at this one, though."

Ben threw the shot back and eyed the older gentleman in front of him. He slammed the glass down and demanded, "Fill it."

The bartender shook his head slowly. "I told you just the one, son."

In a move that would have surprised no one who truly knew him, Ben reached over the bar and grabbed the bartender by his white, collared shirt, the same way he had grabbed his father's only moments before. He yanked the man close to his face, and growled, "I said I'm not your son."

The bartender stared with alarm in his eyes as Ben slowly released him. The man's hands shook now and he was completely paralyzed with fear. Ben was unhinged; there was no room for argument there.

"Fill it," Ben demanded again, and tossed the glass onto the bar where it shattered.

"All right, buddy. Here you go." He filled a new glass and slid it over to Ben. He watched as Ben disappeared into it. He then placed the entire bottle beside the glass in the hopes that it would distract Ben while he slipped away. He hurried to the back office and locked the door, where he quietly called the police.

* * *

"McKenna?" the guard called as he opened the door to Ben's cell. "You made bail. Get out of here."

Ben lifted his head and groaned. He stood and could only speculate about who his father had sent to plead his case. As he shuffled down the long, fluorescent hallway, he wondered what time of day it was—or, more importantly, which day it was. He had nearly two fifths of liquor in his stomach, and he thought seriously about throwing up just to get rid of the nausea.

He rounded the corner and felt the worst kind of fear when he realized his bailers were none other than two of his professors, Bethany Gray and Paul Arthur. *Great.* Ben retrieved his belongings and walked slowly to his professors, contemplating what to say to get out of the load of trouble he was in.

"Jesus," Ben grumbled, rubbing his head.

"Don't say another word," Professor Gray warned with a pointed finger. She was looking over something on a clipboard; she signed the bottom angrily. "Come on," she ordered the clerk in the window, "I know there's more. Give them to me!"

Ben yawned. He headed out the double doors of the station and strained his unadjusted eyes in the bright sun. He stretched to put on his jacket and leaned against the brick wall, waiting for the wrath of his two favorite professors to come down on him like an anvil.

It came only minutes later. Before they could even clear the final step, Professor Gray was yelling at Ben. "Do you have any idea how stupid that was?"

Ben figured she wasn't asking for an answer. He knew how stupid he was.

"I just had to beg—*plead*—for that judge to let you out of there! I had to convince him that you weren't some psycho hoodlum terrorizing innocent old men for no reason. We had to scramble to clean this up to make sure Tanner didn't get wind of it. He'd pull you from the program so quickly you'd be waiting a year before you got another chance at it." She straightened her coat, and sighed in aggravation. It seemed as though she was silently counting to ten, which Ben might have found hilarious if his life weren't dangling on a thin string in front of him. She took another deep breath, adding, "Your father promised to make sure Tanner doesn't find out as long as we gave our word that we would watch you from now on."

"Benjamin, what were you thinking?" Professor Arthur asked more calmly. Clearly this was a good cop/bad cop sort of thing. "I'm trying to understand here, son."

Damn that word, Ben thought.

"It doesn't matter," Professor Arthur said with a wave. "The bar isn't pressing charges, because—well—because that idiot of an old man served you when he shouldn't have. With a little legal mumbo-jumbo and a small payoff, he isn't going to talk."

Ben smirked. He knew well enough that even if the bartender had refused him the first time, they'd still be standing exactly where they were. He would still have lost it and he would still have gone to jail. There was nothing the man could have done to change a bit of it.

"Go home. Sleep," Professor Gray demanded. "You have a therapy session with Dr. Roberta Fields tomorrow."

Ben's eyes lit up like a raging fire.

"Don't speak," she snapped. "You need it, damn it. And don't even think that you'll fill the doctor's hour with silence and BS. You're going to actually talk to this woman. If you want to keep your internship, you'll do exactly what we tell you. We aren't going to allow someone as intelligent as you to act like a raging moron."

"We let ourselves into your apartment and took the liberty of dumping the liquor cabinet you called a kitchen," Professor Arthur added. "You won't be drinking while you're at Weis and Carter."

Ben surrendered, nodding his head.

"We know it's been tough on you, Benjamin. We're here to help with whatever it is you need." Professor Arthur placed his hand on Ben's shoulder. "Get your head together, son."

Ben nodded again, resisting the urge to throw a punch. There was nothing he could say to change their minds and all he really wanted was to be at home. He figured silence was most definitely golden in moments like this.

"Go home," they ordered in unison.

Ben walked the short distance home, thanking the gods above for his free idiot pass. He wondered if it would always be this simple for him. In addition to taking him far, his last name seemed to be a golden ticket to being a flat-out dick most of the time.

He'd go to therapy and jump through all the hoops they asked him to. They had him by the balls, and he knew it. When his internship was over, however, he'd go right back into that bar, finish off a full bottle of whiskey, and then bash the empty glass over the old man's head.

CHAPTER SIXTEEN

On Friday, Dylan hurried along the walk that led to the restaurant where she was to meet her new landlord. Naturally, she was running late, and hoped that he hadn't gotten tired of waiting and left. All of her belongings were packed and ready to move and it would be extremely disappointing to start over in a search for a new place all because she couldn't find an outfit that resembled something a responsible tenant would wear.

She really didn't understand this lunch date of a meeting, anyway. Even Linda and Charlie thought it was completely odd for a landlord to want to meet his future tenant for lunch. Linda thought it was a ploy and had checked all the papers for sadistic madmen in the area who had set up fake rental properties and lured sweet, innocent girls with bright futures to him by requesting a lunch meeting. She was sure Dylan would never be seen again.

"Dylan!" Michael Olerson called to her from just outside the restaurant.

"Great," she mumbled under her breath.

"Hey, Dylan! Wait!"

"Michael, I am so late," she said, while power walking to the door. "I'm sorry. I can't talk right now."

Michael paced her. He opened the door for her, and smiled. He waited for her to run through, and then he followed right behind her.

Still ignoring Michael, Dylan looked out over the room of diners and realized she had no idea what this man looked like. She stood on her tiptoes and craned her neck as she scanned each table and booth, looking for a lone diner.

"Excuse me," Dylan asked a passing waitress, "do you have anyone waiting for someone to join them?"

The waitress shot her a peculiar look. "Um, just that guy behind you," she answered, and rushed away.

Dylan turned and looked at Michael's smiling face. She frowned and looked back out over the sea of people. "Damn," she whispered. "He left."

"Who left?" Michael asked.

"What? Nothing." She sighed heavily. "I mean no one."

Michael stepped next to her. "Who are you looking for, Dylan?"

The waitress came back around. "Do you guys need a table?"

"Yes. A table for two, please," Michael answered. He didn't even look at Dylan to ask if she wanted to join him.

"Oh. No, Michael, I can't stay."

Michael laughed. "I've carried this on long enough."

"Huh?" Dylan asked, slightly annoyed and still looking around the room in the hopes that she might have missed someone.

"You're meeting *me* here, Dylan," Michael said, grabbing her hand to lead her behind the waitress who would show them to their table. "I'm your new landlord."

Dylan stopped and stared at Michael in confusion. "What?"

Michael laughed again as he slid into the booth and picked up a menu. He looked up at Dylan and laughed when she didn't sit down. "I'm sorry. That was really evil of me to stress you out like that. To be fair, though, I have been waiting for a while. Sit down."

Dylan slowly obliged. "*You* own that loft?"

Michael nodded. "I do."

"Why didn't Charlie say anything? He knew I was moving there."

"I don't tell people everything. I bought it a long time ago and kept it for storage. Half the time I even forgot about it."

Dylan fell against the back of the booth. She shook her head, baffled. "I thought I knew all there was to know about you," she added when she was able to control her mouth again.

Michael shrugged. "It was just an investment idea that I put aside when the bar began to pick up."

"So, why are you renting it out now?"

"The economy is poor. The bar's sales have gone down a bit, so I figured now's the time to fix the place up and make some money off of it." He laughed and looked back down to examine his menu. "When the real estate agent said she was meeting a Dylan Mathews, I just about died. I never thought you'd leave your mother."

Dylan nodded. "That's why you went down on the price so quickly." She had wondered why it had been so simple to get the price lower when the real estate agent's phone call had only lasted minutes. She'd figured she would have to bargain. She should have known it was too easy.

"I can't rip you off, Dylan. You know that."

Dylan laughed and picked up a menu. She peered over the top of it and raised an eyebrow at Michael. "So, then, what is this that we're doing today?"

Michael peeked over the top of his menu, eyeing her back. "This is lunch between two friends."

Dylan shook her head and made her selection. The waitress came back with their waters, took their order, and left them alone to talk.

"So, how are things?" Dylan asked awkwardly. "How's Ollie's?"

"Missing its favorite bartender, actually." He sighed and picked up the paper wrapper from his straw. He began to rip it into tiny pieces, rolling them into balls and piling them up on the table. "It's not the same, is all I'm trying to say."

Dylan nodded. She hadn't even considered taking her job back at Ollie's and she really hoped he didn't ask her to come back now. She might feel obligated to if she were living under his roof, so to speak.

"How are you?" he asked, pointing to her.

Dylan had heard that question so often since Ben left that it was beginning to exhaust her. She answered with the same sharp "fine" each time someone asked. As common as a question like that is, she knew what they meant. She almost wished they would just say it: *Hey, Dylan. How are you since you stupidly fell victim to Ben McKenna?*

Michael was different, though. Dylan knew he was probably well aware of the way Ben left her. He wanted to know how she was, though.

"I'm good," Dylan answered. "I'm preparing for my gallery opening in June, my class is great, and I'm finally moving out of my mother's house. I couldn't be better." Okay, so she lied at the end.

"Charlie asked me to go to your opening with him. I've never been to New York before."

"Really? So?"

Michael blushed, something that surprised Dylan almost every time it happened. How could such a tough football player always be so incredibly bashful? "It's up to you. As long as you're okay with it. I don't want to be in the way."

"Michael, of course," Dylan responded. "I'd love it if you came to my opening."

"Then I'll be there."

"Good."

"Are you ready for the wedding?" Michael asked, raising his brow.

"Yes. Are you?"

He shrugged. "I'd still like to walk with you, if you're okay with that."

Dylan nodded slowly as her lips curled into a pleasant smile. "I think that would be nice," she answered. "Besides, Meredith is beginning to get a bit spazzy with the wedding just around the corner. This will make her happy."

"Right," Michael chuckled. "Will you be bringing a date?"

Dylan shook her head. "Nope, stag all the way for me."

"I'm bringing a date," he said with a red face.

"Michael Olerson," Dylan began, "who are you dating?"

Michael laughed in embarrassment. He looked down at his pile of shredded straw paper and laughed awkwardly. "Mary said she would go with me. I thought, why not, you know? She's a nice enough girl."

"Mary? The waitress from Ollie's?" Dylan sat back and smiled. She wished she could find it in her to feel upset. Even the slightest amount of jealousy would let her know that she was capable of moving forward. Sadly, she only felt relief. She couldn't be more pleased by Michael moving on to another girl—someone—*anyone*—other than herself.

"Yep, Mary." He blushed. "She brought me ice after Ben punched me and she helped me clean up after. Since then, we've kind of hit it off."

"She's a lucky girl." Dylan immediately regretted saying it. She could see the look in his eyes, a look that seemed to scream, *Then why didn't you want me, Dylan?*

They ate their food and chatted away, reminiscing, joking, and catching up. Michael didn't ask about Ben and he didn't treat her like a fragile head-case on the brink of a meltdown like everyone else had. They were normal.

As they stepped outside, Michael turned to Dylan and smiled. He fumbled through his pockets and pulled out a silver key. "Here," he said, practically presenting it to her with a chorus of angels and a beaming light, "it's all yours."

Dylan smiled as she took the key to freedom from her new landlord. "Thank you," she said, grinning from ear to ear.

"No parties," he teased.

"Don't worry. My friends and I will just come up to Ollie's and get free alcohol," she said, nudging his arm.

"Funny." He looked down at her and smiled peacefully. "I'm glad it's you moving in there, Dylan."

"Me too." She began to step away from him. She wanted to go call Charlie and tell him to get his muscles and truck ready, but Michael's expression stopped her.

"Listen," he chewed on his lip while he spoke, "I didn't want to bring this up, but—God—I feel like I should."

"What is it?"

"Ben came by before he left for Massachusetts. He apologized for that night and basically told me that he was taking off and no hard feelings."

"Oh," she said, attempting to hide her grief.

"I just felt like you should know that, I guess. I know it's kind of pointless now." He shrugged. "I suppose I just wanted you to know that I don't hate Ben, and if he can admit he was wrong, then so can I. I am sorry for my part in that, Dylan."

Dylan sighed heavily. "Well, thanks, but you're right; it's pointless."

She didn't need to say that this was not a closed wound for her yet. It seemed to be in the air all around her at merely the mention of Ben's name. She could feel the color drain from her face and her body rearrange itself awkwardly. She tried to be strong and appear to be moving on. It didn't always work for her, though.

Seeing her discomfort, Michael leaned closer and said, "I'm always going to be your friend, Dylan." He put one arm around her and looked down. "Always."

"Bye, Michael." She smiled as she turned away from him and quickly walked away.

*   *   *

Ben stretched his arms out over his head, and sighed. "What was that?" he asked sleepily.

"I asked how that made you feel." Dr. Fields said for the second time, possibly the third. "Having such a powerful father?"

"Ah, yes," he remembered, "the F word."

"Yes, that pesky little word that you love so much," she replied.

Ben put his head back against the brown leather couch, a clichéd piece of furniture to have in a therapist's office, he thought. He looked around the room for the tenth time and still couldn't find a clock anywhere. It was a tricky game this woman played, hiding all the clocks so he couldn't know the time. What if she denied her paying patients the full hour? How would they even know if they were being ripped off?

"Where are you, Ben?" she asked in an irritatingly calm voice. "You're thinking about something."

"I'm wondering where all the clocks are," he admitted through a yawn.

"Time is important to you?"

Ben laughed. "Sure."

"What was funny about what I said?"

He laughed again. "Nothing, I guess."

"Are you happy when you laugh, Ben?" She crossed her legs. She had been sitting still for nearly an eternity and Ben had wondered when she would move. It just wasn't human to sit like that for as long as she had.

"Isn't that a cause of laughter?" Ben asked, still looking at her crossed legs. She wasn't attractive like Professor Gray. He just needed to focus on something other than her emotionless face and the clock-less walls.

"No. Not necessarily. In your case, I believe your laughter is a way of masking your discomfort. Would you agree?"

Ben's lips pursed. "Whatever you say."

"You don't agree, then?" Her eyes narrowed in on him. "I'd like to hear your theories."

"How can I have theories about my own feelings?" he asked, laughing again. "Wouldn't I be the one to know the answer? There's nothing theoretical about it."

"So, you believe that you can make sense of all you feel. You don't believe that you need assistance in sorting out your emotions." Dr. Fields looked down at her pad of paper and began to write slowly, like she wanted to be discreet.

Ben felt like he might have met his match in this woman. No one frustrated him this way. It was quite twisted the way she switched up his words and made him think. He opened his mouth and then closed it, chuckling to himself when he realized he had no retort. "Sure," he answered, only because he couldn't allow her to have the last word.

She looked at him steadily. "Let's talk about your mother."

Ben tensed. "Let's not," he replied quickly.

"I haven't brought her up in the last two sessions." She turned in her swivel chair and crossed her other leg. "Shouldn't that count for something?"

"And I thank you for that. Let's not begin now, and we can keep up this entertaining banter we've got going on."

"We don't have to talk about her death. What about her life?"

"Her life was death," Ben answered. "She hasn't been alive for a long time."

"There was never a good time?"

"If there was, it was long before I had the ability to remember."

"How did you cope with that?"

Ben growled in frustration. He looked the doctor in her professional eyes and knew that she would report any difficulties he gave her. He was positive she had been handed a small amount of information about his life; something like, DEAD MOTHER: SUICIDE and ALCOHOL ABUSE. That was all they had on him, though. They knew nothing about the Mathews and, more importantly, they didn't even know Dylan existed. That part of his life was a mystery to the people here.

"Ben?" she asked calmly, leaning in. "Ben, how did you cope with having such a sad mother all your life? Children need to be nurtured. They need love. How did you cope without it?"

Ben looked down at the carpet. It was a god-awful burgundy that reminded him of his high school library. He continued to picture a face he didn't want to think of. The carpet wasn't helping. *Damn this woman*, he thought. He knew how he coped without his mother's attention, of course. He'd had Linda.

He remembered a time when he was five, maybe six. He had fallen from his skateboard doing a trick that Charlie bet him he couldn't do. He scraped his knee and walked it off, vowing never to let anyone see him cry. He hid on the side of the Mathews' house, and wept as he tried to clean up the blood pouring from his busted knee. As he picked the rocks from the wound, he winced from the stinging pain. He jumped as gentle hands wrapped around him. He looked up and saw Linda's sympathetic face. In her hands she'd held a bandage and a washcloth. She said nothing as she sat in front of him and wiped his face, then his knee, and tenderly placed the bandage over the wound.

"There," she'd said, smiling. "Now, next time you try that jump, don't go so fast and try not to hesitate."

Ben had run from her that day, knowing she would never tell a soul he had cried, and knowing, from that moment on, that he could always count on her. He had even ended up mastering the skateboard trick that Charlie bet him he could never do. That part he enjoyed the most.

"Linda," Ben said sadly, without thinking.

Dr. Fields' expression almost registered surprise. She shifted in what Ben assumed passed for excitement. "Who's Linda, Ben?"

Ben smiled. "She's someone who took the place of my real mother sometimes."

"Do you still see her?"

Ben shook his head slowly.

"Why?"

The timer behind her went off with an alarming ding. It seemed to have made even the doctor jump. She must feel like she was finally getting somewhere with him when, because of her own timer, he pulled back again. Ben was sure the next time he came in there would be no timer.

"Time's up," he said, beaming. He stood to his feet and stretched out his arms. "Until we meet again, Doctor."

Dr. Fields sat back in her chair and pointed to him with her silver pen. "We'll start off right there on Monday," she reassured with a small smile.

"Right," he said, flashing a patronizing grin.

He stepped outside her office and raised his eyebrows at his babysitter, Professor Arthur, waiting for him in the waiting room. His two professors had taken turns making sure that he made it to his appointments. He had hoped that after the first two sessions, the hovering would end. No such luck.

Professor Arthur stood and dropped a magazine down onto the table in front of a couch. "All set?" he asked with a smile.

Ben nodded and flung his jacket over his shoulder. "Have a good night," he said, and bolted out the door. The last thing he wanted was more heart to hearts with people trying to look inside his head. If he stayed, the professor was sure to ask more invasive questions, and Ben could only handle one nosy person per day.

As usual, he went home alone. He was always alone.

* * *

When Dylan got home from her lunch date, Linda was waiting for her outside. She was on her knees, hovering over a giant pot filled with soil and flowers. She would say that she was gardening, but Dylan knew better. She was waiting to make sure her daughter wasn't kidnapped and murdered and looking out the window had gotten to be tiresome.

Dylan hopped out of her car and smiled. "Still alive," she teased.

Linda sat up and rolled her eyes. "I see that."

She sat down next to her mother. "You're never going to guess who my new landlord is."

"I haven't a clue."

"Michael Olerson."

Linda sat up, shocked. "You're kidding. He has a way of always popping up in your life, doesn't he?"

Dylan put on a pair of gloves and began to toss the few garden rocks back into the pots they managed to roll out of. She had never understood the way her mother loved to tend to her flowers. Linda said it was relaxing. Dylan thought it was stupid, but she would help her out of obligation. Since she was the only girl, such duties lay heavily on her in an irritatingly sexist way.

There was no point in trying to explain that sexism to her family, though; Linda would only see what she wanted to. When Dylan turned ten, Linda had been ecstatic to present her daughter with an extravagant dollhouse that Dylan had never asked for and had no interest in. It was the kind of a thing that lots of girls would have cried happy tears over. Not Dylan. She was too busy admiring her new easel and charcoals to notice the pink monstrosity behind her.

And her lack of interest in stereotypically feminine things always made the yearning to please her mother that much greater. It would feel disrespectful if she didn't.

"So, you're still moving in, then?" Linda asked curiously.

"Absolutely," Dylan answered quickly.

Linda sighed deeply. "So, then, this is our last night living under the same roof?"

Dylan nodded and frowned. "It would appear so."

Linda sighed again, and stood up. She brushed the dirt from her legs and picked up the hose. As Dylan sat on the ground, staring up at her, she sprayed her daughter in the face and yelled, "Consider this your send-off!"

Dylan screamed and laughed as she ran into the house to hide and dry off. She hopped up the stairs to her bedroom and looked around the near-empty space. For twenty-two years this space had belonged to no one else. She wasn't even sure if it ever would, because they were all positive that Linda would never move from the house Carl had paid for.

She hated that she thought of Ben in that moment and that he went along with her memories in her own bedroom. She hated that she could only seem to focus on those memories now. She imagined the way he had kissed her, held her, laughed with her. Now, she only despised the way his lips would form a genuine smile as he made love to her. He would cup her cheeks, staring into her eyes like he'd never look away, like for the first time he was really seeing someone other than himself.

Dylan's heart seemed to crack away one piece at a time. It was only getting worse. The emptiness he had been able to leave behind consumed her, leaving a tightness in her chest that ached from time to time. Thankfully, she was learning to conceal her pain so that she looked somewhat human to the outside world.

"I come hoseless," Linda teased from behind her. "Hey, how about a cosmo night as a final farewell? Do you think you could spare a Friday evening for your mother?"

"You're handling this mysteriously well, Mom."

Linda sighed, defenseless. "I knew it was coming. If I make it hard on you, then you'll never come back to visit me."

Dylan grinned happily. "Okay, cosmo night it is, but only if we throw a little tequila into the equation. If we're going to do it, we've got to do it right."

Linda wrapped her arms around Dylan and hugged her tightly. "Okay, but when I vomit, you're holding my hair."

Despite her eagerness to be on her own, she would miss her mother. She wouldn't pretend otherwise. "It's a deal," Dylan whispered with tears in her eyes.

CHAPTER SEVENTEEN

Ben coasted through the hallway, staring straight ahead and holding his chin in the air. As he passed each cubicle, he counted in his head to appear as if he knew exactly where he was going. He always made sure his first impressions were his best.

He paid no attention to Nicolc, the latest victim to run out of his room in tears (something he felt somewhat guilty about). She passed him with a stack of papers that she hugged to her chest, and did an obvious about-face as soon as she noticed it was him. As bad as he felt, he couldn't find it in his heart to apologize. That was asking too much of him.

Darius Mason, the attorney he would work under until the fall, had instructed him to "settle in" and return to his corner office when he was ready. Ben was born settled into this role, but he felt it might be necessary to at least see where he would check his emails.

He found his cubicle and set his briefcase down. He dropped into the cheap chair and took in his surroundings. His heart was beating like a gladiator's before a death match. No one would ever know the extent of his nerves, however. His power face was on and he was ready for business.

He knew exactly how he managed to score the position with Darius, Weis and Carter's most vicious, successful attorney. Ben had an overbearing, miserable father, but the perk of his last name would carry him far.

Ben figured he had taken enough "settling in" time and got back to his eager feet. He headed back into Darius's office.

"Did you find everything all right?" Darius asked as Ben returned. "Is your cubicle as small as mine was when I interned here?"

"Was the desk hanging out into the aisle?" Ben answered, chuckling politely.

"No bother. You'll be spending most of your days here with me or running errands, anyway." He dropped a stack of files onto his desk and slid them over to Ben. "First assignment," he announced with a smile.

Ben stared down at the stack hungrily. He smiled and carefully restrained the urge to clap his hands and rub them together. He was nearly salivating at the idea that there was a real case inside that manila folder, just waiting for him to sink his teeth into it.

"You've got that look in you, McKenna. I like it." Darius leaned back in his extravagant leather chair and sighed. "I'm envious. I wish I still got that excited over work."

Ben opened the folder and thought that he had never felt better in his life—other than when he was with Dylan, of course. Nothing could top that. But this was almost that good. This was what he'd been waiting for.

"A little background on this," Darius began, "Jordan Long is an accountant facing fraud and laundering charges. *Allegedly,* our guy swindled a few people out of a couple of bucks."

Ben nodded slowly. "I've heard about this case. This was big news."

"We don't worry about the news, McKenna," Darius said with a chuckle. "What do we worry about?"

"If the prosecution can prove it," Ben answered confidently. "And how we can disprove whatever they find."

"My man!" Darius slapped Ben's arm. "I was hoping you'd add that last part."

Ben laughed. He sat down and carefully thumbed through the information in the file: legal phrases he understood perfectly, a picture of the client, Jordan Long, and three different bank statements, highlighted in yellow.

"Take this with you tonight and do a little homework," Darius instructed. "Tomorrow we have a meeting with Mr. Long and you'll be there. You'll be silent, but you'll be there." He grinned, flashing perfect, white teeth. "It'll be the same drill at Wednesday's arraignment: silent observation. Consider yourself my secret weapon."

Ben chuckled. He watched as Darius practically danced around the room. He wasn't anything like Ben had expected. He seemed like a kid as he picked up a miniature basketball and tossed it into the small net that hung from the back of his door.

"Are you hungry, Ben? We should go across the street to that pub and grab a bite to eat. You'll die a happy man after you've had a burger from that place."

Ben wasn't hungry. He wanted to work, to do what he came there for. It was barely eleven in the morning. He didn't plan on eating for at least another six hours. However, this was a god before him—his deity of law. If the man wanted him to eat a burger, his only reply would be, *Bring on the beef!*

They took a seat along the bar and Ben sighed in relief when Darius ordered a diet soda. Ben ordered water. He wasn't ashamed to tell anyone he wasn't drinking. It was the answers to the questions that would follow his assertion that he was ashamed of.

"So, Ben," Darius began, "how's your father doing?"

Ben tossed the lemon that came with his water onto the bar. He sipped slowly and nodded. "He's good." He really had no clue, but that wasn't a very good answer.

"I never personally got to know him, but I've heard a few things about him. What a shark, man. He sounds fierce."

"Try being his son," Ben replied, laughing. He never enjoyed small talk about his father. It was that law deity thing again, though. Ben would eat, sleep, and breathe however this man wanted him to. He could certainly handle a few off-limit topics of conversation.

"Oh, I bet," Darius said with a laugh. "I bet you learned a lot from him, though. I've already seen that same fierceness in you. I saw the way you looked at that file, Ben. I thought you were going to take a bite out of it. That's why I chose you."

"You chose me, huh?" Ben asked, nearly laughing.

Darius nodded eagerly. "Hell yes! I had to practically wrestle you away from Dick Thompson. That's who your father wanted you to work with in the first place, you know?"

Ben frowned and fell into thought. Darius Mason chose him? "I thought my father set this up," Ben admitted. "I was sure he placed me with you because you're the best."

Darius raised his eyebrows and grinned. "No one sets interns up with me. Sometimes I don't even have an intern because I'm not interested in any of them. I choose who I want, and I chose you because *you're* the best, Ben."

Ben had nothing to say. He had never earned anything on his own, without his father's influence. This was the first time he had felt pride in himself, knowing he had accomplished something alone.

"You know that your GPA is flawless. You came highly recommended by all of your professors," Darius reassured once again. He had to have seen the disbelief in Ben's eyes.

"I'm just not used to getting things without my father's influence. He can be rather persuasive at times, you know?" Ben looked down as his food arrived. "Anyway, let's eat."

"I've heard he's quite a guy, that Warren." Darius shook his head and frowned. "Terrible thing about his heart, though. The poor guy gets married, all is well, and then—bam—heart starts failing him. Sad."

Ben froze and tried not to look confused. He nodded, pursing his lips.

Darius took Ben's discomfort for sadness. "Hey, I'm sorry. You probably don't want to talk about this."

Ben shrugged, attempting to school his face. "It's all right," he assured him.

Darius waved his hands. "Let's eat these burgers. You haven't lived 'til you eat this thing."

Ben looked down at his food and realized that if he hadn't been hungry before, he certainly wasn't the slightest bit interested in the greasy thing in front of him now. "I'm going to go wash up real quick. I'll be back in a minute."

"Hurry up there, McKenna. I'm pretty hungry. I might steal yours if you let it sit here too long."

Ben laughed his fake laugh for what must have been the fiftieth time in an hour. "Feel free," he joked, standing up. He truly didn't get the fuss this guy was making over a burger. It looked like any other burger he had seen before. If he were on speaking terms with Jonah, this would be the first thing he would make fun of Darius for when Jonah called to see how his first day went.

He walked into the bathroom and leaned over the sink. He stared into the mirror as he controlled his breathing. He splashed water on his face until his heart started beating normally again. As he pressed the rough paper towel to his cheeks, it hit him: his father had a heart condition? How "sad" was it, though? It wasn't so sad that Warren had thought it necessary to tell him about it, even at their last encounter. Was Ben really so unimportant that strangers knew of this before he did?

He stood, dabbing the cheap paper over his wet forehead. He took a deep breath and then blew it through his dry lips.

"Shit," he whispered.

* * *

Dylan exhaled as she made a long stroke against her blank canvas. She had been staring at it for hours and now laughed at herself for only coming up with this one meaningless line. She stepped back and brushed the hair from her face, leaving a green streak across her forehead. Despite her lack of ideas, she was happier than she had ever been with this one green line, because it was the first line painted in her new studio.

Everything was unpacked except for a few random things here and there, but already this place was home. Her drawing table was set up in the corner of the room and her easel was just under the giant wall-to-wall window. It was perfect.

She could sense her joy just by looking at the jars of paint in front of her. They were filled with only bright, lively colors, shades she had not used in ages. She finally felt at peace. Still, there was that one hole inside her that Ben had left. She had been able to camouflage it well, but she was sure it would never be filled again.

"Here comes the bride!" Meredith called as she and Charlie stepped through the door to Dylan's new home. No one had ever accused her of not being cheesy enough.

"Don't leave your door unlocked," Charlie scolded with a frown. "That's the first thing I said when I left last night and, here you are, unlocked and vulnerable." He looked down at Meredith, and asked, "Didn't I tell her that? I knew she wouldn't listen."

Meredith nodded and rolled her eyes with a sigh. "Yes, honey, you did tell her that."

"I'm hardly vulnerable," Dylan replied, eyeing the can of pepper spray Charlie left on her table. "And, hello? Do we knock ever?"

Charlie laughed. "Uh, no, we don't. Robbers and rapists don't knock, either. Just in case you were wondering."

"I really wasn't wondering, but thanks." Dylan squinted as she forced a smile that wasn't meant to be pleasant.

Charlie looked back at her through competitive eyes, beginning an immature staring contest. The two had been in countless of these, which they found much easier than shouting. The only problem was they could both go on forever.

"Dylan, we brought you a present for your new place!" Meredith beamed, interrupting the stare down. "Look!"

Dylan smiled. "Oh, it's a picture of you two. Just what I always wanted!"

"It's our engagement photo," Meredith pointed out.

Of course, Dylan had seen that picture multiple times. The picture was by far one of Charlie's cheesiest moments, but just as much a token of his love for his future wife. Only she could get him to dress up and sit in a garden.

Charlie rolled his eyes behind her. He didn't need to say that, like everyone who knew Meredith, he was ready for this wedding to be over and done with.

She placed the frame on a shelf by the window and smiled up at it like it was the greatest thing she'd ever seen. She needed more pictures of her family displayed, anyway; her walls looked a bit bare.

Charlie relaxed into the small, red loveseat that Linda had purchased for Dylan when they went shopping. He shifted comfortably and sank deeper into the soft cushion. "You're spoiled," he said with his eyes narrowed. "Mom never bought me a thing for my apartment."

Dylan smirked. "Well, I am her favorite," she teased. "You should have been a girl. Or, it's not too late to be flamboyantly gay."

Meredith's head jerked up at the word "gay." "Excuse me, I need him to be straight, thank you. That would just be a disaster." She frowned at the thought. "Wouldn't that be the worst thing ever? I mean, 'honey, I'm gay' would quite possibly be the most horrible news to hear on my wedding day."

Charlie and Dylan both stared at Meredith as they attempted to keep up with her strange train of thought. When she turned and realized that they were looking at her with puzzled expressions, she asked, "Charlie, you wouldn't really wait until the day of our wedding to tell me something like that, would you?"

"I don't think you have to worry about that, honey," Charlie said monotonously, as if he were prepared with an answer for any ridiculous question imaginable. "I'm sure I would have realized it a long time ago."

"It's a bad *Lifetime* movie, Meredith," Dylan said, still perplexed. "I was just kidding."

Meredith laughed uncomfortably, her face a bit white. "Maybe we should just wait until after my wedding to say funny things, okay? My mind is running wild with the what-ifs I'd rather not—you know—know if."

"Let's order a pizza," Charlie said, ignoring his fiancée's wondrous ability to think of everything. "I'm hungry."

Dylan groaned. "Charlie."

"What?"

"Leave!"

"Why?"

"Because we're hovering, honey," Meredith intervened. "She wants her alone time. That was the whole point of her moving here."

"We gave it to her last night," he said, dumfounded. "Really, though, did you lock the door last night after I left, like I said?"

"Charlie—God!" Dylan stomped to her door and flung it open. "Seriously!"

Charlie laughed and stood up. "Okay, okay. We're leaving."

"The place looks great, Dylan!" Meredith called as she pulled Charlie's hand.

"Lock it!" Charlie yelled as Dylan slammed the door in his face.

To satisfy her protective brother, she locked the knob and twisted the bolt. She stood, waiting next to the door for what she knew would be coming in any second.

"Thank you!" she heard Charlie call from the other side.

She shook her head and laughed as she headed back to her easel. Not even Charlie's Bridezilla of a fiancée could keep him too busy to drive her crazy. Because of the aggravation his smothering caused, Dylan thanked the heavens above that Brandon lived in California, far away from her. She suspected that it was only a matter of time before he showed up with a state of the art security system.

Dylan stared at her green line once again. She sighed and crossed her arms, staring at this one, irrelevant line that she had grown to love simply because of its meaning: freedom.

"Well, that's all she wrote for today, I suppose," Dylan announced to know one, and scooped up her brushes. She put her things back into their places and washed the one dirty brush under the tap water.

Her phone rang loudly, making her just about jump out of her skin. "Hell," she growled in frustration and stomped over to retrieve the ringing disturbance.

"Hello?" she answered the foreign number. "Hello?" she asked again, impatient when the caller didn't respond quickly enough. Her hands were still wet, causing her to hold the phone awkwardly.

"Hello. Ms. Mathews?" a male voice asked.

"Who's this?" she asked.

"I apologize for any interruptions, but my name is Lorenz Fuller."

"Yes?" Dylan snapped, ready to end the call. "How can I help you?"

"Yes, I run a department here at the Boston Institute of Art Education. Ms. Mathews, did I catch you at a bad time?"

Dylan blindly sank onto the loveseat behind her, hoping she had the placement of her furniture locked into her memory by now, but not really caring. A bruised rear end was the last of her concerns; this was the art school of all art schools. A phone call like this didn't come very often.

"No. I'm sorry. You have my full attention." She giggled nervously.

"I should hope so," he said with a small chuckle. "I've been in touch with an old instructor of yours, a Scarlet Hudson? She thinks very highly of you and your work. I came across your number through her."

Her nervous heart sputtered in her chest with the many possibilities for his call. "Yes, I know Scarlet," Dylan answered carefully.

Scarlet was Dylan's favorite teacher and had been the one to get her the job at the school she taught at now. She was always very free-spirited, smoking on school grounds and pushing for self-exploration. As long as an artist believed and felt what they were creating, that was enough for Scarlet. She'd never had to say it out loud: Dylan knew she was her prized student. It wasn't a shock to Dylan that Scarlet thought of her for whatever this man was seeking.

"We've been looking for a new instructor here at the school and, while I've had many applicants, I'm just not sure that they have what I'm looking for."

"Which is?" Dylan asked, making sure he was saying what she thought.

"Ah—well—*you*, Ms. Mathews," he said simply. "I believe we're looking for you."

"Oh?" she asked with the very limited amount of air left in her lungs.

"I've seen a few pieces of yours—only what Scarlet was able to send me. I'd love to see your work in person." He paused for a minute, possibly out of courtesy. Dylan was just about speechless on the other end. He had to have known it. "I was wondering, might I see a small showcase before I make an offer?"

"Really?" Dylan asked, stunned.

"That is if you're even interested in the position. I probably should have asked if you would even consider moving across the country. Though I assure you, the pay will be much higher than what you receive now."

"Yes!" Dylan shouted a bit too enthusiastically. She decided to bring it down a notch or two. "I mean, yes," she said in a quieter, more reserved voice. She was still sure it was far too late to recover, though.

"Perfect! When can we meet? I'll come to you."

"Oh. Well, I have a gallery showing in New York on June twelfth. Would that be too late for you?"

"Not at all. I was hoping you'd say that actually. Scarlet mentioned it, but I didn't want to overwhelm you."

"I'm really looking forward to meeting you, Mr. Fuller."

"Likewise," he replied. "I'll be in touch."

The call ended and Dylan sank back into the loveseat. She sighed deeply when she realized exactly what this decision would involve: another move that her mother would never get over and a very short distance between herself and Ben. On the other hand, this was an offer that wouldn't come twice.

CHAPTER EIGHTEEN

"So what are you going to do with that information, Ben?" Dr. Fields asked in a comforting voice. "Have you given any thought to how you will approach this with your father?"

Ben sighed deeply, still miffed at this talented woman who could pull things out of his tightly locked emotional vault. "I haven't thought about it."

"But it is weighing heavily on you. That's obvious, or you wouldn't have brought it up." She jotted down something on her pad, a familiar move of hers that always seemed random and discreet. She looked back up and noticed his tightened jaw. "What is it?"

"I brought it up because you already knew. I know Arthur or Gray told you." He laughed. "I'm not stupid."

"Do you feel that people think you're stupid?" she asked, avoiding the bit about Ben's professors sharing information with her.

"Do I strike you as someone who is insecure about his intelligence?" Ben asked through a burst of laughter. "Jesus, I'm afraid of showing my feelings, not about what people think of me. It was an expression, you know?"

"Finally, you admit that you're frightened when your feelings are revealed." She didn't smile, but something told Ben that inside she was gloating. "Let's touch on that."

Fuck, Ben thought. This woman was a genius. He couldn't help but to grin at her.

"What hurts the most? We've been tiptoeing around this other family of yours: the mother, Linda, and the best friend, Jonah. Who else is there?" She wasn't tiptoeing around anything now. She was full-on stomping through his brain to get the answers. "Come on, Ben. This stays here; you know that. I only report your cooperation and progress."

Ben groaned and pressed the back of his head against the leather couch. "There's Linda, Brandon, Charlie, Hugh, Jonah, and," he prepared himself to even say her name, "Dylan. She's a girl."

"And the father?" Dr. Fields asked without seeming to notice his discomfort at Dylan's name. He was still able to mislead her a little. "What about the father of this family?"

"He died of cancer years ago," Ben answered. "He—I never talk about him. There isn't much to say. He was good to me and he died. The end."

"You found refuge in this family. They were good to you when your real family wasn't." She had nailed it on the head. "You push them away because they make you feel too loved?"

Ben shook his head. "That's not why."

"Then why?"

"Because I don't deserve them," he blurted without thinking.

"Just like your real parents never deserved you," she returned.

"No they didn't. My father, during the little bit of time he was there, only molded me to be him, and that wasn't any kind of bonding. My sick, neglected mother always pushed me to the side and, when I went to the Mathews' home, I was accepted without question. There was always a plate set for me, always presents under the tree. I was included, whether I was there or not."

"Out of pity perhaps?" she asked as she leaned forward, pushing harder.

Ben shook his head. "No, no. It was because they wanted me there. They wanted me to be a part of their family. They were always so natural about it." He sighed shamefully and closed his eyes. "I hurt one of them."

"The girl?" she asked, nonchalantly. She acted as if it were a completely normal thing to be so incredibly accurate. "Dylan?"

"Jesus," he whispered as he stared at her with a puzzled expression. "You're good, you know that?"

Dr. Fields lifted her chin to the wall behind him. It was filled with certificates and awards of every kind that Psychology had to offer. "It's confirmed in frames."

"And you're sarcastic," he added with a pointed finger.

"You respond to sarcasm, I've noticed," she admitted.

Ben smiled in disbelief. "Is this what they call a 'breakthrough' in your little Psychology Club?"

Dr. Fields smirked for the first time ever. "Yes."

"Great," Ben said, leaning his head back against the couch.

"We're not done, though. We're going to cover this family and the girl." Dr. Fields swiveled around in her chair and pushed the stop button on the timer, clearly not wanting any disruptions. "This is why I always schedule you last."

*   *   *

"Dylan?" Jonah stepped into his mother's house and laughed at all the bags on the floor. It was obvious his sister and mother intended for him to do all the heavy lifting when they left for the hotel later that evening. Of course, them staying with Meredith at the hotel overnight meant that the men had the Mathews' home all to themselves, promising a great night and one seriously hung-over groom the following day.

He sniffed the air and sighed at the aromas of dinner that filled the kitchen. "What are you making? It smells good."

Dylan appeared with an apron wrapped around her waist, looking like a Stepford Wife in the making. "Umm, Thanksgiving dinner, I guess?"

"In May?" Jonah laughed.

She smiled and shrugged. "Everyone is home again so I thought we'd celebrate. Besides, I had a craving."

"I didn't know you could cook like this," Jonah said, looking in each pan and allowing all the mouthwatering steam to escape. "It better be as good as it looks and smells, damn it. Now I'm all excited."

"That's the point, dummy. Besides, you'll lie to me and eat it anyway. I'm your twin; that's what we do for each other."

Jonah watched his happy sister. It was the first time in a long time that she had looked content. The few random times that he had seen her since the Ben blowup had left him worried to the point of sleepless fear. Now, she seemed to have mostly returned to the familiar Dylan he had always known. He didn't say it out loud, though. She would punch him.

"Knock it off," Dylan warned as she hunched over the stove and added mini marshmallows to her yams.

Jonah watched the back of her head, wondering how the hell she knew he was staring at her. "Knock what off?" he asked with amusement. "What am I doing?"

Dylan placed a glass lid over her casserole pan and placed the dish into the oven. After she closed the door, she turned to eyeball her twin with her arms folded against her chest. "There are going to be a few ground rules if you think you're going to eat any of this food."

"Okay," Jonah replied hesitantly and crossed his own arms, attempting to even the playing field she had set up. It didn't work, though. She still made him feel like a miniature version of himself.

"Rule number one: you are not to stare at me like that. I get enough of those looks from Mom and Charlie and I want to strangle them as it is." She didn't even wait for a reply before adding, "Number two: you are not allowed to ask about security systems, extra bolts, mace, or fire alarms for my apartment. I'm not a total moron and I do know how to take care of myself, understand? And, dear Lord, rule number three: if you even try to call me *Weed*, I'm going to punch you so hard in the balls, you'll be my twin *sister* for the rest of your life, got it? That name is retired."

Jonah's mouth opened and closed, with no response for the verbal ass-kicking he had just received.

Dylan smiled wickedly with a satisfied look in her eyes as she wiped her hands on her striped apron. "Please spread the word to your brothers. Thank you." She turned back around and began to crumble bacon over her green bean casserole.

Suddenly, Brandon walked in, followed by Charlie and Hugh. Jonah's wide eyes looked them all over as they stared at his blank face.

"What the hell is wrong with you?" Brandon asked Jonah as he dropped his bags on the floor. "You look like someone just punched you in the balls."

Jonah laughed, snapping out of his trance at Brandon's extremely apt choice of words. "I think someone just did," he answered with a chuckle.

They were all there again, warming Linda's heart as she walked into the kitchen to greet them. "My babies are home," she announced proudly. She hugged each one, stopping to run her fingers over Hugh's smooth face.

"After we eat I'm taking you ladies to the hotel," Brandon said charmingly.

"And then we're going to drown ourselves in the shitload of alcohol I picked up last week," Hugh said with a grin.

Linda pointed a scolding finger and wagged it around the half-circle her sons stood in. "No, no. Meredith would kill you all if you got him drunk before her wedding day. Don't do anything stupid."

Jonah gasped with a grin and placed his hand against his chest. "Mother, I am insulted."

"Who said anything about Charlie?" Hugh added with an identical smile. "He can go to the hotel with the girls, for all I care!"

Charlie frowned. "Mom, it's my last night of freedom."

"What an awful thing to say," Linda answered. "Your father never said anything like that before our wedding day."

In unison, the boys all snickered and turned away, most likely knowing something their poor mother didn't. Carl Mathews had the wondrous ability to be two men at once: a kind and doting husband, and a man's man with stories about his youth that weren't family-appropriate.

"He didn't!" Linda snapped, possibly having heard a story or two herself.

"I'm sure he didn't," Brandon appeased, and slapped his laughing brothers on the arms.

"Let's eat," Dylan practically sang with a casserole dish in her oven mitts. She stared at them all and felt the need to pat her own back for the impressed expressions on her family's faces.

*   *   *

The next morning, Meredith stood over her bridesmaids and demanded they all wake up to assist in the impossible task of calming her jittery nerves. Bridezilla seemed to be gone and in its place was a timid little bride-to-be, wide-eyed and white-faced.

To no one's surprise, the song "Chapel of Love" was played repeatedly. Dylan was teetering on the edge of losing her mind and had seriously considered throwing Meredith's sister's iPod out the damn window. It was beyond tacky, and entirely expected, but, for only a minute, a nice break from that ridiculous *My Best Friend's Wedding* song that they had played over and over the night before. Dylan stuck to her guns when someone recommended that they lip-sync into hairbrushes.

Dylan watched as Linda tried not to look on edge, but she was terrified at the potential state of her house due to the text message that Jonah had sent her early in the morning, instructing her not to go home until her sons gave her the "okay."

Clearly they'd had a good night and woken up too late to clean and hide the evidence of the night before. Knowing her brothers, Dylan could only imagine what her poor mother could walk into; a stripper pole and leftover exotic dancers seemed most plausible. Empty cans and bottles wouldn't be enough to scare the boys into warning their mother.

Through it all, though, Dylan had jitters of her own, and they came from a lingering question that she couldn't get out of her mind. Would Ben surprise everyone and grace them with his unreliable presence? Over and over again she practiced what she would say—or not say—if she happened to run into him. Each time left her sick to her stomach, hoping to God he didn't bring a date to add an extra jab of pain.

Meredith was a vision of perfection while she waited for her wedding party to line up and make their way down the aisle to where Charlie waited. Her smile was enormous with the excitement of the day that she had longed for her entire life. She squeezed her pink-and-white-rose bouquet in a white-knuckled death grip. No one dared comment on it, though.

Just before Dylan and Michael made their entrance, Dylan blew Meredith a kiss and smiled extra widely as she waved her pink bouquet. "See you at the end, sister," she whispered as the double doors closed behind them. *Let's get this over with*, was what she had really wanted to say.

Michael locked his arm with hers and smiled tenderly as he looked down at Dylan's happy face. "You are the most beautiful girl in the room," he whispered.

"You're not supposed to say that, Michael," Dylan scolded with a smirk.

"I'm sure I'm not the only one here who thinks so. I'm just the only one with enough nerve to tell you."

"There's a bride here, you know. It's not my day for compliments." Dylan elbowed him, forcing a quiet chuckle from his throat and a snide look from Mary as they passed her along the way; it was a look Dylan decided to pretend she didn't see.

The two finished their walk, and Dylan winked at Charlie as she headed to her place in line.

*   *   *

Ben's nerves were as twisted as they had ever been in his life. He could not remember a time when anything had managed to make him feel so sick. Dr. Fields thought this was a good idea and, despite his own better judgment, he trusted her immensely. He could still hear the words she used: "family," and something about "healing." Whatever. His round-trip ticket was for one day, so he had an excuse to leave without getting into too much of a dramatic conversation. Jetlag was the least of his worries.

He wasn't disappointed when he found that he was late and could only stand at the white double doors in the back and watch the ceremony out of sight. If he were to walk in, the entire church would surely turn to stare at him. This was Meredith's day. Maybe he could just watch, leave a card, and duck out without being noticed at all. He'd never promised Dr. Fields that he would speak to anyone.

Ben leaned against the door as he peeked around the edge to watch in secrecy. They'd gone overboard with the flowers, the amount of pink was atrocious, and the golden harp was over-the-top and ridiculous.

None of that mattered to him, though. Not when he noticed Dylan shining in the room, wearing a light pink, strapless gown that looked perfect against her skin. She took his breath away.

He watched as the soft light from an enormous candle behind her sparkled through a wisp of her hair, giving it that famous auburn glow. He sighed as he remembered the golden skin that curved over her perfect shoulders and slender neck. He chuckled as she pressed her finger to her eye, trying to conceal an escaping tear.

He pried his eyes from her and looked at Charlie. *He is so hung-over*, Ben thought with amusement. He watched as Charlie looked near strangulation in a tuxedo that he clearly loathed with every fiber of his being. Charlie gave a small sway and closed his eyes quickly, on the brink of either passing out or throwing up, Ben imagined.

"Hang in there, brother. If you don't, she's going to make you pay for the rest of your life," Ben whispered so low that only he could hear.

Brandon, Hugh, and Jonah were in no better shape. They looked like death as they all fidgeted behind their brother and tried not to vomit. A slight gleam of sweat on Hugh's forehead told Ben that he was the closest to bolting to the bathroom. It occurred to him that he had missed a good night.

The vows, of course, were written by the bride and groom. Ben could hardly hold in his airline breakfast as he listened to Meredith's simpering description of a man who was definitely not the Charlie he knew. Of course, Dylan could describe him in ways that no one would believe, either, so it wasn't fair of him to judge.

It must have been the sobs in between each word that irritated him. Charlie spoke quietly and, if Ben had been a crazy person, he would have believed that a tear really had fallen from Charlie's eye as well. The giant of all men fallen to his doom.

As the new Mr. and Mrs. Mathews were happily presented, Ben allowed himself another glance at Dylan and found that familiar lump in his throat as she smiled the beaming smile she had once given him ... while she locked arms with Michael Olerson. He was sure he deserved that. All the same, it was his sickening cue to leave.

He'd made his exit from the church, managing to remain unseen, and now he only needed to leave the card with the enormous check inside and be on his happy way. Before that, though, he had to sneak onto the golf course, find the reception tent, and move as discreetly as possible.

* * *

All of the grandiose wedding dramatics were finally coming to an end and Dylan could at last see the light at the end of the sappy tunnel she had been trapped in for months. It wasn't that she wasn't happy for the new couple, but she had seen enough tears and smiles to last her a lifetime. Over the course of her nine-month-long bridesmaid ordeal, she had managed to make several promises to herself regarding her own wedding, the most important of which was that she had come to the conclusion that elopement was the best way to go.

"Dylan, hold my flowers," Meredith barked rabidly. "Here. Like this, Dylan! You're going to squish the petals."

Dylan smiled graciously, and patiently took the bouquet from her new sister. "I need a drink," she whispered to Jonah, who closed his eyes and nodded in sympathy.

"I need a bathroom and a cold washcloth," Jonah murmured through a smile full of teeth. "I don't think the wedding photos are going to look as great if the groom has puke on his shoulder. I'm just saying."

"Just a few more, everyone!" the photographer yelled to the group. "Then you can all go get those drinks you've been promised."

"Thank God," Charlie groaned without thinking. "I mean, oh damn," he corrected when Meredith shot him a warning look.

The final shutter clicks sounded and the group was at last released to make their way to the reception tent and finish the celebration off with ease.

Inside the tent, the night took off without a hitch. All but Jonah seemed to conquer their hangovers. The laughter and dancing roared through the white canopy, making the evening a successful one.

Dylan watched from her table with amusement. She drank her cold beer in a champagne flute in order to appease Meredith, who felt that elegant dresses and bottles of beer did not mix. No Ben, she noticed. Her ambivalence to that observation was enough to annoy her for the rest of her life.

She couldn't deny that a twinge of stinging sadness had shot through her when she watched Meredith dance with her father. *I used to be a daddy's girl*, she thought.

"Dance with me," Hugh demanded with a grin. Dylan was sure he had sensed her brief moment of self-pity. "I won't tell anyone we're related."

Dylan chuckled, adding a last-minute eye roll, and grabbed his hand. "I'm sure no one could tell," she pointed out sarcastically.

"I get the next one!" Brandon hollered to Hugh as he led Dylan to the floor.

He smiled when the band began the slow tune that was once their parents' song.

Dylan loved dancing with her brothers. It was one of her fondest memories—at first she had hated it, but after years of special occasions and Linda's constant insistence, she found that there was no one she would rather dance with than a Mathews man.

Hugh twirled her around and she giggled.

"You look pretty tonight. Do you know that?" Hugh asked as he pulled her back to him. "I can't believe how beautiful you've turned out, Weed—shit—sorry—Dylan."

Dylan couldn't help but laugh. He was trying, and she would always give her airhead brother the benefit of the doubt. "Thanks. Now stop," she demanded quickly.

"Okay," he said, understanding that the line of mush was dangerously close to being crossed.

"Really, though, thank you, Hugh," Dylan said tenderly, and then trusted him completely as he dipped her with an enormous grin.

* * *

Jonah stood outside the tent, hidden from view, and tried to breathe deeply. If he were to lose it at any point tonight he would never hear the end of it from his brothers, who insisted that he was the lightweight of the bunch.

As he rounded a corner, he stopped short at a familiar silhouette hovering deep in the shadows, spying on the ongoing party inside. It was rather obvious what had drawn his attention.

Jonah looked through a small opening and watched as Hugh glided with his sister over the dance floor. She really did look stunning in the twinkle lights that hung from the ceiling. It was a long way from her usual ripped jeans and T-shirts.

She smiled as Hugh dipped her and handed her off to a smiling Charlie, who wasted no time twirling her around.

Brandon laughed and threw his arms in the air, impatiently waiting for his turn to dance with his little sister. Jonah knew he should probably get in there and join the traditional fight. This was something they did on every special occasion and Linda would notice his absence. He was already in enough hot water with her.

The game was naturally a crowd pleaser, but Jonah always felt it was Dylan that created the audience. He was merely a prop. It was unintentional, but she simply stole the show everywhere she went, even at weddings.

"She looks pretty, doesn't she?" Jonah said to Ben's back.

Ben didn't seem surprised to hear his voice. He didn't take his eyes from Dylan as he softly confirmed, "Yes."

"Inside and out," Jonah replied, feeling a bit of pride as he said it. "She's the best of all of us, isn't she?"

Ben nodded and sighed as he hung his head low. "Is she happy?" he asked with a shaky breath.

"I think she's getting there." Jonah took a step closer before adding, "Why don't you go in and ask her yourself? I can't speak for Brandon, or even Hugh, but I'm sure there are a few people who would like to see you."

Ben shook his head and stepped backward. "I should get going. I'll only ruin the night."

"Well, you'll never know unless you try," Jonah said, carefully considering his boundaries.

Ben lifted his chin as the laughter from the crowd inside grew louder. Brandon had managed to steal Dylan away from Charlie, and guided her through the crowds, far away from any others who might have wanted to steal her.

Dylan beamed with joy as she and Brandon danced and laughed. She radiated happiness. She looked oblivious—like any sorrow she'd had before had disappeared the moment Hugh asked her dance.

Jonah watched in astonishment as Ben brushed away a tear. It was so quick that he thought his eyes had played a trick on him, but he knew it had been real.

"Hand her over, Mathews!" Michael's voice bellowed from inside. He pulled Dylan from Brandon's grasp and spun her into the crook of his arm.

"Brothers only, Olerson," Brandon teased. "Last time I checked you weren't included in that!"

"And thank God for it," Michael replied quickly. "Trust me, I would never want to be her brother. But as owner of the roof she lives under, I am entitled to at least two dances."

Dylan shrugged and happily allowed Michael to whisk her away.

Jonah noticed Ben's wide-eyed look just before he started to back away. "Ben, wait. Don't go yet. Let me at least run in and get my mom."

"No. I can't. I'm sorry, Jonah," he said, and stepped closer to his awaiting cab.

"Ben?" Charlie stepped out of the tent and took a step toward the cab. "Ben, wait."

"Congratulations," Ben said with a simple shrug. "I'm happy for you, brother. Really."

"You don't have to go," Charlie assured.

"Hey, don't tell her I was here, okay? I don't want her to be upset." Ben looked into the tent once more and a peaceful expression stole over his face. "I don't want that smile to go away, and I have a tendency to make that happen."

"Okay," Jonah said regretfully, as they watched Ben duck into the cab and close the door.

"Do you see it now?" Charlie asked Jonah. "This is about him. It was never about our sister."

"Yeah," Jonah began in wonder, "I think he really does love her."

CHAPTER NINETEEN

Dylan sat quietly in her mother's kitchen. She contemplated last night and tried to decide how she felt about Ben's absence.

"Morning," Jonah grumbled from behind her. "Coffee."

Dylan looked her brother over with a raised brow. "Put clothes on," she demanded at the sight of his boxer briefs.

"Shut it," he answered.

"Are you still hung-over from the other night? I didn't see you drink at all at the reception."

Jonah nodded as he poured himself a cup of coffee. "I fell in love with a stripper. She stole my heart, my wallet, and possibly a necklace of Mom's. Her name is Sparkle."

"Of course it is," Dylan replied, stifling laughter. She seriously wondered how much of this story she wanted to hear.

"What are you doing here, anyway? Don't you have your own place now?" Jonah asked as he sipped his coffee. "I'd like to see it today. I promise, no alarms, mace, or guard dogs."

Dylan sighed. "I'm trying to figure out how to tell Mom that I may or may not have a job offer in Boston."

Jonah's eyes widened and he chuckled. "Yep. That'll do it."

"Do what?" Dylan asked, glaring suspiciously.

"Send her straight over the edge," he answered. "Then again, she has to let go eventually, I suppose."

"Yeah, tell her that," Dylan replied, deciding that particular bomb would have to wait to be dropped.

She didn't even know if the offer would come. Lorenz Fuller could dislike her work, and she had learned her lesson: things that seemed too good to be true usually were.

"You know," Jonah began as he rested in the chair beside her, "Boston is right next to Cambridge."

"That did cross my mind." Dylan stirred her coffee to avoid his stare. "It wouldn't make a difference, Jonah."

"Sure it would," he said quickly.

"No. It wouldn't." Dylan glanced up to see the battle in Jonah's eyes. He was debating something, she could tell. She didn't want to know what. "Just drop it, Jonah. The issue is a dead horse and I'm sick of beating it, you know?"

Jonah groaned. "I hate being in the middle of this shit. You know that. But I've been on the sidelines for so long now; I think I should be able to say what I think."

"What sidelines?" Dylan asked incredulously.

"C'mon, Dylan, you think I didn't know about the two of you?" Jonah asked with frustration in his voice. "He's my best friend. I saw the way he looked at you. I knew when he came up to your room, and I saw you guys on New Year's Eve."

"Oh," was all she could manage.

"He loves you. I really believe that. And it's so crazy because this is Ben we're talking about. But, then again, it's not so crazy, because I'm pretty sure it's always been you. I think he just freaked out."

"Don't dredge all this up. Just stop it." Dylan stood up, afraid she was going to cry.

"I hate being in the middle of this. You have no idea how bad this sucks." Jonah sounded like he was in pain.

Dylan shot him a look of warning and snapped, "I have no idea? Seriously, Jonah?"

Jonah threw his hands up in defense. "Okay. That was a pretty stupid thing for me to say," he admitted. "I'm sorry."

Dylan retreated. She had been ready to punch him in the nose. "Please, just drop it."

As Dylan walked away from him, Jonah called after her. "He was at the reception last night. I found him outside watching you."

She closed her eyes, which sent a tear down her cheek. She felt relief that her back was all Jonah could see in her moment of weakness.

"I don't care," she lied, and walked away.

*   *   *

Ben did an awkward dance in front of his father's white mansion for what seemed like hours. He put one foot on the stone step that led to the porch, and then immediately took it down when his chest stung with a nervousness that had become all too familiar since his first visit to Phoenix back in December.

Life had been much simpler before that memorable trip. He was convinced that his life would have been the same as it had ever been if he hadn't allowed his mother to guilt him into coming.

Without that trip, he would never have had Dylan, though.

He jumped when the door finally opened and a petite blonde stepped out. She smiled warmly, and Ben knew instantly who she was. He also realized that the picture of her he'd had in his head was sadly inaccurate.

"Hello," she said. "You must be Ben."

"You must be Jackie," Ben replied carefully.

"Come in," she said with a pleasant smile. She opened the door wide and held it there until Ben stepped in.

Ben looked around at the grandness of the room before him. It was only the foyer, but Ben could imagine what the rest of the home looked like. It was white, clean, and full of expensive décor. It was the yin to Ruth's yang. His mother's home had looked like an expensive version of Hell. This place looked like an expensive version of Heaven. Fitting, he thought.

"I was just putting lunch on," she spoke from behind him. "Are you hungry?"

Ben noticed two round faces peeking at him from just around the other side of a wall. Their porcelain cheeks shined with a tint of pink as they stared at him bashfully. His new *sisters*, he figured.

Ben turned to shake his head uncomfortably at Jackie. "No, thank you. I'd rather just see my father, if that's all right with you."

"Of course," she said, and motioned with her chin up to the grand staircase before them. "He's in bed, but he should be awake. It's the fourth set of doors on the right. Don't mind the mess."

"Thank you," Ben replied, and made his way up.

The room was dark and reminded him eerily of the way his mother's room had looked when he found her dead. The sun gleamed through the window and shot across the room, touching everything in its path.

Medical machines had been set up all around the bed, cords running to and from each piece of equipment, tangling on top of the carpet and finally running under the bed in an attempt at discretion.

Ben had never seen his father so fragile. He was barely noticeable, tucked under the white sheets. He looked old—much older than the middle-aged man he had seen only a few months before.

"Dad," Ben whispered, nearly choking on the word.

Warren's eyes fluttered weakly.

Ben sat down on the bed, carefully finding a place that wouldn't disrupt his father, if there was such a place. "Sir, it's me, Benjamin."

"I know. I'm not blind," Warren whispered, his voice raspy. "You should be working," he scolded tiredly. "What are you doing in New York?"

Ben stifled his anger. He shouldn't have been surprised that his father would worry about his internship, no matter what the circumstances.

"Darius gave me a bit of time off. He assured me that I can come back when I've dealt with—you know—whatever this is." It was hard to even look at him. Was he dying?

Warren gave a weakened wave. "He's a pompous moron. I never wanted you working under him. That's just proof that he's a sap of a man."

Ben chuckled. "He's not a sap. He's taught me a lot in a very short time, actually. And he happens to have an enormous amount of respect for you."

Warren gave another weak wave, followed by a sickening groan. "I'm happy you're here, anyway. I have something for you. Go to that hutch over there," he said, pointing. "There's a box I need you to get."

Ben did as he was told and brought back the wooden box. He placed it down next to his father and waited for the next order. There would always be another command.

"Don't open it until you leave," Warren demanded.

"Okay," Ben agreed in barely a whisper.

"So, how are you?"

Ben smirked as he leaned over to fix his father's pillow. "Terrible. And you?"

"Dying," Warren admitted with a chuckle.

"That sucks, Dad."

"Yes." Warren sighed. "Have you seen the crying young lady that you chased out of your apartment that morning?"

Ben laughed, remembering all too well what he was talking about. "Yes. I see her, but she wants me dead, so I try not to speak to her."

"Are there any women out there that want you alive, son?"

"No. Well, maybe one," Ben joked. "But I ruined that and she's with someone else. She even lives with him now."

"That must be the Mathews girl. Jonah's twin, right?" he asked as if he had been there all along.

"Dylan," Ben confirmed. He couldn't help show his bewilderment.

"You're surprised I know a bit about your life?" Warren asked with a smile. "I should have been closer, I suppose. Maybe this is karma for my mishaps as a father. I do know things, though, Benjamin."

"Yes, then. I'm talking about Dylan."

Warren's eyes closed. "Then why are you wasting time here with me?" he asked faintly. "You should be groveling at her feet and begging for another chance."

"It's too late for that."

Warren's eyes slowly opened. "It's never too late, son. I'm dying proof of that."

Ben nodded, and wiped a tear from his eye. He was thankful his father didn't see it. God only knew when the real Warren McKenna would come back and yell at him for being so weak.

Ben sat and watched his father sleep for some time. There had been no discussion about their fight. Neither of them needed to point it out. A peace had fallen over them, and Ben was finally relaxed at his father's side.

Ben grabbed his box and looked at Warren's face once more before he left. He felt no need to wake him for a long, drawn out goodbye. There was a stillness inside his usually raging head, and he was content to keep wordless.

As Ben approached the front door, he was stopped by Jackie's voice. "It took him three rough drafts before he finally felt happy enough with that letter," she said from behind him.

Ben nodded and smiled. "I'm sure," he agreed quietly.

"I'm trying to make him as comfortable as possible. I hope you know that," she said desperately. "This was never about money. I have enough of that."

Ben turned to face her with compassion. "I believe you. I'd rather not do this with you right now, though. I can only handle so many heart-to-hearts in one day. Please understand."

Jackie smiled as she let out a sigh of relief. "I'm married to the older version of you, Ben. I think I understand a thing or two about how you operate."

Ben couldn't help but laugh. "Thank you." He looked back up the stairs and said, "Take care of him."

"I promise," she said with such sincerity that Ben would never question it again. "Would you like that lunch now? You've been up there for so long it may as well be dinner."

"I have another stop I need to make before I head back home. But I do appreciate the offer."

"The offer will always stand. I hope you come back to visit soon."

"Of course," he said, and walked outside into the sun.

He sat down a few steps away from the porch and placed the box in his lap. He just couldn't wait another minute to see what his father had in store for him.

Inside were papers, medals, awards, and certificates, each with Ben's name stamped in calligraphy at the top. The box seemed bottomless; it was filled with every achievement Ben had ever earned. At the top of the pile rested a small piece of paper with words scrawled in a messy version of his father's handwriting.

Benjamin,

You are a better man than I could ever hope to be. Please know that and remember it when you think of me.

Always, Your father, Warren McKenna

Ben's eyes welled with unexpected tears. His face fell into his hands and he sobbed as he sat on the steps that led to his father's porch. In that moment, it felt like an invisible boulder had been lifted from his chest and he knew that every word his father had written was genuine and true.

He should have raced back into that room and told him that he loved him, too. He couldn't. Like him, Warren despised emotional overload. He knew that Ben loved him, though. He didn't need any words to confirm that.

Ben collected his wooden box and walked down the stone steps. He didn't belong there anymore. He belonged somewhere else. He had one more stop to make and a promise to fulfill.

CHAPTER TWENTY

Dylan's hands shook violently with every guest that walked into her showroom. Every piece that she presented seemed to call out "amateur!" whenever an onlooker glanced at it.

She remained somewhat hidden while she watched a man and woman point and nod at the piece she'd painted only weeks before. It was an abstract painting with colors she thought were right at the time, but seriously questioned now.

"Oh, God, when is this going to be over?" she asked her mother, taking a shaky breath.

Linda smiled obliviously as she sipped her champagne. "What do you mean, baby? I'm having a wonderful time. I love it here. I feel so classy."

"That's great." Dylan pulled the flute from her giggly mother's hand and downed the contents. "Why would I ever agree to this?"

"Because you're one of the most gifted artists I've ever known," a voice answered from behind her.

"Scarlet!" Dylan beamed as she wrapped her arms around her former teacher's neck. "I can't believe you're here!"

"Like I'd miss this, dummy," she said with a bright smile.

Scarlet was a true hippie with the dreads and recycled shoes to prove it. Only, tonight she seemed a bit more sleek and presentable than usual. She still smelled like patchouli oil, though.

"This is quite a turnout," Scarlet noticed.

"They're paid actors," Hugh teased, and then dodged a slap from Brandon.

"It looks like people are starting to clear out," Meredith pointed out over her champagne flute.

"Has anything sold?" Charlie asked.

"Oh, yes! Norman said that several pieces have been claimed, and there are a few that are pending," Scarlet answered. "You really should have agreed to higher prices, Dylan."

"Yeah, sis," Jonah cut in, "make us all rich so I can quit school and give Mom's bank account a rest."

"You'll be doing that regardless," Linda said with a stern look. "I don't think my bank account can handle another bar tab."

"You can always get a job as a bartender, Jonah," Michael taunted.

"He'd drink you dry," Hugh scoffed.

"You're all driving me crazy!" Dylan snapped, and fled before she strangled them one by one. She couldn't handle the usual Mathews banter. Not tonight, anyway.

As she rushed away from her crazy family, she was stopped by a small man with salt-and-pepper hair. "Ms. Mathews?"

"Mr. Fuller?" Dylan confirmed breathlessly. She decided now was a great time to control her rampant nerves. "I'm so happy you made it."

"I am as well, Ms. Mathews." He looked around and smiled. "However, I've seen enough."

Ouch. "Well, I appreciate you taking the time to come here," she began disappointedly.

Lorenz Fuller laughed wickedly. "Ms. Mathews, we need to work on your pessimism. I fear you are your own worst enemy at times."

"I'm not following," Dylan said without caring about sounding proper.

"I'm offering you the position!" he exclaimed with a grin. "I knew I was right about you after I received your credentials, and this gallery only proves it. I love being right," he added with a wink.

Dazed, Dylan walked away with a mass of instructions about how to contact him and when she could start. She had to put that behind her for now and concentrate on the exciting moment at hand.

It was a like living in a dream and she wondered when it would all collapse into a nightmare. Yes, more pessimism.

Dylan walked back to her family and tried to greet them with a smile. They had all showed up, supporting her in every way, despite their busy lives. No one could ask for a better group standing behind them, and here she was acting like a vicious brat.

"Why are you taking that down?" Dylan asked as Brandon pulled her favorite painting from the wall. Even she could hear the urgency in her own voice.

"Uh, someone bought it," Brandon said, as if the answer were obvious. "Norman told me to pull it when the showing was coming to an end and take it to the back to be wrapped. He said to do this one first."

"Oh," she said with a sense of sadness. "Just give me a minute with this one, okay?"

Brandon shrugged. "Sure. Mom bought a painting that reminded her of Dad. It was the one with the orange moon. I'll get that one first. Oh, and don't try and argue with her. She said it's her motherly duty or something."

Dylan gave a mechanical "Okay" and didn't take her eyes from her painting. She had thought long and hard about letting this one go, but knew it was one of the best pieces she had ever done. She wasn't surprised it had been claimed.

She lightly traced her fingers over the man that reminded her of Ben, and felt her eyes fill at the memory that seemed so long ago now. The stars that hung over the entangled couple were brighter than she remembered, and she secretly felt a certain serenity knowing that they would never dim.

"That one was our best sale tonight," Norman said as he approached. "There was something of a battle over it, so it went well beyond the asking price."

"That's great," Dylan replied monotonously.

Brandon returned with a cautious grin. "May I take it now? Have you had your moment?"

Dylan tried to shake off the possessiveness she was feeling. She smiled at her brother, and even added a "Yes, jerk" to sound more content with her loss.

* * *

Ben watched Dylan from the sidewalk on MacDougal Street, just in front of the building she stood in. The gallery had large windows, making it easy for him to spy without being seen.

He laughed as she raced around, and he wanted more than anything to kiss her flushed cheeks. She was nervous for reasons that he could only chalk up to her insecurities. From the outside, her night looked like a success.

"Are you ever going to go inside?" Brandon asked from out of nowhere. "This stalking thing is getting a little creepy, man."

"Is that mine?" Ben asked, nodding at the painting in Brandon's hands.

Brandon looked down and gave the piece a small tap. "I think so. Norman said the buyer would be waiting right where you are."

Ben pulled the painting from Brandon's hands and felt a twinge of happiness rush through him. He couldn't have her in real life, but he could certainly savor her art.

"Maybe someday you'll stop sneaking around and actually come say hello," Brandon said sincerely. "There are a few people inside who would like to see you, you know?"

Ben nodded. "Are you one of them?"

Brandon chuckled. "Nah, you're not my type."

Ben laughed quietly. That was enough to let him know that he had been forgiven. "Just tell her I said congratulations, okay?"

"Tell me yourself," Dylan said quietly from the front doors of the building.

Stunned, Ben's eyes widened. "I didn't mean for you to see me. I just—"

Dylan looked down at the painting in his hand. "May I?" she asked and reached for the wrapped piece. She unfolded part of it and peeked inside to find the man and woman intertwined in an almost kiss. "You bought this," she said, her voice thick with emotions he couldn't name.

"It reminded me of—" he shrugged, "—you know. I promised you I'd buy something." He tried to sound casual but failed miserably.

"Thank you," she said.

"Anyway, I have to get going," he began. "You look beautiful."

Dylan nodded slowly, like she was contemplating something. She looked at him with confusion and something else that Ben could not quite decipher.

In an awkward, unexpected hug that stunned even him, he pulled her to him and held her there. His hand lay flat across the small of her back as he drew her in closer, pressing against her. He held her too tight for too long, but still he could not find it in him to let her go. He smelled her hair against his better judgment, knowing what her scent would do to him. It was arousing and humiliating, but the world was right again as the reality of her consumed him for a brief moment.

He would have held her forever, but the sound of a group exiting the building forced him to release her too quickly. Only then did he see the tears in her eyes. He couldn't see her cry again; that wasn't why he came.

"Ben?" Linda asked, both shock and happiness in her voice.

"Hey," Charlie said, grabbing Ben's hand and holding it with a manly firmness. "It's good to see you."

"Hello, Ben," Meredith said, her genuine smile a peace offering.

"McKenna," Michael Olerson greeted, and looked from Ben to a clearly shaken Dylan.

Ben shook Michael's hand and seriously considered punching his face or congratulating him on being the better man. He took the high road with a nod of the head.

Brandon, Hugh, and Jonah only smiled with easy looks, but Ben understood what that meant. He preferred for them not to speak anyway.

"So," he began, looking away, "I just wanted to come and buy a painting, like I promised. Congratulations again." His jaw tightened and his eyebrows furrowed. "Bye, Dylan."

Dylan said nothing as he forced himself to walk away, carrying his new painting in one hand, the other shoved in his pocket.

He hated himself for the pain he'd unleashed on her, whether he meant to do it or not. It was unbearable to watch her cry, knowing he was the cause.

He could hardly feel sorry for himself as the rain began to beat down on his head; it only added a nice dramatic effect to his misery. He shielded his painting with its dustcover and turned it inward against his body.

He shook his head as he walked. He wanted so badly to erase his mistakes—to erase all the ways he had hurt Dylan. He was nothing without her, but she was so much better off without him. That was the reality of it all.

"Ben!" he heard as he stood at a crosswalk. "Ben!"

He swung around and stared at the figure running toward him. Jonah grew closer and closer as he waved his arms in the air and yelled his name. "Ben, stop!"

The rain splashed around him and his hair was sticking to his forehead, but all he could think about was protecting the piece of Dylan he carried under his arm. "Go back, Jonah!" he demanded. "Go be with your family!"

Jonah yanked the painting from Ben's arm. "You're my family, too, asshole."

Ben pulled the painting back, locked in a standoff with his friend. "What are you doing?"

"I'll take care of this for you! Stop it, Ben!" Jonah yelled.

"Stop what?" Ben's confusion grew by the minute. "What are you doing, Jonah?"

Jonah ripped the painting back from Ben's death grip. "Washington Square Hotel, room twenty-seven," he said with a sopping wet face. "Stop being a dumbass, Ben."

Ben stared, processing Jonah's words.

"She just may be the only person in the world you're ever going to love," Jonah yelled over the pouring rain. "You're never going to have another chance at it. Go, Ben!"

Ben chewed the inside of his cheek. Ben had always believed that Jonah didn't have a single deep thought in his shallow head. Now, here he was, telling Ben to go get Dylan.

"But she's with Olerson now. They live together."

Jonah snorted and grinned at his confused friend. "No," he said, shaking his head. "You couldn't be more off base. Dylan rents her loft from him, but she lives in it all by herself, alone and *single*."

Ben's chest filled with relief. "She's not with him?" he asked with joy. This time he just needed to make sure he'd heard Jonah correctly.

"She never even considered it," Jonah answered with a smirk. "She won't admit this, but she misses you. Stop being so stupid and go fix this so I don't have to chase you down like a dramatic loser again."

He didn't wait for Ben to respond. He turned away from him and walked back the way he'd come, shielding Ben's beloved painting as promised. He disappeared into the downpour, and Ben watched him the whole way.

The "walk" sign blinked, warning Ben to cross or forever hold his peace. He waited, looking back down MacDougal Street, then ahead of him again. Behind him was Dylan, pure happiness. Ahead of him was an agony-filled, lonely life. There was no choice.

He sprinted through the rain, hitting people with his shoulders, tearing through the crowds of Lower Manhattan. He bolted across an intersection without even looking for a sign that told him to go. He ran for his life as he stomped through puddles, getting even more soaked.

He found her hotel on Waverly and burst through the double doors of the dimly lit building, bypassing every form of security that tried to stop him as he hopped onto a closing elevator. If he stopped and allowed the front desk to call her room, it was quite possible she would turn him away. He had to surprise her, catch her off guard and knock on her door himself.

An old woman with blue hair and a small dog tucked under her arm stared at him curiously. "Are you all right?" she asked in a delicate voice.

Ben tried to catch his breath as he laughed. He nodded and smiled at the petite old lady.

"Is it a girl?" she asked, smiling. "It's always a girl."

"Isn't it?" Ben gasped, out of breath.

"How can I help?" she asked with excitement.

"You can keep security off me," Ben suggested with a grin. "That would help."

"I will try." She beamed.

The doors slid open and Ben took off down the hallway. He stopped at Dylan's room and leaned against the door with his hand. He caught his breath and realized he had no clue what he wanted to say, or how to get it out.

He paced as he ran his hands over his wet hair and straightened out his drenched clothes. He was a coward. It seemed as if that realization had smacked him in the face a lot more in the past year of his life.

The door swung open and Dylan's face peered out. "What are you doing?" she asked sternly.

"Hey," he said, nearly leaping backward.

She looked him up and down, eyeing his wet clothes and hair. "What do you want?" she asked, keeping the door opened just enough for her head.

"I wanted to—"

"Yes? You wanted to what, Ben?" Dylan asked pointedly. She *would* make this difficult for him.

"I don't have any excuses for anything I've done, but if I could just have another chance ... I would make it up to you, or at least try." He surprised even himself when he exhaled and waited for her to respond.

"Ben," Dylan began. "Now isn't—"

Ben put his hand up and placed it against the door. He leaned closer to her face, and pleaded, "Don't say that now isn't a good time. *Please.*"

When she didn't say anything, Ben desperately blurted, "I'm going to quit school and my internship. I'm moving back to Phoenix to be close to you. You mean more to me than anything else."

Clearly stunned, Dylan turned her face from his. She closed her eyes, sending a tear rolling over her cheek that ripped a piece of Ben's heart out as it fell.

"Okay," Ben said with a nod. "I'm sorry. I just couldn't go through the rest of my life without saying that to you."

"I hate you," she finally whispered.

"I know," he whispered in return.

Suddenly, her head whipped up to meet Ben's stare. This was not the face that he had come to know over the years. This was something entirely different, something he had never seen in her before. The wrath in her eyes almost knocked the wind out of Ben, who stared back, completely helpless.

"You don't *know*," she said as she took a step out of her hotel room and into the hallway. "You don't have a fucking clue. You don't *know* because you are always too busy deciding how everything affects *you*, Ben!"

"Dylan ..."

"No! You don't get to speak anymore, understand? It's my turn to speak and it's your turn to listen. And when I'm done, you are going to leave. You never get to speak to me again, get it?" She jabbed her finger into his wet chest and pushed him until his back was against the wall behind him, until he had nowhere else to go.

"You are the most selfish man that I have ever met. You never deserved me, my family, your family, or anyone else who has followed you around as if you were the greatest thing on the fucking planet. All you have ever done is tell people exactly what they want to hear to keep them all worshipping you. I gave you all of me—every ounce. I shared a part of myself that I have never shared with anyone and you broke that, Ben. And now you want to destroy the greatest night of my life, too? Aren't you done? Was that notch in your belt that you just *had* to have not enough for you?"

As Ben's mouth began to open so that he could tell her no, not her, she was never—*ever*—a notch, Dylan quieted him once more: "No. I know the answer to that question and I don't want to hear your bullshit lies anymore. Leave me alone, Ben."

She retreated back into her room. She didn't even give him a second glance. She just left him standing there, his back against the wall, exactly where she had pushed him. As the door slammed behind her, the reality of all that she said crept over him in a way that he had never experienced before. He deserved every bit of it, too.

Ben exhaled and wiped away another tear that had managed to escape. He fumbled with the inside pocket of his jacket and pulled out the rain-soaked envelope that he had kept with him for reasons that he only now understood. He bent down and slid the envelope under the door that separated him from Dylan. Before he could bring himself to walk away from her one last time, he placed his open hand against the door, and mouthed the words "I love you," praying that she could somehow feel it.

Crushed and dejected, he made his way out of the hotel. He would never again feel this way about another human being. He didn't want anyone else. He never would.

*   *   *

Dylan stared at the door as she took her first breath in what seemed like a suffocatingly long time, a result of the invisible Ben-sized boulder that sat on her chest. She couldn't believe all of the things that she had just said to him, and it had even taken her a few seconds to remember how she ended up sitting on the floor. It was like an out of body experience that had left her reeling, breathless as she gasped for air through her relentless tears. She couldn't feel any regret for all of the things that had flowed from her lips while she so obviously stung him to the core.

She glared down at the envelope that slid from the hallway and wondered when and how she would bring herself to open it. Did she truly want to know its contents? No. It would only suck her in. She was already on the fence, teetering on the edge of running after him to scream how much she loved him. If she opened it now, she'd never regain the strength that she had just shown.

She stood and walked away from the envelope—as far as the room would allow her to go—and decided that a cup of tea was the best thing for her, a substitute for calling her mother, of course. Besides, the tea would not say a single obnoxious word.

As she dipped the teabag into her mug of microwaved water, the rain outside pounded away, sounding like a drum line. The downpour cascaded down the window in sheets.

She crept closer to the window and could not believe the sight before her. The storm was unyielding, the wind and rain striking with all of nature's power. She sipped from her mug and watched the blank, New York streets below. The only occupants were the papers that blew wildly over the pavement. She watched as one landed in a puddle and paused mid-sip when she noticed the figure standing like a statue above it.

Despite the sad fact that she'd know those feet and the legs anywhere, she felt her eyes travel up along his body until they met his eyes, staring her way.

Dylan gasped and jumped to the side of the window, out of Ben's view. She was petrified. She couldn't look at him again. If she did, she would surely allow her weak side to come out.

Ben McKenna was standing in the pouring rain!

Dylan's eyes scanned the room and landed on the envelope that was still on the floor. In a matter of seconds, she was on her knees above it, staring until her curious side won out.

She carefully pulled the envelope open, taking note of how old it actually was. It was fragile from the rain and could have ripped to nothing before she even knew what it held inside. But when she pulled the letter out, she noticed instantly that the handwriting matched her father's, and the sudden cry that erupted from her sent a ringing through her ears.

"Oh my God," she whispered, as she tried to calm her shaky hands.

It had been years since she had seen that writing but, even now, she would know it anywhere. It was an unsteady version that told her immediately he had written it when he was at his weakest, just before he passed away.

She pulled the envelope to her face and breathed it in as if it were her father himself. With a trembling hand, she drew it back and began to read the words her father had written—words that she had gone so long without knowing.

Ben,

Sometimes in life we get these rare opportunities to say things to people that we love. I am happy that you saw one here, and I understand why you chose to stay away. You are like a son to me, as I am like a father to you. Please do not ever be sorry for saying how you feel. I think that people come into each other's lives because of fate, to learn something that they could never have known on their own. You are in our family for a reason. How it unfolds from here is up to you. Just know that you are worthy of what you want and what I someday hope that you are man enough to have. It would have been an honor to witness it, I must admit. You are a good person, son. I have known it from the moment that you showed up on my doorstep. You have a great big heart in that chest of yours and I think that someday you are going to know how to use it. Please don't wait too long. She's quite a girl, if I do say so myself. I know that she will probably always love you, but I taught her to be strong and she won't wait forever. Be good, Ben. Be the man that won't let anyone else's demons get in the way of what he wants and what he knows to be right.

I'll never be too far away,

Carl Mathews

* * *

"Ben!" Dylan called into the pouring rain that fell ruthlessly around her.

As he slowly came into view, she finally saw how cold he looked, his blue lips trembling. It was pathetic, downright pitiful and degrading. But she couldn't buy into it or even feel sorry for him.

"What is this?" she screamed through the loud, heavy rain. "Why would you give me this?"

Ben seemed to think long and hard—or maybe he was just stunned by the fact that she had come down at all.

"You're using my father now? You think the fact that he wrote you a letter a decade ago might make me think that you're not the asshole that you continually prove yourself to be?"

"Christ, Dylan," he said, laughing a little, as he moved a few steps closer, "I would never do that. I would never *use* him."

"Then what, Ben? What is this supposed to tell me?"

"Didn't you read it?"

Frustrated, Dylan shook the open letter in her hand. "Obviously!"

"Okay." Ben inched closer, careful as he spoke. "He knew that you loved me, even then."

"What was he talking about when he said that you shouldn't be sorry?"

"In the letter that I wrote to him first—"

"You wrote him a letter?" she interrupted, dumfounded.

Ben nodded slowly, but said nothing.

"What did it say?"

He smiled, reminding her of the person she'd seen only in small glimpses. Over the last few months she had often wondered if that person ever truly existed or if it was someone he only pretended to be. She thought she had made up her mind about the answer, but seeing his peaceful face before her once more made her question it all over again.

"I told him that I loved him like a father, thanked him for everything, and I said that I would miss him."

Dylan felt her mouth fall open as she tried to process it all. "I—I don't know what to say, Ben. I didn't know any of this."

Ben took another cautious step toward her, but Dylan put her hand up to stop him. "Stay there," she demanded. "I can talk to you from right where you are."

He smiled, appearing to understand that she might be wavering. That smile would be the death of her, of course. Her stony facade was fading fast and he could read every hint that she unintentionally gave him.

She could hate him for how perfect he was, for how handsome and lucky he had always been. He got everything he wanted and, if she gave in to him tonight, that would only prove her theory more. It was an agonizing decision. She could cross the distance between them and slide into his arms, or she could throw the letter at his feet—the precious letter written in her father's writing—and leave him outside, this time forever.

"I think he always knew that you were the one for me, Dylan. I told him as much in my letter. And I felt bad because," he took another cautious step toward her, "I said that as much as I loved him, I was glad he wasn't my real father."

"What? Why did you say that?"

She watched as the sincerity in Ben's expression grew. "I didn't want you to be my sister, Dylan. I never loved you like a sister. I loved you in an entirely different way and ..."

"And he knew." She finished his sentence as the realization consumed her, filling her with her father's last words of wisdom. "He always knew."

Ben nodded slowly and took another step toward her. "I've learned so much about myself, Dylan. You wouldn't believe what I've been through. I know now that it all led me here, so that I can tell you that I'm never going to run again. If you let me, I'll spend forever making it up to you."

It only took two more steps before he was right in front of her and pulling her into his arms. She could feel the desperation inside of him as he held her tightly. He *needed* her and she was too stunned to resist him again.

"I'm sorry," he whispered into her ear. "I'm so sorry, Dylan."

Dylan pulled back and forced herself to look into Ben's eyes while she breathed deeply through the rain. She allowed her hands to travel up his chest and along the wet skin of his neck, until she reached his cheeks. She held his face in her hands and saw the vulnerable man that he was beneath her touch.

"I have always loved you," he said as she stared at him in wonder. "Even if you make me go away, just know that I will never stop. I will love you for the rest of my life."

Dylan didn't need to hear another word. She moved with an urgency that she had never felt before; she gasped before pressing her lips to his. As if they had never been apart, Ben slid his tongue into her mouth and tightened his grip on her, urging her legs up and wrapping them around his waist securely.

Dylan's hands grasped at the back of his neck while he carried her back into the hotel and quickly headed to the elevator. They didn't notice they had an audience and they wouldn't have cared even if they had. Once inside, Ben fumbled against the wall until he found the button that would send them to Dylan's floor. As the elevator rose, Ben pushed Dylan against the wall and kissed her with a determination that nearly left her without breath.

When the familiar *ding* sounded, Ben carried Dylan to her room and set her down with her back against the door. He placed his hands on each side of her head while he nipped at her neck and waited for her to find the keycard in her wet clothes. Dylan pulled the card from her back pocket and kissed Ben as she reached behind her and unlocked the door at last. They fell into the room and slammed the door behind them.

Dylan walked backward and watched as Ben pulled his wet jacket and shirt from his body, and tossed them both onto the floor. He didn't take his eyes off her as he followed closely, his bare chest heaving. She stopped in front of the couch and smiled as Ben closed the gap between them.

She continued to look into his eyes as she freed him from his belt and then his pants, before pushing him down onto the couch. She lifted her soaking wet shirt above her head as he watched her with wide eyes. She let her pants fall to the floor and stepped out of them slowly, taking pleasure in the way Ben swallowed hard and looked at her as if she were the only person in the world.

She carefully straddled his lap and slowly leaned forward to kiss his neck. Inhaling him was sweeter than she remembered, and it sent a warmth rushing through her body that seemed to burst as it shook her to the core.

"I love you," she whispered in his ear.

They didn't waste another moment. She had him out of his boxer briefs in a matter of seconds. It had been too long for them both and they were more eager to be together than they could have ever imagined.

Ben cupped her cheeks in his hands. He smiled adoringly as he grabbed her hips and made his way inside her. "I love you," he whispered.

Dylan threw her head back and groaned with a long, exultant breath. "I know," she said with a certainty that would never falter again.

They made love throughout the night, and then drifted off to sleep. They remained entangled in each other for hours until Dylan awoke in Ben's arms the following morning, just before sunrise. He whispered that he loved her and made love to her again.

When they left the hotel together in the afternoon, Ben grabbed Dylan's hand as they stepped out into the city. He held it tightly and proudly, even smiling when she glanced his way in astonishment. All barriers were down and, Dylan knew, this time, they would stay down. Ben had made peace with himself.

Epilogue

Dylan painted a long, black line down the white wall and stepped back to look at it.

"What's that going to be?" Ben asked as he carried a box full of dishes past her.

"I don't know," she said happily. "But it's the first line in our apartment."

Ben set the box down, wrapped his arms around her waist, and kissed the slender part of her neck. "Then it's a masterpiece. Leave it alone."

"Stop groping my sister," Jonah demanded breathlessly as he carried a heavy box. Only he could be roped into helping them move. "I didn't come across the country to watch that."

"You might need to leave then," Ben taunted as he turned Dylan around and pulled her closer.

"I'm going to get some food. Jesus," Jonah groaned and headed out the door.

"I have paint all over me, Ben," Dylan complained with a hint of laughter in her voice.

"I like it when you have paint all over you," he murmured against her skin. "I'll meet you in our new bedroom in about three minutes. Keep the paint on."

Dylan smiled coyly and turned to head to the bedroom.

"Turn off your cell phone," he demanded as he swatted her bottom. "If your mom calls one more time I'm going to lose my mind, and she seems to always call right when we're in the middle of my favorite moments."

"You're lucky she didn't move to Massachusetts with us," Dylan replied as she got sidetracked and dug into a random box. "Thank God Meredith is pregnant. That should keep my mother busy for a little while."

Ben suppressed a smile. "Meredith's baby bump is pretty cute. I imagined you with one and I kinda liked it."

Dylan spun around and narrowed her eyes in a glare. "Meredith has hemorrhoids right now, Ben. Do you think that's cute?"

"Well, I don't want to imagine those," he scoffed with a grimace. "When I give you a baby bump, don't tell me everything, okay?"

"Deal," she replied quickly, and unwrapped a photo of Carl. "Just so you know, whenever that does happen, the entire Mathews family will relocate. We might want to put that off for a while."

"I'm just happy I don't have to worry about Brandon walking in on us naked and killing me." Ben grinned mischievously. "Speaking of naked, why are your clothes still on?"

"Because you wanted to talk about baby bumps," she said, and put down her father's photo. "I'm going."

"Three minutes!" Ben reminded as she walked away.

Dylan shook her head as she headed into their new bedroom. It was all *theirs*. He was hers. What a wondrous thing to say!

Sidetracked again, she began to pull clothes out of another box until she noticed the painting on the bed. Her heart stopped and a smile spread across her face when she realized what it was: the painting she had given Ben when they were children.

She picked it up and stared at it, remembering every brushstroke as if it were yesterday. She had been so nervous.

"Ben?" she called to him, but still did not take her eyes from the painting of two children under a red heart. "Ben, where did you get this?"

When he didn't answer, she turned to find him, but she stopped at the sight of him in the doorway. He was on one knee with a look on his face that she would never forget.

"Turn it over," he said simply.

Despite her lack of breath and pounding heart, she did as she was told. Her hands shook as she read the two words painted on the back: MARRY ME.

"Well?" he asked uneasily when she didn't answer.

Dylan finally pulled herself from the two words in front of her, and made her way over to him. She knelt down to him and smiled at the ring in his hand.

Through falling tears and a quivering chin, she managed to nod her head and throw her arms around his neck, knowing that life with him was meant to be and she would embrace it always.

They would always belong to each other.

The End

Acknowledgements

To my children—my entire world wrapped up into two handsome boys—thank you for sticking to the *unless you're on fire* rule from the other side of my office door.

To my husband, Marcus, thank you for always believing in me and reminding me constantly that this wild imagination of mine does, indeed, have a purpose.

To my inspiring father and step-mother, Cathy, who always urge me to see my future, thank you for your not-so-subtle pushes.

To my extraordinary sister and witty brother in-law, Christian and Mike, thank you one million times and more for always being by my side from way over there.

To my big brother and sister in-law, Maury and Rochelle, thank you for just being you and always lifting me up when I forget who I am.

To my silly sisters, Karen and Shannon, thank you for always listening to my constant babble; I'd be lost without you.

To my darling in-laws, Tom, Carol, Matty, Mitch, and Mallory, I don't know how I made it without you for the first twenty-one years of my life.

To my many nieces and nephews, Auntie loves you! To the Souden, Edwards, Schirr, and Stange families, I adore you all so much; thank you for the memories and great laughs.

To my precious Ballaghs, Milams, Ocwiejas, Rouses, and Wojciechowskis, yours are friendships that I could never go without.

To Ashley and Amanda, a huge thanks for your expertise, my friends.

To our brilliant leader, Sherry, and the fabulous consultants at the Oakland University Writing Center, THANK YOU!

To the fearless Jillian Dodd and the ever-patient Beth Suit, you have truly made my dreams come true.

To Michelle at Indie Book Covers, thank you for gracing my cover with your extraordinary talent.

I owe a great deal of gratitude to all reviewers and bloggers that take the time to spread the word for authors. Without these wonderful people, many novels would go unnoticed in today's tough literary competition. In the beginning, I had a lot of help from these fabulous ladies. So, a very special thanks to: Erin from the Autumn Review, A Love Affair with Books, Swept Away by Romance, Merryways, RapidReviewer, The Book Tart, Bookslapped, A is for Alpha B is for Books, Sory from Poppybook, Lost to Books, Jenee's Book Blog, Laura YA Indie Princess, and Book Hooking.

Also, a huge thank you to Brandee's Book Endings for your help in getting Under the Orange Moon up and running.

Last, but certainly never the least, thank you to all the past, present, and future readers; I am so thankful to be able to share this story with you.

Adrienne Frances

ADRIENNE
FRANCES

Adrienne Frances spends her time as a writing consultant at a
university near her home.
In her spare time, she loves to be with her husband and two sons,
who have made her exactly who she is today.
Writing is a passion that she has appreciated for as long as she
can remember.
She believes that a wild imagination is a terrible thing to waste
and should be captured and brought to life by all that are blessed
to have one.

For more information about Adrienne:
www.adriennefrances.com

Made in the USA
Charleston, SC
06 January 2015